Extraordinary praise for

BEFORE SHE KNEW HIM

"Mr. Swanson unfolds this creepy story with the assurance and economy of a master. Surprises follow one another with inevitability, until the final electrifying jolt." —*Wall Street Journal*

"In Peter Swanson's expert hands, one woman's discerning observation at a quiet suburban dinner party unfolds into a gripping, twisty, psychologically complex thriller. I could not put it down."
—Alafair Burke, *New York Times*
bestselling author of *The Wife*

"[A] neatly knotted suspense story."
—*The New York Times Book Review*

"Compelling, creepy, and psychologically astute, this is stylish thriller writing at its very best." — *The Guardian* (UK)

"A twisty, fast-paced tale that depicts picket-fence suburbia's seamy, murderous underside. . . . Swanson is at his best in exploring the kinship—or what some see as the kinship—between artist and killer, one of the themes of Swanson's great model and forebear, Patricia Highsmith. . . . A dark, quick-moving, suspenseful story." —*Kirkus Reviews*

"It is deliciously good—dry, intelligent, perfectly paced, [and] there is more than a touch of the Barbara Vines about the delicately played out, deliciously dark relationship that develops between Hen and Matthew. . . . This is Swanson's best thriller yet."
—*The Observer* (UK)

"There's a neat twist at the end, but the real surprise is the way characters are allowed to grieve their losses, a luxury not always allowed in stories of this type. For a fast-paced thriller, *Before She Knew Him* achieves an impressive significance in its pauses." —*BookPage*

"A cornucopia of carnage and craziness, *Before She Knew Him* simultaneously disturbs and delights."

—*The Free Lance-Star*

"A wicked thriller that does not disappoint. . . . Another gem that pulls the reader in and never lets go, even as the story comes to a close. This is a book that will keep you up at night and haunt your thoughts. A fun, chilling read."

—*Manhattan Book Review*

"Woven into this twisty-turny murder thriller is mental illness and the instability it causes. Maybe worse than not being able to rely on yourself is that other people might not believe you. How can they be sure you're not being paranoid, or manic, or obsessive?"

—*The Big Thrill*

"Plenty of suspense and surprises. . . . This intense and sinister thriller builds to a shocking conclusion as the bizarre relationship between a woman and her killer neighbor plays out."

—Shelf Awareness

"What would happen if a serial killer met the perfect confidant, someone who would never be believed if they revealed his secrets? Nothing good. . . . Swanson has crafted another bar-raising psychological thriller with this tense, unexpected spin on serial killers and those obsessed with them."

—*Booklist*

"The narrative trickery is bold, but reined-in. . . . As in all his best work, Swanson is equally beguiling when conjuring up the mind of a sociopath and the middle-class Eden that harbors him."

—*The Sunday Times* (UK)

"[Swanson] knows how to ration his twists and where in the narrative to place them, devoting just the right amount of time to exploring the ramifications of each new development before spinning the story off in an ominous new direction. . . . De Palma, or Hitchcock, . . . would kill for the film rights."

—*The National* (UK)

"A must-read. . . . A shocking, addictive mystery with a classic crime twist. . . . Swanson is a master." —Crime by the Book

"Engagingly original. . . . This [is a] multilayered mystery that brims with duplicity, betrayal and revenge—all bubbling slowly to the surface. . . . Swanson has a bent for revenge and murder. Fans won't be disappointed." —USA Today

"Intelligent, twisty, stylish, startling. . . . No matter how well you know someone, you can never fully know what's in their heart and mind. *Eight Perfect Murders* proves the point. Which is what makes it perfectly creepy."

—New York Journal of Books

"An homage to classic mystery stories that offers both the charms of a puzzle mystery and the bleak atmosphere of a noir. . . . The flawed main characters are well developed, the New England settings are vividly drawn, and the twists keep coming in this suspenseful, ingeniously plotted tale."

—St. Louis Post-Dispatch

Praise for

ALL THE BEAUTIFUL LIES

"Swanson's fourth psychological thriller is a gripping exploration of delusion and deceit; sure to please readers of Laura Lippman's stand-alones." —Booklist

"Suspense lovers will devour this deliciously duplicitous read, which is chock-full of twists, turns, lust, greed, and dishonesty." —Library Journal

"An explosive mix of seductions, obsessions, and dark secrets." —New York Journal of Books

"Gripping . . . [Alice's] past is peppered with secrets and the damage is revealed in a split narrative between now and then, culminating in an edge of the seat ending."

—*Sunday Post* (UK)

"*All the Beautiful Lies* has a very rich texture which the reader gets to see only gradually, so cleverly it is disguised."

—Thriller Books Journal

Praise for

HER EVERY FEAR

"Most readers won't anticipate the Hitchcockian twists and turns in this standout suspense tale." —*Washington Post*

"Chapter by chapter, the text peels back layers to reveal a pathological relationship between Kate's cousin and a long-ago acquaintance that's reminiscent of a folie à deux out of Patricia Highsmith. . . . By then, readers, privy to much Kate doesn't know, may be experiencing their own anxiety."

—*Wall Street Journal*

"Peter Swanson tells the engaging story of a woman battling severe anxiety who decides to radically change her life—and the horrifying results that follow—in *Her Every Fear*. . . . An effective and compulsive thriller." —*St. Louis Post-Dispatch*

"An excellent whodunit with a magical appeal for the mystery thriller lover." —*Seattle Book Review*

"[It] has 'movie adaptation' written all over it. It has an alluring location, a fragile yet resilient protagonist, and a thoroughly Hitchcockian storyline, replete with the requisite false starts and plot twists. . . . High tension, lightning-fast pacing and psychological drama in spades." —*BookPage*

Praise for

THE GIRL WITH A CLOCK FOR A HEART

"*The Girl with a Clock for a Heart* is a twisty, sexy, electric thrill ride and an absolute blast from start to finish."

—Dennis Lehane, *New York Times* bestselling author of *Since We Fell*

"The pace is fast . . . and the plot genuinely twisty. . . . [It is] seemingly pre-measured for the movies . . . often to good effect; all in all, a quick, deft, promising first crime novel."

—*Kirkus Reviews*

"[A] roller coaster thrill-fest of a ride, filled with deliciously wicked moments of mystery, murder, and mayhem, double-cross and deception. A cerebral noir thriller debut."

—*New York Journal of Books*

"*The Girl with a Clock for a Heart* is an edge-of-your-seat psychological thriller that dares you to turn the next page, but it's much more dangerous than that. . . . This novel burns faster and hotter than a lit fuse, and you'll be feeling its heat long after the explosive ending."

—Wiley Cash, *New York Times* bestselling author of *The Last Ballad*

"Swanson gives readers an adrenaline rush through all the hairpin turns." —*Publishers Weekly*

"The book has pace to burn. It feels like a throwback to Ross Macdonald's flawed but relentless work. . . . Glimmers with bright and original moments." —*USA Today*

Also by Peter Swanson

EIGHT PERFECT MURDERS
ALL THE BEAUTIFUL LIES
HER EVERY FEAR
THE KIND WORTH KILLING
THE GIRL WITH A CLOCK FOR A HEART

PETER
SWANSON

BEFORE
SHE
KNEW
HIM

A NOVEL

WILLIAM MORROW
An Imprint of HarperCollinsPublishers

BEFORE SHE KNEW HIM. Copyright © 2019 by Peter Swanson. All rights reserved. Printed in the United States of America. No part of this book may be used or reproduced in any manner whatsoever without written permission except in the case of brief quotations embodied in critical articles and reviews. For information, address HarperCollins Publishers, 195 Broadway, New York, NY 10007.

First William Morrow mass market printing: December 2020
First William Morrow paperback printing: February 2020
First William Morrow hardcover printing: March 2019

Print Edition ISBN: 978-0-06-302329-1
Digital Edition ISBN: 978-0-06-283817-9

Cover photographs © restyler/Shutterstock (woman); © Miloje/ Shutterstock (texture)
Photograph on title page and part title pages by Rawpixel.com/ Shutterstock, Inc.
Author photograph © Jim Ferguson

William Morrow and HarperCollins are registered trademarks of HarperCollins Publishers in the United States of America and other countries.

20 21 22 23 24   CPI   10 9 8 7 6 5 4 3 2 1

To three generations of the Galleranis
(but especially to Meghan)

BEFORE SHE KNEW HIM

PART 1

WITNESS

CHAPTER 1

The two couples met at a neighborhood block party, the third Saturday in September.

Hen hadn't wanted to go, but Lloyd convinced her. "It's just down the street. If you hate it, you can turn around and come straight back."

"That's exactly what I can't do," Hen said. "I need to stay at least an hour or else people will notice."

"They really won't."

"They really will. I can't just look around at my new neighbors, then turn and leave."

"I'm not going if you don't go."

"Fine," Hen said, calling his bluff, knowing that he'd go alone if pressed.

Lloyd was silent for a moment. He was in front of the living room bookshelf, rearranging. They had closed on a single-family in West Dartford at the beginning of July, during one of the worst heat waves in Massachusetts history. Two months later, the weather had cooled, and Hen was beginning to feel that the house was theirs. The furniture was all in the right rooms, paintings were hung on the wall, and Vinegar, their Maine coon, had started to occasionally come up from the basement where he'd been hiding.

"What if I ask you to come with me as a favor?"

Favor was an unacknowledged code word between them, a gambit Lloyd usually used only when Hen was unwell. In the past, it was how he sometimes roused her from the bed in the morning.

"Don't do it for you. Do it for me. It's a favor."

She occasionally resented the word and the way Lloyd used it, but she also understood that it was reserved for times when Lloyd thought it was important. Important for both of them.

"Okay. I'll come," she said, and Lloyd turned from the bookshelf, smiling.

"I apologize in advance if it's awful," he said.

Saturday was sunny and blustery. Sporadic gusts of wind ripped at the plastic tablecloth, weighted down with bowls of pasta salad, chips, endless hummus and pita. Dartford was a well-heeled commuter suburb forty-five minutes from Boston, but West Dartford, separated from the rest of the town by the Scituate River, had smaller houses spaced closer together, all built for the workers from a long-defunct mill that had recently been turned into artist studios. The converted mill was one of the reasons that Lloyd and Hen had picked this location. Hen could have her own studio that was walking distance from home, and Lloyd could take the commuter rail—the station was also walking distance—into Boston for his job. They'd still need only one car, the mortgage was less than what they'd been paying in Cambridge, and they'd practically be in the country, away from it all.

But standing at the block party, dominated by young hip couples, almost all with children, it didn't feel all that different from their previous neighborhood. A woman named Claire Murray—the same woman who had hand-delivered the block party invite—introduced Hen and Lloyd around. Invariably, conversations broke out along gender lines: Hen found herself explaining her name—"short for Henrietta"—at least three times and that she was a full-time artist another three times—and told two of the women that, no, she didn't have any children yet. Only one, a darkly freckled redhead wearing a T-shirt with the logo of a preschool, asked Hen if she planned on having children. "We'll see," Hen lied.

It was a relief when, after eating some pretty delicious pasta salad and half a dry cheeseburger, Hen and Lloyd found themselves back together, conversing with what appeared to be the only other childless couple at the party, Matthew and Mira Dolamore, who turned out to live in the Dutch Colonial immediately next to theirs.

"They must have been built at the same time, don't you think?" Lloyd asked.

"All the houses on this street were," Matthew said, rubbing at the space between his lower lip and his chin. When he took his finger away, Hen saw that he had a scar there, like Harrison Ford. He was handsome, Hen thought, not Harrison Ford handsome, but good-looking in the sense that all his features—thick brown hair, pale blue eyes, square jawline—were the features of a good-looking man, yet they all added up to something less than their parts. He stood stiffly, a dress shirt tucked into unstylish high-waisted jeans. He reminded Hen of a mannequin, with his broad shoulders and his large, knuckly hands. Later, when they all had dinner together, she would decide that he was one of those harmless, cheery men, the type of person you'd be happy to see but would never think of when they weren't around.

Much later she'd realize how wrong that first impression was. But on that bright Saturday afternoon, Hen was just happy that Lloyd was back by her side, conversing, and she wouldn't have to fend for herself.

Mira, about half the size of her tall husband, moved in closer to Hen. "You don't have children, either," she said, more a statement than a question, and Hen realized that their new neighbors had undoubtedly spied on them as they moved in back in July. It was strange that they hadn't come over and introduced themselves.

"No, no children."

"I think we're the only couples on this street who don't." She laughed nervously. Hen decided that Mira was the physical opposite of her husband, that her features—a slightly too large nose, a low hairline, wide hips—added up to someone far more attractive than her husband.

"What do you do?" Hen asked, immediately annoyed at herself for instantly relying on that particular question.

The four talked for another twenty minutes or so. Matthew was a history teacher at a private high school three towns over, and Mira was a sales rep for an educational software company, which meant, she said several times, that she spent more time traveling than she did at home. "You'll have to keep an eye on Matthew," she said. "Tell me what he gets up to when I'm away." The nervous laugh again. Hen should have hated her, but somehow she didn't. Maybe the move really had mellowed her, but it was more likely the effect of her current meds. Another burst of wind, colder now, came down the street, rustling the still-green trees, and Hen pulled her cardigan around her body and shivered.

"Cold?" Matthew asked.

"Always," Hen said, then added, "I think I might head on back . . ."

Lloyd smiled at her. "I'll come with you," he said, then turned to Matthew and Mira. "Believe it or not, we're still unpacking. Nice meeting you both."

"Nice meeting you, Lloyd," Matthew said. "And you, too, Hen. Is it short—"

"Henrietta, yes, but no one, except for my birth certificate, has ever called me that. It's always been Hen."

"Let's get together sometime. Maybe cook out, if it's not too late." This was from Mira, and they all agreed, in vague responses that made Hen decide that it was never going to happen.

So Hen was surprised when, a week later, Mira ran out from her front door as Hen was walking home from her studio.

"Hen, hi," Mira said.

As usual, after spending an afternoon working, Hen felt spacey, in a good way. "Hi, Miri," she responded, realizing right away that she'd gotten the name wrong. Her neighbor didn't correct her.

"I was going to drop by this evening but I saw you coming down the street. Can you come over for dinner this weekend?"

"Um," Hen said, delaying.

"Friday or Saturday, it doesn't matter," Mira said. "Sunday even works for us."

Hen knew she wasn't going to get out of this, especially now that three possible nights had been offered up. She and Lloyd had no specific plans that weekend, so she picked Saturday night and asked what they could bring.

"Just yourselves. Yay. Is there anything you can't eat?"

"No, we eat everything," Hen said, neglecting to tell her about Lloyd's phobia of any meat that came attached to a bone.

They settled on seven o'clock on Saturday, and Hen informed Lloyd when he came home that night.

"Okay," he said. "New friends. You up for it?"

Hen laughed. "Not really, but it will be nice to have a meal cooked for us. We'll be dull and they'll never invite us back."

She and Lloyd arrived exactly at seven, armed with a bottle of red and a bottle of white. Hen wore her green-checked dress with tights on underneath. Lloyd, who'd showered at least, was wearing jeans and a Bon Iver T-shirt that he sometimes wore when he went running. They were taken to the living room—the layout was identical to theirs—where they all sat around a low coffee table, arrayed with enough appetizers to feed a small party. Hen and Lloyd sat on a beige leather couch, while Matthew and Mira sat in matching chairs. The room was very white and sterile, incredibly clean. There were interesting prints hanging on the walls, but Hen thought she recognized them from Crate and Barrel.

They made small talk for about fifteen minutes. Hen was aware that they hadn't been offered a drink—was this a nondrinking house?—but didn't particularly mind, except she was thinking of Lloyd. But just as Mira was asking if Hen was going to be part of the upcoming Open Studios, Matthew stood and said, "Can I get anyone a drink?"

"What are the choices?" Lloyd asked, a little too eagerly.

"Wine, beer."

"I'll have a beer," Lloyd said, while Hen and Mira each asked for a glass of white wine.

Matthew left the room, and Mira asked again about Open Studios.

"I don't know," Hen said. "I just got my space set up, like yesterday. It seems strange to suddenly have people parade through."

"You should do it," Lloyd said.

"Yeah, you should," Mira said.

"Have you been to Open Studios before?" Hen asked Mira.

"Yeah. Every year we've been here. I go, anyway. Sometimes Matthew does. It's fun, you should definitely do it. You might even sell something. That's where I bought these prints."

Mira indicated the framed prints on the wall, and Hen felt bad for thinking they'd come from a furniture store. Matthew returned with the drinks, Hen noticing that he'd brought a can of ginger ale for himself.

"Tell us about your art," Mira said.

It was not Hen's favorite thing, explaining her profession, but she did her best, and Lloyd, always her champion, jumped in and took over. Since college, Hen had been a printmaker, first in woodblocks and later using copper or zinc plates. For years, she created works of pure imagination: grotesque, surreal tableaus, usually with a caption. These illustrations were made to look like they came from books, often terrifying children's books that didn't exist except in her mind. She'd been fairly successful all through her twenties, selected for several group shows and even profiled in a New England arts magazine, but she'd always had to supplement her income by working in art supply stores and sometimes as a framer for a prominent Boston painter in the South End. All that changed when she'd been approached by a children's book author to create actual illustrations for the first chapter book in a proposed fantasy series. She'd taken the job, the book had done well, and that had led her to an agent, and now she was a full-time children's illustrator who only occasionally created an original piece of art. She didn't mind. Secretly, she felt happy these days to be told what her compositions should be. Her current cocktail of meds, which included a mood stabilizer, an antidepressant, and something that apparently boosted the antidepressant's effects, had kept Hen's bipolar disorder from rearing its ugly head going on two years, but she did feel that it had also removed all of her creative impulses. She could still do the pieces—still loved the work, really—but rarely had an idea these days for something original. Not that she told any of this to Mira and Matthew. Mira was mostly interested in the fantasy books, since she'd heard of them, and was promising to buy the first in the series. Matthew asked her several questions about her artistic process, leaning in and listening intently to her answers.

They eventually moved to the dining room, where the food had been set up on warming plates on a sideboard: mashed potatoes, drumsticks in a bright yellow sauce, a green salad.

"This was how my grandparents used to serve food," Hen said. "On a sideboard."

"Where are they from?" Mira asked.

Hen explained that her father was British and her mother American and how they'd moved back and forth between Bath in England and Albany in New York during her childhood.

"I thought you had an accent," Mira said.

"Really? I thought I didn't."

"It's mild."

"Are you from . . . ?"

"I'm from California, but my parents were both from the north of England, by way of Pakistan, and they acted very British. All our meals, including breakfast, were served from a sideboard in the dining room."

"I like it," Hen said.

Conversation at dinner was fine but never really kicked into anything lively. It was a lot of talk about their respective jobs, the neighborhood, the ridiculously overpriced housing market. Whenever Matthew spoke it was to ask more questions, usually of Hen. She realized, after he'd asked her if she'd survived the block party, that he was fairly perceptive. Lloyd, hoping to turn the conversation to sports, asked Matthew if he did any coaching at Sussex Hall. Matthew said he didn't ("the only sport I was ever good at was badminton"). Hen, who, right out of college, had spent a disastrous three months trying to teach a preschool art class, asked him if he found teaching to be emotionally draining, and he said that the first two years were hard. "But now I love it. I love the students, learning about their lives, watching them change so much from freshman year to senior year." Hen could sense Lloyd, steadily working his way through several glasses of wine, stifling yawns.

After dessert—a warm rice pudding with raisins and cardamom—Hen said that they should be going, that they were driving the next morning to Lloyd's parents' house. True, but they weren't leaving until late morning, at the earliest.

The two couples stood in the front hallway, Hen saying again how much she loved the way they'd decorated the house.

"Oh, we should give you a tour," Mira said. "We should've done it earlier."

Surprisingly, Lloyd agreed, and Mira took them through the renovated kitchen, showed them the deck they'd added off the back of the house, and then brought them both into Matthew's downstairs office. It was a room so different from the light colors and clean lines of the rest of the house that Hen felt it was like walking into an entirely different house, maybe even a different time. The walls were papered in a dark green with a faint crosshatch pattern, the floor was covered in a well-worn Persian, and the room was dominated by an enormous glass-fronted cabinet filled with books and framed photographs. There was one small desk in the study, with a leather-padded chair; the only other place to sit was a corduroy sofa. Nothing in the room seemed remotely modern, and every available space was taken up by knickknacks or framed pictures, all in black and white. Hen, drawn to small objects and anything old, took two steps into the room and couldn't stop herself from saying, "Oh."

"This is all Matthew," Mira said.

Hen turned back and smiled, noticing that Matthew, who'd been doing the dishes through most of the tour, now stood nervously in the doorway. Hen felt awkward, like they were being shown something far more private than a study. "I love it," she said. "So many interesting things."

"I'm a collector," Matthew said. "Mira is the . . . what's the opposite of collector? A thrower-outer?"

There was a fireplace, and Lloyd was asking if it worked as Hen scanned the objects along the mantel. It was an odd assortment—a small brass snake, wooden candlesticks, a miniature portrait of a dog, an illuminated globe, and, in the middle, a trophy, the figure of a fencer in mid-lunge on top of its silver pedestal. For one terrible moment Hen thought she might faint. Her vision blurred, and her legs felt as though water were rushing through them, then she gathered herself. *It's probably just a coincidence,* she said to herself, stepping forward to look at the inscription on the base of the trophy. THIRD PLACE ÉPÉE, she read, then, in smaller script, it looked like JUNIOR OLYMPICS and a date she couldn't make out. She didn't want to get too close to it. She turned and, in what she hoped was a normal voice, asked Matthew, "Do you fence?"

"God, no," he said. "I just liked the trophy. I bought it from a yard sale."

"You okay, Hen?" Lloyd asked, looking with alarm at her face. "You look kind of pale."

"Oh, yes, I'm fine. Tired, I think."

The two couples congregated again in the front hall to say their good-byes. Hen could feel the blood moving back into her face. *It was just a fencing trophy— there must be thousands of them,* she told herself, as she praised the dinner again and thanked them for the tour, all while Lloyd had one hand on the doorknob, trying to escape. Mira swept in and kissed Hen on the cheek, while Matthew, behind her, smiled and said good-bye. She might have been imagining it, but Hen thought he seemed to be intently watching her.

Back outside in the cold damp air, after the Dola-mores' door had clicked shut, Lloyd turned to Hen and said, "You okay? What was that about?"

"Oh, it was nothing. I just got a little faint. It was warm in there, wasn't it?"

"Not really," Lloyd said.

They were already at their door, and Hen wanted to walk a little bit longer in the night air, but she knew Lloyd was eager to get inside and check to see if the Red Sox game was still on.

Lying in bed later, Lloyd asleep next to her, Hen told herself that it had been a ridiculous thought to have, that the world was full of fencing trophies, and that they probably all looked the same. *But it's not ridiculous, is it? Matthew teaches at Sussex Hall, and that's where Dustin Miller went to high school.*

CHAPTER 2

After Mira fell asleep, Matthew got up and went down to his study. He stood in the same place that the woman from next door had stood, about four feet from the fireplace, and stared at the trophy, trying to read its inscription. He could barely make out the date and place, and he had perfect eyesight, and he already knew what the inscription read. Still, she might have been able to read it. He'd been stupid—stupid and arrogant—to have the trophy just sitting there in the center of the mantelpiece for anyone to see. Still, what were the goddamn chances of someone actually making that connection?

She had, though, hadn't she?

Just looking at her, he could tell she had been ready to faint. He thought she was going to and wondered if her not-so-bright husband would be quick enough to catch her before she dropped.

Matthew felt the knot in his chest that he felt when he was anxious. He thought of it as a baby's fist, tightening and untightening. He did some jumping jacks to make it go away, and after he was done, he told himself he'd need to get rid of the trophy altogether, just hide it away.

That thought filled him with something he imagined was what grief felt like.

"IT WENT WELL, I think," Mira said again the next morning. "I really liked Hen."

"It'd be interesting to see her art," Matthew said.

"I know, right? Let's go to Open Studios. Do you know when it is?"

Matthew got on his phone to check what weekend was Open Studios, while Mira started to pull items out of the refrigerator to make breakfast. It was one of their few routines, a large, hot breakfast on Sunday mornings.

After eating scrambled eggs and hash browns made from leftover mashed potatoes, Matthew told Mira he had lesson plans to work on and went into his study, shutting the door. He stood for a moment in the dark room, breathing in the air, picturing how Hen had looked in his room. She was small, and dark, and pretty. Brown hair and large brown eyes, and slightly elfin features. The thought that she knew what he had done to Dustin Miller—even if she just suspected—filled him with both a feeling of terror and a feeling of something close to giddiness. Had that been why he kept the fencing trophy in the first place? Had he wanted someone else to know what he'd done? He picked it up. He would need to get rid of it now, that much was obvious. But did he need to get rid of it at this exact moment? Would the police be arriving at his house today? It was possible. And what about the engraved cigarette lighter that he kept in his desk drawer? Would anyone connect that with Bob Shirley? A tremor of sorrow coursed through Matthew. Their new neighbor was going to be responsible for his getting rid of his most prized possessions.

He breathed slowly through his nose, then thought of a way to get the souvenirs out of the house but not entirely gone from his life.

He went to the basement and found a cardboard box that seemed about the right size. He passed Mira on his way back to the study; she'd changed into yoga pants and an old T-shirt.

"You going for a walk?" he asked.

"No, just doing my yoga program on TV. What's the box for?"

He told her that he wanted to return some of the history textbooks he'd accumulated over the past few years back to Sussex Hall.

"You're going there today?" she asked.

"I thought I would. Give me an excuse to get out of the house."

"It's Sunday. You can bring them in tomorrow, can't you?"

"I was actually going to try and get some of my lesson planning done there as well. Write some dates on the whiteboard."

Mira shrugged.

"Come if you want. We can walk around the pond afterward."

"Okay, maybe," she said, and walked toward the living room. He watched her. He'd always loved her walk, the way she rose a little on her toes with each step. She'd told him that between the ages of five and thirteen the only thing she'd cared about was ballet, but that her dream had been crushed by her inability to grow much beyond five feet tall. She'd been a gymnast in high school, and she could still do a back handspring.

Back in the study, he wrapped the Junior Olympics

fencing trophy in newspaper and put it in the bottom of the box. He added Bob Shirley's lighter, the pair of Vuarnet sunglasses he'd taken from Jay Saravan's BMW, and, finally, the battered schoolboy's copy of *Treasure Island* that had belonged to Alan Manso.

He then hunted down several history texts lying around his study—books he no longer used in any of his classes—and piled them on top of the four souvenirs. Then he taped up the box and went to tell Mira he was going to school.

She'd just finished her yoga, and the living room was warm and smelled of her sweat, but not in a bad way.

"I'm off," Matthew said. "Should I wait for you?"

"No, that's okay. I have plenty to do here. How long are you going to be?"

"Not long at all," he said, grabbing the car keys and his sunglasses. He stood for a moment in the foyer trying to think if he'd gotten everything. Standing there, he realized that Hen or her husband, Lloyd, might be out in front of their house, or looking out the window. They'd said they were going somewhere, but what if they were back and saw him leaving with a box? Would it be obvious he was getting rid of the trophy? Fortunately, his driveway was on the opposite side of the house from theirs. He'd be visible to them for all of about ten seconds as he left the front door and turned toward his car. He could risk it.

It was warm outside, more like a midsummer day than late in September. Across the street Jim Mills was mowing his lawn again, even though it had been only a few days since he'd last done it, and the smell of cut grass and gasoline filled the air, making Matthew slightly ill. It had been one of his jobs as a kid, mowing the back lawn of his parents' house. His nose would run, and his hands would itch from the vibration of the push mower, and on wet days, the cut grass would clump underneath the mower and stick to his shins. He got into his Fiat and turned on the air conditioner. He put the box next to him on the passenger seat. Because of the smell of the lawn mower he'd barely even thought about Hen or Lloyd spotting him with the box. Probably a good thing that he didn't cast a guilty look toward their house.

It was a twenty-minute drive to Sussex Hall, a private high school with about seven hundred students, half of whom boarded and half who came from the surrounding wealthy towns of this part of Massachusetts. Built on a hill, all the buildings of Sussex Hall, except for the newish gym, were constructed from brick at the turn of the previous century. Matthew did not always love being a teacher, but he did love the Sussex campus, with its Gothic dormitories and its nondenominational stone chapel. He parked in a faculty spot even though it was Sunday and he could park anywhere. He entered Warburg Hall through the back door, using his own set of keys, and went straight down the narrow stairwell to the basement. As one of his extra duties, Matthew had taken on stewardship of the history textbooks, most of which were shelved in one of the closeted storage spaces in the finished basement. But he also had a key to the older section of the basement, filled with the extra lawn chairs used for graduation ceremonies and, behind those, the discarded furnishings—blackboards, mostly, and old school chairs. There was also a stack of boxes in the far corner that contained the original cutlery from the dining hall. It was there that he slid his box of mementos, sure that they would never be disturbed or found, even if someone were looking for them. And even if someone did find the box, he'd made sure to wipe any fingerprints off all the items, and he'd checked that his name was not in any of the old textbooks.

Back upstairs, after washing his hands in the faculty bathroom, Matthew went to his classroom to work on his lesson plans for the week. Most of his classes were ones he'd taught dozens of times, but this semester he'd agreed to do a senior seminar on the Cold War, and he needed to brush up. This week they were focusing on postwar reorganization. He'd been at his desk nearly an hour when he heard the loud metallic screech of the back door opening, then a timid "Anyone here?"

He stepped out of the room into the dim hallway and shouted, "Hello."

Michelle Brine came up the stairs, said, "Thank God. I hate being here alone on weekends. It gives me the creeps."

He wasn't surprised to see Michelle here. It was her second year teaching, and he was amazed she'd survived the first. Timid, mousy, and imbued with the honest belief that her students cared about history, she had faltered, frequently crying, through her first year. Matthew had taken her under his wing, offering up his lesson plans, his strategies for discipline, and then, toward the end of the spring semester, his thoughts on her personal life as well, coaching her through her relationship with her asshole of a boyfriend.

"I'm so glad I'm not the only one panicking and coming in here on a Sunday. I'm so behind already." She had followed Matthew back to his classroom. She wore jeans, something she never did while teaching, but he recognized her black blouse, buttoned to the top button, as something she sometimes wore with a skirt while teaching.

"It's nice in here on weekends, don't you think?"

"I hate it when I'm the only one. How long are you staying?"

"I was getting ready to leave, actually."

"Oh no," she said, unzipping her backpack. "Can you look at something real quick? It's something I'm planning with my sophomores."

After he'd gone over one of her lesson plans that had the students creating their own mock Constitution—"Maybe teach them the actual Constitution first," he'd suggested—she'd instantly launched into a new story about her boyfriend, Scott, how he'd played a gig with his band two nights ago and didn't get home until three in the morning. She went to look at his phone while he was sleeping in, and he'd changed his passcode.

"That doesn't sound good," Matthew said.

"I know. I know. He's cheating on me, isn't he?"

"Tell me exactly what he said when you called him out on it."

Matthew, who'd already texted Mira to tell her he was running a little late, leaned back behind his desk and did one of the things he was very good at doing. He listened to a woman.

CHAPTER 3

On Sunday Hen considered calling the police tip line or trying to get in touch with the lead detective in charge of the homicide of Dustin Miller—it was two and a half years ago now—but she knew if she was going to notify the police, she'd have to tell Lloyd, and she didn't want to do that quite yet.

Instead, after coffee and breakfast, when Lloyd went out for a run, she sat down with her laptop and typed "Dustin Miller death" into the search engine. As soon as the string of articles appeared on her screen, Hen felt a surge of nausea and excitement. Three years earlier, Hen had agreed to a med switch recommended by a new psychopharmacologist she'd gotten when Lloyd had switched jobs and their health insurance had changed. It had sent her into a manic period during which, along with the upside of getting a ton of work done, she became obsessed with the homicide of Dustin Miller, who had lived in Hen and Lloyd's old neighborhood. She'd actually been on a walk in the Huron Village section of Cambridge when she'd seen the EMTs wheeling a gurney topped with a body bag out of the Victorian down the street from her house. She'd stopped and stared, watched as more police cars and unmarked vehicles arrived and then two tall men in gray suits.

It was on the news that night, the suspected homicide of a recent Boston College graduate who'd been found dead in his home. At first, Lloyd, shocked as she was by the proximity of the crime, had been as interested as Hen. But as time wore on, as more details emerged, and as it became clear that the police, despite "promising leads," had not identified a single suspect, Hen found herself more and more obsessed, poring over every detail the police released and walking by the rose-colored Victorian several times a day. There had been no signs of a forced entry, and Hen assumed that whoever had killed Dustin had probably known him. He'd been found tied to a chair, asphyxiated by a plastic bag secured over his head with duct tape. There had been a few items missing from the house, including his wallet, a laptop, plus a trophy he'd received from the Junior Olympics of fencing. He hadn't fenced at Boston College—he'd played tennis—but he'd been a fencer at Sussex Hall, the private school outside of Boston he'd attended from sixth grade through twelfth.

Dustin had left behind a Facebook page, and Hen spent hours looking at it, not just his previous posts and pictures, but what friends had written since his death. Most of those comments were attached to his last post, a picture he'd taken of his street—Hen's street—the pear trees in blossom, a pink streaky sky above the roofs of the houses. In the corner of the photograph, a woman wearing a short skirt was walking away from Dustin. The caption read, "God, I love my new street." Hen went back and forth trying to figure out if he was simply referring to the blossoming trees, the pretty houses, and the spring in the air or the leggy girl caught in the picture.

"You're a guy, Lloyd. What do you think he meant by this picture? Was he talking about the girl?"

Lloyd had looked at the Facebook page for five seconds, before saying, "What does it matter?"

"He took that picture probably just hours before he was killed."

"You think the picture had something to do with why he was killed?"

"No, I didn't say that. It's just . . . you don't find it creepy?"

"I do. I find it very creepy, and that's why I don't want to spend all this time thinking about it and talking about it. I don't think you should, either."

Ever since she'd been old enough to pick out her own library books, Hen had always had a morbid streak, a preoccupation with death. She had never considered it any kind of liability—she'd won several art awards in high school with her dark, disturbing illustrations—but in her freshman year at Camden College, she'd had her first manic episode, cycling rapidly through bouts of wild self-confidence and crushing insecurity. She couldn't sleep, staying up late obsessively rewatching her season one DVDs of *Twin Peaks*. She'd fall asleep at dawn and started missing her morning classes. She had constant bad thoughts, her mind a fever of death-related imagery. She imagined elaborate acts of suicide and chewed her nails till they bled. Around this time, Sarah Harvey, another freshman on the hall, came down with the flu, becoming so ill she had to return home for the semester. A rumor went through Winthrop Hall that

Sarah's roommate, Daphne Myers, had purposely left the windows open in their shared room in order to try to make Sarah sicker. Hen became fixated on Daphne—she hadn't liked her from the moment they'd met on day one of freshman orientation—and convinced herself that Daphne hadn't been just trying to make Sarah sicker; she'd been trying to kill her roommate. It made perfect sense. Tall, blond, dead-eyed Daphne, a psychology major, was a psychopath.

Hen decided that her purpose—the reason she'd been placed at Camden at that particular time—was to discover the truth about Daphne. She began to watch her all the time, and the more she watched her, the more she came to believe that Daphne was an evil human being. In November, Daphne, who'd gotten friendlier and friendlier toward Hen—*Very suspicious,* Hen thought—told Hen that she was switching from psychology to fine arts and asked her what professors she recommended. She even showed Hen one of her art pieces, a pen-and-ink drawing that, to Hen, seemed like a brazen copy of Hen's exact style. It was a deliberate provocation, and Hen went first to her academic adviser and then to the local police, saying that she felt her life was in danger from Daphne Myers, who had already tried to murder Sarah Harvey. At both meetings, Hen had broken into hysterical tears. Her parents were notified, and Hen's mother arranged to visit, but before she arrived, Hen, at three in the morning, her skin electric with anxiety, her mind a buzz saw of terrible thoughts, went outside of Winthrop Hall in only an oversized T-shirt and threw a paving stone through Daphne's window. When Daphne peered out through the busted window, Hen charged her, slicing open a wrist on a piece of jagged glass. Hen was treated at the emergency room, then admitted to a psychiatric hospital, where she stayed for ten days, emerging with a diagnosis of bipolar 1 and a protective order banning her from coming within five hundred yards of Daphne Myers. She was charged with criminal assault.

Hen's father, a lawyer, tried to talk the family of Daphne Myers into dropping the charge, but they refused. In the end a plea agreement was struck, Hen agreeing to continued psychiatric treatment and community service. She also agreed, very willingly, to leave Camden and to never make contact with Daphne again. Her father asked the judge to seal the testimonies, and the judge agreed, but not before several local news outlets had picked up on the story. Daphne, to her credit, never spoke to reporters, and neither did Hen, of course, and the story eventually died, despite one feature article titled "Cat Fight Between College Freshmen at Camden College Turns Deadly."

"I was sure it was schizophrenia," her mother said, driving Hen back to upstate New York, "because of your uncle. But turns out you're just batshit crazy like everyone else in this family." She'd laughed, then apologized. It was what she did.

After a year back at home—six months spent in a hole so deep and so black she thought she'd never feel joy again, and six months in a gradual return to normalcy—she'd enrolled at the State University of New York at Oneonta. It was there that one of the professors introduced her to engraving, and she felt as though she'd found her life's purpose.

Lloyd, who knew all about the disaster that was Hen's freshman year at Camden, brought it up to her as she was becoming more and more obsessed with the death of Dustin Miller.

"It's different," Hen said, irritation making the skin of her chest and neck flush red.

"How is it different?"

"This is an actual crime, on *our* street. I'm not trying to persecute someone. I'm not paranoid."

"But you're a little manic right now, I can tell."

Later, when things got worse, Hen started to believe that Lloyd had somehow pushed a magic button when he used the word *manic* to her, that it began the three-month period during which she started to study every unsolved homicide in New England for the past ten years, looking for a connection with Dustin Miller. It was also during this time that she'd gotten into an argument with her shift manager at the art supply store where she worked part-time. She stopped going to work, telling Lloyd that she'd be a full-time artist. He said he thought they could swing it, but wanted her to at least give her notice at the store.

"You might need a reference one of these days," he said. "I just don't think you should burn this bridge."

"You're right," Hen said, but she couldn't bring herself to call the store. She simply stopped leaving the house, immersing herself in work and studying unsolved murders (she was now looking outside of New England for possible leads). Then one day in November she woke up late and confused, her body aching, and drained of any desire to ever create a piece of art. Lloyd came home to find her still in bed. He tried to talk with her but she wouldn't stop crying.

"We'll get through this," he promised. "But I need you to do me a favor, okay?"

"Okay."

"If you feel suicidal you need to let me know. You can't leave me, no matter what. You need to stay alive."

Hen promised Lloyd that she wouldn't leave him, and in the end, she kept her promise. For two months she lived in a world of dread and anxiety, her only constructive thoughts ones in which she imagined the way she'd kill herself. But she'd made a promise to Lloyd, even though down deep she knew he would be better off without her. Finally, after a day in which she'd gotten behind the wheel of their shared car with a plan to drive to the North Shore and drown herself in the ocean, she told Lloyd, when he'd returned from work, that she needed to be in the hospital. He drove her to the emergency room that night.

Hen spent two weeks in a psychiatric ward, then another two weeks in outpatient care, receiving, along with a new cocktail of meds, a series of electroconvulsive treatments. She began to feel better—not immediately, but over time. Her old world—a desire to create art, to see friends, to plan trips—returned. Over time, the terrible episode receded into the past. She was receiving more offers for illustrations than she had time to do, and her fixation on Dustin Miller, on unsolved murders in general, disappeared. One of the benefits of the electroconvulsive therapy was that her memory of the whole episode was hazy at best, and some of it was completely gone. She and Lloyd, who had always considered having children, made a final decision to not have any. Instead, they agreed to move out of Cambridge and find a larger house somewhere in the country.

Hen finished her coffee, grown cold in the mug. Now that she'd reacquainted herself with the Dustin Miller case, she was more convinced than she'd been the night before that her new neighbor was Dustin's killer. Most of what she'd read was old news, but there had been a large *Boston Globe* feature on the unsolved murder that had run in July, back when Hen was orchestrating the exhausting move ("We're never moving again, you realize that?" Lloyd had said), and she'd somehow missed it. There wasn't a whole lot of new information in the feature, but it included some details about Dustin's time at Sussex Hall, during which he'd been accused of sexually assaulting a fellow student. Either Hen had forgotten this detail or it was only being revealed now. No, she thought, there was no way she would've forgotten it. Not a chance. It made everything fall into place. The alleged sexual assault took place during that year's Junior Olympics of fencing, held in St. Louis, Missouri. Her neighbor Matthew Dolamore, a teacher at Sussex Hall, obviously knew Dustin—he'd probably been one of his teachers. Maybe Matthew knew that the sexual assault—never proven—had actually happened. Five years later, he murdered Dustin out of revenge, or a sense of justice, and took the fencing trophy. It was ludicrous, somehow, but also entirely possible. Hen needed to see the trophy, however, and make sure it had the correct date and place. Then, and only then, she would call the police. It was her duty, right? Maybe she could even do it anonymously.

Hen shut down her computer and stepped out onto her screened front porch, glancing toward the Dolamores' house next door. There was no car in the driveway, but, like their own house, there was a single-car garage at the end of the drive. Still, she remembered seeing a smallish, dark car there the night before. How was she going to find out the truth about the fencing trophy? She could try to sneak into the house while Matthew and Mira were away, or better yet, she could get herself invited over by Mira again. Maybe she'd send her an email, asking if she could take a look around their house again, to get some ideas about decorating. They had the same layout, after all.

It was warm outside, warmer than it was inside the house. Hen pulled off her sweater, sat on one of the rocking chairs, and tilted her face to the sun. She was in that position when Lloyd returned, dripping with sweat and breathing heavily from his run.

"I love it here," he said, as he held on to the porch railing and stretched out his legs.

"This house or this town?" Hen said.

"Both," he said. "How about you?"

"Both as well," she said, and stood up. The warm breeze held the smell of someone's cookout, and Hen was suddenly hungry.

CHAPTER 4

Mira rarely went into his office, but Matthew found her there on Sunday night. She was brushing her teeth, looking at the books on the shelf.

"I need something new to read," she said, foam flying in specks off her lips. "Sorry," she said, and left the office.

She came back, toothbrush discarded. Her hair was pushed back under a headband, and her skin was clean of makeup, still shiny from the moisturizer she put on her face every night.

"How about this one?" Matthew said, handing her *The Pillars of the Earth*.

"It's so long," she said. "Plus I need a paperback."

"What time's your flight?" Matthew asked. He'd just remembered she was leaving the next day for Charlotte.

"Not till three in the afternoon. I have the whole morning free."

"Have you read *The Daughter of Time*?" Matthew handed her an old beat-up paperback; on the cover was a toppled chess piece, the king.

"What's it about?"

"It's a mystery novel, but it's about Richard the Third."

"Okay," Mira said. "I like it. It's small." She flipped open the front page. "Who's Christine Truesdale?"

"I don't know. I bought it used."

Mira, reading the handwritten inscription, said, "'Christine Truesdale. Finished March 17, 1999. Five stars.' Well, she liked it, anyway."

"You'll love it. It's very good."

"Hey, what happened to your trophy?" Mira said, looking at the mantelpiece where Dustin Miller's fencing trophy had taken center stage. Matthew had replaced it with a mounted replica of the Rosetta stone he'd bought at the British Museum.

He said, "I just got sick of it, I guess. Thought I'd switch it out."

Mira stepped forward and touched the Rosetta stone. "Hen from next door was pretty interested in that trophy, did you notice?"

"I didn't, no."

"Maybe she was a fencer."

Later, in bed, they both read their books, Mira starting *The Daughter of Time* while Matthew was finishing *A Distant Mirror,* probably the third time he'd read it. He loved all history, but nothing stirred him so much as the Middle Ages, something about the ubiquity of death, the cheapness of life, the rawness and aliveness of that time.

"You think we'll see them again?" Mira suddenly said.

Matthew knew she was talking about the neighbors, about Lloyd and Hen, but he said, "Who?"

"Hen and Lloyd, from next door."

"I'm sure we'll see them again. Plenty. They live right next door."

"You know what I mean. Socially."

Matthew and Mira had very few arguments—neither of them was remotely confrontational—but Mira did frequently bring up the fact that she wished they had more friends. She'd never brought it up when they'd been actively trying to have children, but she did now—quite often—after they'd decided that a child was not going to happen.

"I don't know. It wasn't the most sparkling evening, was it?" He felt bad as soon as he said the words.

"What? You didn't think it was?"

"It was fun. It was fine. It just wasn't . . . there wasn't necessarily a spark."

Mira rubbed a finger against her temple. "I thought I had a spark with Hen. A little bit, anyway. She was really interesting, didn't you think?"

"I did. You should get together with her. We don't need to do things as a couple, always."

"Yes, I know. It would be nice if it worked out, though."

"Ask her to lunch sometime," Matthew said.

"I will," Mira said, then added, "You were not a fan of Lloyd, huh?"

"Eh," Matthew said. "He was okay. Struck me as a poor match for Hen. He lucked out there."

"You always say that."

"I'm usually right."

They went back to reading. As usual, Mira put her book on her bedside table first, turned her lamp off, and curled into Matthew. "I don't know where I'd be without you," she said, as she did every night, at least whenever they were in bed together. It was her way of saying good night. Also, it was a kind of a prayer, Matthew thought. He'd almost mentioned that to her once, but realized that it made him sound like he was calling himself a god.

Matthew kept reading until Mira had fallen asleep. It took her only about ten minutes. She would curl away from him, and her breathing would slow, and, more often than not, she would mutter unintelligible words to herself. Matthew shut his own book, turned off his lamp, and lay on his back. The room was a hazy gray, never completely black like the bedroom he'd slept in for the first seventeen years of his life. He was wide-awake; he always was when he started the process of falling to sleep. It was his favorite time of the day, and he considered his options, considered what story he would recount to himself as he fell asleep. Lately, it had been one of two. In the first, he'd travel back in time—one year ago, almost exactly—to when he'd driven down to New Jersey and murdered Bob Shirley in the apartment he kept secret from his wife. Bob, a town selectman who'd been friends with his father, had been old and weak, and Matthew had knelt on his chest while clamping down on his mouth and nose. The other story he'd been telling to himself of late had been what he'd do with his fellow teacher Michelle's boyfriend if he ever figured out how to be alone with him. That was really the bedtime story he'd been telling himself the most. But tonight, because of the fencing trophy—and what it had felt like handling it again after all these years—he decided to tell himself an oldie but a goodie. The story of Dustin Miller.

Matthew had thought about killing Dustin ever since Courtney Cheigh accused him of rape while the two had been on a trip to St. Louis for a fencing tournament. Some teachers at the time had actually sided with Dustin, while most held back, saying they needed to hear both sides, but Matthew, who'd despised that cocky, insignificant shit even when he'd had him in freshman American history, knew that Dustin was guilty. And he knew that, one day, he would mete out justice. Time was on his side—it always was—and after Dustin had graduated from Boston College, he'd conveniently posted on his Facebook page the actual address of the apartment in Cambridge that his parents, no doubt, were renting for him.

All through late winter and into early spring, Matthew spent time in Huron Village, watching Dustin. He did this only when Mira was away on business. He grew a beard, something he often did in the winter months, and wore a scally cap, and he never let Dustin get a good look at him. The closest call came one night at the Village Inn, the only bar in that part of Cambridge and a place that Dustin sometimes showed up at on Thursday nights. Matthew was in one of the back booths, drinking a ginger ale, when Dustin came in, clearly looking for someone, scanning all the customers. But Matthew felt Dustin's eyes pass right over him. He was looking for a female, either a particular one or just an available one. He settled at the bar, where he ordered a pint of beer and watched the hockey game on the television mounted in the corner.

The close call gave Matthew an idea of how he could kill his former student. Two weeks later—Mira was in Kansas City—Matthew returned to the Village Inn on a Thursday night. He didn't go in, but sat in his car across the street doing the *Boston Globe* crossword and keeping an eye on the entrance to the bar. Just before ten

Dustin, walking a little unsteadily, made his way down the street and pushed his way through the doorway into the Village Inn.

What happened next was a series of extraordinarily lucky events. Recounting them to himself made Matthew's skin tighten and his breathing quicken. It was like watching a suspenseful film for the second time and still feeling excitement even though you knew the outcome. Matthew, skirting through backyards, made it, unnoticed, to the rear of the condo-ized Victorian that Dustin lived in. He was on the second floor and there was a rear balcony. It wasn't easy, but Matthew stood on the railing of the first-floor deck and hoisted himself onto Dustin's balcony. He had hoped the back entrance was unlocked and it was. Matthew, wearing gloves and a balaclava, entered Dustin's apartment. He took a quick look around so that he knew the layout, then looked for a hiding place. He had hoped for a closet with an alcove, but the two closets in the apartment were both packed with junk—Dustin was one of those phonies with a tidy apartment that was only tidy because he'd shoved all his belongings out of sight. Matthew hid underneath Dustin's platform bed. And he waited, hoping that Dustin, when he returned, would be alone.

Not only did he return alone, but he also returned drunk. Matthew, under the bed, could hear the slam of the front door, the heavy footsteps, and then Dustin was in the bathroom just next to the bedroom taking a long, forceful piss. He was talking to himself—Matthew picked up, among other things, a protracted "Jesus Christ" as he emptied his bladder—and then Dustin went into the living room. Matthew expected to hear the television turn on, but there was nothing. Just silence.

He made himself wait for an hour, at least, then Matthew slid out from under the bed and stepped quietly into the living room, carrying his backpack with him.

Dustin was passed out on a reclining chair, still dressed, one hand holding the remote as though he had meant to turn on the television. It was a perfect situation. In Matthew's bag was a roll of duct tape, a stun gun, several plastic bags, even a jackknife, although the last thing Matthew wanted to do was cause any blood to spill.

Holding his stun gun in his left hand, just in case, Matthew duct-taped Dustin's legs to the footrest of the recliner, all while Dustin continued to sleep. He stirred awake only after a piece of tape had been wrapped around his chest and upper arms. "What the fuck?" he said, and Matthew hit him with a volt from the stun gun that doubled as a flashlight. While Dustin recovered, Matthew duct-taped over his mouth, then secured his head to the headrest. It was a handsome head, with blond floppy hair, the dimpled chin, the flawless skin. He was the worst kind of predator, one with the face of an angel.

Matthew turned the flashlight toward his own face, and when Dustin's eyes had adjusted and showed what Matthew interpreted as a flash of recognition, he said, "This is for Courtney." Then he pulled the bag over Dustin's head, taped it around his neck, and watched him die.

Afterward, Matthew spent a little bit of time in Dustin's apartment, looking for something to call his own. He'd already decided that it would make sense to take Dustin's wallet, plus his laptop, just to make it look like a robbery. But those he'd get rid of right away, unload them in some dumpster or landfill many miles away. No, he wanted something for himself, something he could keep. In Dustin's bedroom, he spotted it. A fencing trophy, sandwiched between a can of Axe body spray and a bottle of mouthwash. He lifted the dusty trophy and in the dim light was able to make out that it was actually from the trip he'd been on when he'd raped Courtney Cheigh. Just holding the trophy, Matthew knew he had to have it.

He left the way he'd come. It was a cold spring night and there was no one about. He got back into his car and drove to West Dartford, making sure he never exceeded the speed limit.

Somehow, thinking back to that almost magical night, Matthew finally started to relax. He spun onto his stomach and slid a hand down between his legs. It was how he liked to fall asleep; it was how he'd been falling asleep for as many years as he could remember, holding on to himself the way a climber might hold on to an outcropping of rock. Mira stirred next to him, mumbling words he couldn't understand. He was glad she was leaving tomorrow. Maybe it was time to start a new project in earnest. It had been a while. At the very least he could maybe arrange to see his brother while Mira was away. *That* had been a while as well, and Matthew worried that Richard, who knew that Mira didn't really like him, might think Matthew didn't, either. He'd check in with him tomorrow, see if he was free. He'd make himself pork chops. Yes, he was kind of glad that Mira was leaving. He was always glad when she left, but he was always glad when she came back. And wasn't that the definition of a happy marriage?

CHAPTER 5

She was under deadline—two new illustrations for a chapter book—but Hen spent Monday morning sitting on the west side of the house, sketching a little, but mostly looking out the window toward what she could see of the Dolamores' place.

The driveway was empty, and Hen assumed that Matthew had taken his car to Sussex Hall to teach. What Hen was waiting to see was if she could spot Mira leaving in her own car, a car she probably kept in the garage, not visible from Hen's vantage point. Mira had probably already left, even though Hen had been keeping an eye on her neighbors since about eight in the morning. Still, if Hen could actually see Mira drive away, then she would know with certainty that the house was empty. She could check and see if they'd locked their back door, the one that led directly into the kitchen. And if they hadn't? Well, entering the house, going to look at the trophy—how long would that take? Thirty seconds at most. Maybe the trophy would be from 1953, and then Hen could take a big breath and forget the whole thing. But what if the trophy was from the year that Dustin Miller was a ranked Junior Olympian? Either way, she needed to know for sure.

Hen stood and did some stretching exercises. She was not a patient person—never had been, really—and the waiting was exhausting. What if she just went over there and knocked on the door? If there wasn't any answer, and if she could see no sign of a second car, then she could test the doors. But what if Mira *was* home? What would she say to her? Well, she could always just tell her she was dropping by to thank her for having them over to dinner. It would be a weird thing to do, but it wouldn't be suspicious, exactly, would it? It's not like Mira would be telling Matthew later over dinner that "that nosy woman from next door came over to try and break into the house, but I was there and she had to make up some lame story about thanking us for dinner." Besides, Hen could come up with a better story than that. What if she told her she was dropping over because she wanted to get another look at the way they'd decorated their house? That she was trying to get ideas for their place? It was a better plan all around. If Mira was home, she'd probably be flattered, and Hen would be given a second tour. She'd be demonstrably nosy about everything, so that by the time she got to the trophy it wouldn't look suspicious when she went right up and read what was on it.

Deciding this was a good plan—and now hoping that Mira actually was home—Hen changed into jeans and a long-sleeved shirt, and went back downstairs. Walking toward the front door, she spotted Vinegar scooting along the baseboards, and her heart sped up. Lloyd's cat—she always thought of Vinegar, who merely tolerated Hen but loved Lloyd, as her husband's cat—stopped and looked at Hen.

"You scared the shit out of me, Vinnie," she said, and the cat meowed back plaintively.

Feeling guilty, Hen went down to the basement to check Vinegar's food bowl, which was empty, and his litter box, which was full. She amended the situation, and Vinegar even rubbed against Hen's ankles while she dished out the dry food.

Back upstairs, Hen had a moment when she couldn't remember what she'd been doing when she'd been interrupted by the cat, but then remembered. She breathed deeply, wondering again if it was a smart decision, but then stepped through her front door and walked to her neighbors' house.

She rang the bell, deciding too late that she should have brought something as a thank-you gift for dinner—a bag of muffins or something—but then the door was swinging open, and there was Mira, smiling.

"Hi, Hen," she said.

"Mira, hi. I hope you don't mind my just dropping by, but I was going to email, then decided how ridiculous it is to email someone when they live right next door to you. So I just came over. Is this a good time?"

"It is. Come in." Mira held open the door. She was wearing yoga pants and a threadbare University of New Hampshire T-shirt.

"I'm sorry to barge in," Hen said. "Were you working out?"

Mira smiled, her upper gums visible. "Ha, no! I'm packing. I'm going on a business trip this afternoon."

"Sorry. Please keep packing. I'll come back some other time."

Hen was backing up, but Mira shut the front door.

"Don't worry about it. I'm pretty much done, and my taxi's not coming until one. It's not a problem at all. Can I get you something? Some coffee?"

"Actually, Mira, I came by because I was hoping to get another look around your house. It's just . . . I got back to our place on Saturday night and it looked so plain, and now I'm just nonstop thinking about decorating ideas and where to put furniture. And since we have essentially the same house . . ."

"I get it. Happy to show you around again. Let me run up and change, and I'll give you the grand tour without the bored husbands looking on."

"Thank you. Perfect."

"You sure you don't want coffee? It's already made, in the kitchen. You can help yourself."

Mira turned and bounded up the stairs. Hen felt guilty for barging in, especially since Mira—who had been dressed beautifully on Saturday night—was probably one of those women who hated being seen in regular clothes. But then Hen reminded herself that she was on a mission. She entered the kitchen. The coffee did smell good, and there was a clean mug next to the coffee-pot, so she poured herself a cup. It was some sort of flavored brew, hazelnut or vanilla, the type of thing she would never buy for herself but enjoyed when she had it at someone else's house. She leaned against the granite countertop and looked at the clean, stylish kitchen. It was like looking at something in a catalog, everything perfectly in tune with the current kitchen fads. It had some sort of cork flooring, subway tile backsplashes, simple white cabinets, and stainless steel appliances. The kitchen in Hen's house had ornate rustic cabinets and a linoleum floor that had probably been white once upon a time, and it had come with a mustard-yellow refrigerator. Hen actually loved the vintage-y fridge but despised the rest of it. Still, if she changed it around she'd do something more exciting than what Mira had done with her kitchen.

"Oh, good. You got coffee." Mira was entering the kitchen. She hadn't changed, exactly, but she'd put on a sweatshirt—also with a UNH logo—over her shirt. It wasn't cold in the house, and Hen quickly decided that Mira was being modest, covering up just how much the well-worn T-shirt had revealed of her body.

"I did. It's delicious. Where are you flying to?"

Mira hesitated for a brief moment, then said, "Charlotte, North Carolina."

"Oh," Hen said, unable to come up with anything to say about that particular location.

"You know, I almost forgot where I was going. It's always the same. I stay at a Marriott that's near the airport and right next to a Chili's or an Outback."

"You don't like it?"

"No, I love it. It's just . . . it's not glamorous. You tell people you travel a lot for work and they think you're jetting around, living the life."

"I know you already told me, but you sell . . . educational software, right?"

"To school systems mainly. Charlotte is one of my biggest clients. I'm there a lot."

"Matthew doesn't mind?"

"That I'm away a lot? He says he does, but who knows? I'd hate it if it were the reverse. I don't like being alone, and I just don't think he minds it."

"So it all works out," Hen proclaimed, putting down her mug of coffee.

"Shall we do the tour again? Want to see upstairs?"

"Sure," Hen said. "If I'm not intruding."

They went so slowly through the house, Mira clearly thrilled to be able to talk about every design decision, that Hen began to worry they'd never make it back to Matthew's office. Upstairs, they looked at the master bedroom, Mira saying, "I think it's really important where you place the bed. Have you noticed the morning light that the bedrooms get?"

Hen said she had, but only because it woke her up at an ungodly hour.

They looked at the guest room, twin beds plus a quilt on the wall that looked Indian to Hen, and then they entered the third upstairs room, a room toward the front of the house with a sloped ceiling. The walls were painted a bright, cheery yellow. On top of a table were a sewing machine and a few stacks of fabric.

"My craft room, but, honestly, I never really use it," Mira said. "It was going to be a nursery, but . . ."

"You tried to have children?" Hen asked.

"We did. For about three years. It just never happened, and now we're okay with it. It makes life easier, not having kids, don't you think?"

"I do. Definitely easier."

"Not that . . . Are you planning—"

"No, it's off the table."

"Can I ask why?" Mira said.

Hen was surprised by the question, but not annoyed. "I have health problems—" she started.

"Oh, I didn't mean to pry."

"No, you didn't. I'm . . . I suffer from depression and, honestly, I'm just not willing to go off my medication, which I would need to do if I got pregnant. I'm also not sure that I want to pass along my brain to the next generation." She laughed to let Mira know it was okay to laugh as well.

"I'm so surprised," Mira said. "You seem like a really happy person."

"I'm doing really well now," Hen said, thinking, *I am a happy person, always have been. But that's just my personality, which has nothing to do with this broken brain that periodically and very convincingly tells me that I'm a worthless person who doesn't deserve to live.*

Then Mira said, "My grandfather, who I was very close to, was depressed, too."

"Yeah?" Hen said. One result of her decision to always be open about her mental illness was that people always seemed to have a story of their own, ranging from the trivial to the tragic.

"He killed himself when I was fourteen."

"Oh, no. I'm sorry, Mira."

"It was a long time ago. I tell myself that he was sick and that the sickness killed him."

"That's a good way to think about it," Hen said, and found herself warming up to Mira. It was a habit of Hen's, and not one she was proud of, that she was often interested only in people who'd suffered in some way.

They moved downstairs, looking again at the kitchen, Hen making sure to ask lots of questions about everything so that when they got to Matthew's office she wouldn't look too interested in what Matthew kept on his mantelpiece. After leaving the kitchen, and pausing briefly in the dining area, Hen was hoping they'd turn right toward the office at the back of the house, but they went through the living room first, Mira explaining in detail how they'd knocked out the wall to the foyer to open up the space. When they finally got to the office, Mira said, "Nothing in here, of course, has anything to do with me. This is Matthew's domain."

"I want to see how big the desk is, because we need to buy one ourselves."

They stepped into the room, Hen shocked all over again by how different it was from the rest of the rooms. Her eyes went immediately to the mantelpiece, noticing straightaway that the fencing trophy was no longer there. In its place was a flat wedge of rock with writing on it glued to a stand. Hen tried not to stare and let her vision sweep around the room, to see if the trophy had been moved.

"Do you want me to get a measuring tape for the desk?" Mira asked.

"Sure. Why not?"

Hen listened as Mira went up the stairs, probably to her craft area. She went closer to where the trophy had been. For a brief moment, she considered the possibility that she'd been confused the night of the dinner party, that she'd seen it somewhere else, but, no, she was sure it had been there, centered above the fireplace. It had been moved.

He'd moved it because he'd seen her looking at it. He knew she knew.

And Hen was sure now that Matthew had killed his former student. She was as sure of it as she'd have been if the fencing trophy had Dustin Miller's name on it.

"I found it," Mira said, coming back into the room with the measuring tape. She pulled out a length of the yellow tape, and it snapped back. Both Hen and Mira jumped, then laughed. Together they measured the desk.

CHAPTER 6

Matthew made himself a pork chop for dinner the way he liked it: a little salt and pepper, then cooked in the cast-iron pan with butter. Boiled potatoes on the side, and steamed broccoli. He put a heaping spoonful of applesauce right on top of the pork chop.

He ate the meal with a glass of milk while he watched the local news. Another private school, one in the western part of the state, had just admitted that seven former teachers had sexually abused students in the 1980s. Sussex Hall, as far as Matthew knew, had never employed any such teacher. There had been the scandal with William Roth, a first-year English teacher, who quit after he became romantically involved with one of the senior girls. This had been only a few years after girls were first admitted to Sussex Hall, and most of the older teachers blamed the incident on *that* fact, rather than William's inability to control himself. It turned out okay in the end. William Roth left the school, and Maggie Allen, who never lodged a formal complaint, went on to graduate at the top of her class.

After dinner, Matthew's brother, Richard, came over. Matthew had told him that Mira was out of town, and

Richard was taking advantage of her absence. There had been a time in the past when Richard and Mira could occasionally be in the same room together, but that time was long gone.

"Have a drink with me," Richard said, as Matthew poured him a large Scotch and soda, the same drink their father used to love.

"No, thanks," Matthew said.

They sat in Matthew's study. He knew it didn't make sense, but having Richard over to his study felt less like a breach of Mira's trust than having Richard in one of the rooms that Mira had designed.

"I was thinking about you last week," Richard said.

"Oh yeah?"

Richard leaned forward and pushed his hand through his hair. He had a widow's peak, another similarity with Dad, although Richard's hair looked like it hadn't been washed in a couple of days.

"I was, uh, driving down Merrimack Avenue, and I was at that four-way stop for about five minutes because a whole gaggle of *your* students were jogging by. Jesus Christ, Mattie. What was that, the girls' cross-country team?"

"I don't know. Were they in uniform?"

"Green, right? Half of them were in those tight little shorts. How do you stand it? Jesus, the flesh on them. I thought I was going to have a heart attack right then and there."

"I don't think of them that way. They're my students, and they're children."

"Exactly. You ever notice how even the fat on young girls looks hot? I mean, how do they do it?"

Matthew was able to change the conversation for a

little while, and they talked about their childhood, about Mom and Dad. It was the only reason Matthew even kept Richard in his life anymore, so that they could reminisce. They shared a history, a miserable history with miserable parents, and because of that they were bonded together. When Matthew had first started dating Mira, he had tried to explain the sophisticated cruelty with which his father had treated his mother, but could never explain it to her in a way she would get it. His father had very slowly shredded his mother's self-worth and confidence, reducing her to something that was only vaguely human. Porter Dolamore had a gift; he was a master torturer, someone with so much patience that he could remove just a tiny strip of skin from his victim every day, keeping the victim alive and in pain. Natalia Dolamore did the only thing she could to survive. She became the woman that Porter always thought she was, bedding half the married men in town. It was how she got her revenge, but it took its toll as well. She was a different woman after Porter died at the age of fifty. Quiet and morose, hardly ever leaving the house. She died herself three years after her husband was gone.

Richard had three more drinks after his first one, but Matthew made sure to mix the last one with far more soda than Scotch. He wanted Richard to leave. There was no way he could bear his presence for the entire night.

Before Richard left, he surprised Matthew by saying, "I saw your new neighbor."

"I have two new neighbors, Lloyd and Henrietta. They're married."

"I didn't see Lloyd, but I did see Henrietta."

"She goes by Hen."

"She looks like she'd be up for it," Richard said, his tongue actually darting out to touch his upper lip.

"Why do you say that?" Matthew asked. He was actually interested in Richard's response because he wanted to understand where it was coming from. Like their father, Richard saw every woman who came within his range of vision as a sexual object, just a piece of meat. The difference between Richard and their father was that their father had actually occasionally caught his prey. With Richard, Matthew believed it was just talk. If he actually ever got his hands on a woman, Matthew didn't think Richard would even know what to do.

"You can just tell," Richard said. "Look at the clothes she wears."

"When did you even see her?"

"When I came by a few weeks ago. She was out front, sitting on the porch with her legs up on the railing. I could see right up her skirt, saw the inside of her thigh. She saw me looking and didn't even flinch. She'd give it up in a second, let me tell you."

"I think you're wrong about that," Matthew said. "And I think you should probably leave. It's my bedtime."

"You offended?"

"No, not offended, Richard, but you sound just like Dad."

"He understood women."

"And you think you understand women? I'm the one who's happily married. That's more than you can say, and that's more than Dad could ever say."

"Calm down, Matthew. I'm just talking. Don't take it so seriously. Except for your neighbor. Take her seriously. She is going to be trouble." He raised his voice on the last word, spacing out the vowel sounds. Matthew, beginning to get an upset stomach, made Richard leave.

THE NEXT DAY, MATTHEW, still feeling a little queasy from time spent with his brother, had an unsettling moment with one of the students in his favorite class, the advanced senior seminar on the Cold War. The class met after lunch. Matthew finished his turkey and cheese sandwich and moved the desks around so that they formed a circle. There were only eight students in his seminar, and not only had they picked the subject to study at the beginning of the course, but Matthew had them present many of the topics. Today they were talking about the Yalta Conference, and Hilary Margolis, probably the brightest girl in this year's senior class, was leading the discussion. Matthew was sitting directly across from her, and as Hilary talked, she nervously uncrossed and recrossed her legs under her desk, and Matthew, unintentionally, saw up her dark green skirt, catching glimpses of her inner thigh and a flash of plain white underwear. It was the type of thing that Matthew saw on a daily basis—the girls at the school sometimes seemed oblivious of their young bodies, the flimsiness of their clothes—but, for some reason, seeing it right after a visit from Richard made Matthew think about it differently. He heard Richard's voice in his head—*she's up for it*—and even briefly imagined how soft the skin of Hilary's thigh must be. He felt the blood rising up through his chest into his neck and caught Justin Knudsen eyeing him with just a little bit of concern.

At the end of the day, Matthew sat in his Fiat in the school's parking lot. He blamed Richard for the way he'd looked at his student and for the thoughts that went through his head. He should never have had him over last night. Just because he was his brother didn't mean they needed to spend time together. They had zero in common.

Trying to calm down, he thought about what he might cook for dinner that night, and he decided he'd drive over to the fish market and buy a nice piece of center-cut cod, then he'd go to the grocery store and pick up Ritz crackers for the topping. It was his favorite way to cook fish, but Mira was not a fan, preferring salmon with a spicy Asian glaze.

He started his car, just as Michelle Brine was hustling across the asphalt toward her own car. She heard the Fiat's engine catch and turned her head, smiled at Matthew, and came over.

He rolled down the window.

"I wanted to thank you," she said. "Yesterday, I actually gave a full class lecture on the basics of the Constitution. I thought they'd go to sleep, but I think it was okay. I had them do their mock Constitution today, and it went great. They seemed really into it."

"I'm glad."

"*And* I used your tip to get Ben Gimbel to shut up, and it actually worked."

"Which tip?"

"He was talking, and instead of telling him to be quiet, I just stopped talking myself and stared at him. The rest of the class got on his case. It was something else." A warm gust of wind blew some of Michelle's long hair in through the car window. She gathered it up and refastened it at the back of her head.

"What about Scott?"

"Oh, God. It's been nonstop. I accused him of hiding

his phone from me, so he gave me his new code and said he only changed it because he saw some suspicious-looking kids"—she made quotation mark signs with her hands—"watching him punch in his code at the coffee shop. And then he handed me the phone and told me to check out anything I wanted to check out, but this was twenty-four hours after his gig, so he could have deleted anything he wanted to."

"Do you actually think he's cheating on you?"

"I don't know. Maybe. Probably." Matthew watched tears well up in her eyes.

"If he is, he doesn't deserve you."

"I know, I know. Look, I don't want to . . . You should probably get going."

"It's okay. Mira's out of town again. Just me for the week."

"Oh." Michelle's face flushed slightly. Matthew sometimes wondered if Michelle was secretly in love with him.

"I should get going anyway," he said. "Dinner to cook, lessons to plan, TV to binge-watch."

Michelle laughed, started to ask him what television shows he was watching, then stopped herself and backed away. "*Michelle,* stop blabbing," she said, still laughing. "Have a nice night, Matthew. Thanks again."

Driving home, the sun low in the sky, Matthew was, at least, relieved to be thinking about something other than his neighbor Hen and the way she'd looked when she'd seen the fencing trophy. Now he was thinking about Michelle's boyfriend, Scott, and how it was pretty clear that he really was cheating on Michelle. Where there's smoke, there's fire, he told himself. You don't change the passcode on your phone without having a reason. Matthew had never actually met Scott, but he'd seen pictures of him on Michelle's Facebook page. He was pale, with a sharp, bladelike nose and a full reddish beard. Unless Matthew remembered wrong, in one picture he'd seen Scott was wearing a T-shirt advertising his own band, the C-Beams. How hard would it be to confirm that Scott was a cheater? Then how hard would it be to liberate Michelle from the creep? The very thought excited Matthew. He could feel the adrenaline in his system, and he began to tap out the drumbeat from the radio on his steering wheel. He'd been living in the past for too long now, and it was time to create a new memory. Scott might be a worthwhile candidate.

Back at home, he made himself dinner, stupidly leaving the fish under the broiler for a little too long so that the Ritz cracker topping blackened a little. It still tasted good, though, and instead of eating in front of the television, he ate in his study, watching videos posted on the C-Beams' website. Their events page said that they were playing on Thursday night at the Owl's Head Tavern, practically walking distance from his house, and Matthew told himself that if he could ascertain that Michelle wasn't going to be there, he'd go by himself, get a look at Scott, see what he could see.

CHAPTER 7

I t was late afternoon, the worst time of the day for Hen, her creative low point when her energy flagged and she didn't know what to do with herself. It was too early to start thinking about dinner, and if she read, she'd fall asleep, and if she slept too long, she'd feel irritated and spacey for the rest of the evening. Today, however, she was pacing, trying to figure out what to do about her neighbor. One thing she could do would be to just call the Cambridge police and tell them what she had seen. It would sound crazy, but what if Matthew Dolamore had already been a suspect? What if her sighting of the fencing trophy would push them toward a deeper investigation, would allow them to get a search warrant? Who knew, maybe there was physical evidence at the scene of the crime—maybe even DNA—and that would convict him.

She went so far as to look up the Cambridge Police Department telephone number, but couldn't bring herself to call. There wasn't enough.

Her phone buzzed. Lloyd, texting her that he was on the commuter train, which meant that he'd be home in an hour. She went to the living room couch with her sketchbook, turned to a blank page, closed her eyes for thirty seconds, then drew the fencing trophy exactly as she remembered it, even writing the words she was sure she'd seen. THIRD PLACE ÉPÉE. JUNIOR OLYMPICS. Then she stared at her drawing. It looked correct to her: a fencer in mid-lunge on top of a circular pedestal. Hen went and got her laptop, bringing it back to the couch. She searched for "Junior Olympics fencing trophy." The images from the search were disheartening; first of all, there weren't many, and second, some of the trophies that were shown were trophy cups. But one picture did catch her eye, a teenage girl beaming at the camera and holding a trophy that looked very much like the one she'd seen on Matthew's mantelpiece. The photograph came from a local news website, attached to a story from eight years earlier: "Lubbock High School Sophomore Wins First Place at the Junior Olympics of Fencing." Hen enlarged the photograph, but it was too pixelated for her to see any writing on its base. But it did convince her that the trophy she'd seen at her neighbors' had come from the same event.

Lloyd arrived home, and Hen was startled. It felt like he'd only just texted her to let her know he was on the way.

He grabbed himself a Lagunitas from the refrigerator, poured it into his favorite beer glass, and settled down on the chair opposite Hen. "How was your day?" he asked.

"Fine. Did some work, took a walk."

"You go to the studio?"

"I didn't, but I'll go tomorrow." Hen was surprised to realize that she wasn't going to tell Lloyd that she'd been to the neighbors' house, that she'd toured the rooms again. It would only make him worry.

"How about your day?" she asked.

"Unremarkable," he said, then went on to explain the back-and-forth with an annoying client. Lloyd worked in public relations. "For my sins," he always said whenever anyone asked him what he did; Hen was never really sure what exactly he meant by that, especially since Lloyd loved his job. He'd recently been promoted to the head of social media marketing for his small firm, and he'd landed their biggest client, an up-and-coming microbrewery from just outside of Boston that was about to expand nationally.

"Wanna eat out?" Lloyd said after finishing his beer. "We have leftovers, too."

"Remind me again?"

"Chili and cornbread."

"Oh, right. It's up to you. I'm happy either way."

It was a warm night and they ended up walking into what amounted to West Dartford's center. There was a Congregational church, a convenience store, a café that was open for breakfast and lunch, and a tavern called the Owl's Head that served food and had occasional live music. There were seats available at the bar of the Owl's Head, and Hen and Lloyd each got a beer. He ordered a veggie burger and Hen got a bowl of clam chowder. The bartender, a tall, stoop-shouldered man with a handlebar mustache, remembered their names from the last time they'd been there. He even remembered the name of the microbrewery that Lloyd represented and said he'd checked out their website. The food came, and the baseball game began—the Red Sox were playing the Orioles, with whom they were currently tied in the standings, five games left in the season. Hen looked around the small bar, made to look older than it was, she thought, but cozy nonetheless, with brick walls, tap pulls made from polished wood, and even two taxidermied owls, one on either end of the bar. She wondered how many times she'd come here in the future, and the thought filled her with sudden gratitude. Her life was good. She'd come through foul weather and torrential rain to stand in the sun. Something about the feeling made her say to Lloyd, "I have a confession."

"Uh-oh," he said, but kept his eye on the game.

"Remember you said I was acting strange at our neighbors' house, at Matthew and Mira's?"

"When were you acting strange?"

"At the end when we were looking at Matthew's study."

Lloyd turned and looked at Hen. "I remember. You looked faint."

"It's because I saw something . . . Remember I asked about the fencing trophy on the mantelpiece?"

"Kind of."

"Do you remember Dustin Miller?"

Lloyd took a sip of his beer. "Of course."

"It wasn't reported immediately, but the police did reveal that one of the things missing from Dustin Miller's house on the night he was killed was a fencing trophy."

"Uh-huh."

"And do you remember where Dustin Miller went to high school?"

"Did he go to Sussex Hall?"

"He did."

"I don't know, Hen. That's a stretch."

"You don't even know—"

"You think that Matthew, our neighbor, killed Dustin

Miller and he took the fencing trophy and put it on his mantelpiece in his study?"

"It was a Junior Olympics fencing trophy—it said that right on it, and that was where Dustin Miller got the trophy from. And one more thing—let me finish. There was an accusation of sexual assault against Dustin Miller while he was at Sussex Hall. What if Matthew somehow knew or suspected Dustin was guilty? That would give him a motive for killing his ex-student."

"Not really," Lloyd said, swiveling his stool so that he was now completely facing Hen. He lowered his voice. "Even if he thought he got away with sexual assault, that wouldn't mean he would *murder* him. And take a trophy as what, a souvenir?"

"All I'm saying is it's a possibility."

"It would be a huge coincidence."

"Why would it be a huge coincidence? *Someone* killed Dustin Miller."

"No, it would be a huge coincidence that we lived on the same street as the victim, then moved to the same street as the murderer."

"Okay, yes, that is a coincidence."

They were both quiet for a moment. The Red Sox game had just been called for a rain delay, and groundskeepers were pulling a tarp onto the diamond. Hen instinctively looked toward the large front windows of the tavern to see if it was raining yet in West Dartford.

"To be honest," Lloyd said, "I'm more concerned right now with you than with whether our neighbor killed Dustin Miller."

"I'm fine. I promise."

"You weren't fine last time you became obsessed with Dustin Miller."

"No, I wasn't, but this is different. Also, when I was looking at the trophy, I could sense Matthew's eyes on me. It was like he knew I knew."

"Great."

"There's one other thing," Hen said.

"Okay."

"I went to their house today, and Mira was there. I asked her if I could look around again, try and get some decorating ideas."

"Seriously?"

"It wasn't entirely a lie. I did want to see their house again, even though I really wanted to see the trophy."

"And she let you in?"

"She did. She was really happy to see me."

"And so you saw the trophy again, and it had Dustin Miller's name on it."

"Not quite. It was *gone,* Lloyd. Matthew had moved it or gotten rid of it—either way, it's because he saw I was looking at it. I'm not being paranoid or obsessive, and I don't feel manic, but I *know*. Our neighbor killed Dustin Miller."

Lloyd was quiet for a moment, clearly thinking. Hen knew how his mind worked and knew that he was considering everything Hen had just said, and that he was also considering, as he always did, Hen's state of mental health. It was how he processed their world together, their marriage. Hen loved him, and she truly believed that if it weren't for Lloyd Harding, her life would be far worse. But because of all the times she'd relied on him for care, he now treated her with kid gloves. It had been that way ever since her last episode when they'd lived in Cambridge. He checked on her mood constantly, monitored her eating and drinking, made sure she was sleeping okay. She appreciated it—and loved him for it—but sometimes she missed the Lloyd she'd first known when they'd each answered an ad to move into a six-bedroom house in Winter Hill in Somerville. They were both recent college graduates, Hen starting a program—one she never finished—at Lesley University in art therapy, and Lloyd tending bar and working an unpaid internship in public television. They'd immediately bonded, mostly because the other four residents of the damp, drafty house were like a coven of vegan shut-ins. The house smelled of patchouli and body odor, and every item in the "animal-free" fridge was labeled with a note of ownership. Lloyd and Hen formed their own alternative unit, smoking cigarettes together on the unsafe balcony and buying food, including dairy-based milk, together.

There had been an instant attraction, at least from Hen's side. He was tall and skinny, with a bad haircut, but he had beautiful pale brown eyes and he always smelled nice, like coffee and cinnamon. But Hen was dating one of her fellow students, a very sincere comic book artist from the Midwest, and Lloyd was technically still with his college girlfriend, then in Moldova with the Peace Corps. When Hen and Lloyd first slept together, after a warm evening spent on the balcony with a gallon jug of Burgundy and a pack of American Spirits, it was almost combative, as though they were rushing to complete the act before the guilt stopped them. Afterward, they both swore it would never happen again. But two weeks later, a day before Lloyd's girlfriend—who'd suddenly quit the Peace Corps—was set to arrive, Lloyd crawled into

Hen's bed, with beer on his breath and tears in his eyes, and stripped Hen from the boxers and T-shirt she slept in. That night was the first time she'd had an orgasm just from intercourse. Lloyd left the bedroom having never spoken a word.

It was six months until they were officially together. By that point they'd both broken off from their respective partners—Hen did it easily, Lloyd not so much— and they'd abandoned the semi-commune in Winter Hill and both moved to separate cohousing situations that were only marginally better. In some ways, it was a stressful, terrible time for Hen. Lloyd, guilt-ridden over his college girlfriend, took out some of his self-loathing on Hen. They had many drunken fights and lots of frenetic sex, sometimes simultaneously. Hen wasn't happy, but, even now, she could remember that time so clearly, in the way that she couldn't always remember the years of contented happiness—marred only by her bouts of manic depression—that came later. And there had been a dangerous edge to Lloyd at that time. He'd been a good guy, but he was confrontational, sometimes belligerent, and always willing to call Hen out on her bullshit. Also, back then, when they'd had sex there was always a moment when Lloyd would take control. She could feel him objectifying her, and instead of it making her feel bad, it made her feel good, as though something was freed up between them. But ever since her first bout of depression that led to her dropping out of Lesley, that side of Lloyd had disappeared. He'd become a caretaker, overly aware of Hen's condition. These days they didn't argue, and when they had sex it was reverential, almost. She had mentioned that to her best friend, Charlotte, now married with four kids, and Charlotte

had laughed and said that dull sex had nothing whatsoever to do with Hen's mental health and everything to
do with the institution of marriage.

Sitting at the Owl's Head, Lloyd carefully figuring
out what to say, Hen imagined the Lloyd she'd first met
and what he would tell her. He'd tell her she was nuts, of
course, and that she was imagining things. But he would
never say that now, even if he thought it. When he did
speak, he said, "Maybe the best thing to do would be to
just make an anonymous call to the police and mention
your suspicions. And then be done with it. Either they
look into it or they don't. But it's not going to do you any
good trying to investigate if our neighbor is a homicidal
maniac."

"I did think of that."

"It will only work if you drop it once you make the
call."

"I know. It's probably the best thing to do. But what
do you *think*? Am I crazy or am I onto something? They
were at Sussex Hall together. He had a fencing trophy,
then got rid of it after I saw it."

Lloyd was quiet again for a moment. The Red Sox
game was still delayed, and rain was now pattering
against the windows of the tavern. They should have
brought umbrellas.

"Honestly, I think it's all a coincidence, honey. He
probably moves things around in that office all the time.
But make the call if you want, then stop thinking about
it, okay? It can't be good for you."

CHAPTER 8

On Thursday in the teacher's lounge, Matthew asked Michelle if she was going to see her boyfriend's band that night.

"God, no. I have sixty papers to grade. Why?"

"You know I live walking distance from the Owl's Head?"

"I did know that. Are you going?"

"I was thinking about it."

"Why?" Michelle said, and then laughed, instinctively putting her hand over her mouth, something that Matthew had noticed she always did when she spontaneously laughed. "I didn't mean that, really . . . they're a good band. It's just—"

"You didn't think they were my kind of thing?"

"I suppose so."

Dylan Hembree, one of the English teachers, entered the lounge and went straight for the coffee. Matthew noticed that the front zipper of his trousers was halfway down and wondered if he'd just taught a class in that state.

"It was just that I was thinking of eating out tonight," Matthew said to Michelle, "since I've been cooking for myself all week, and then I remembered that the C-Beams were playing at the Owl's Head."

"How's the food there?" Michelle asked. "I've only been there for drinks."

"Pretty good. I like their chicken potpie."

"You two going to Owl's Head to see Scott's band?" This was from Dylan, who'd gotten his coffee and was now edging in on their conversation.

"Probably not me," Michelle said, at the same time Matthew said, "Check your zipper, Dylan."

"Oh, thanks, dude." Dylan put his coffee down on the very edge of the collapsible card table that held the coffee maker. "Arrgh, embarrassing," he said as he zipped up his fly.

"I taught an entire day once with a poppy seed between my front teeth," Michelle said.

"I was going to get an early dinner at the Owl's Head," Matthew said directly to Dylan, "and I knew that Michelle's boyfriend's band was playing, so I wanted to know if I'd see her there."

"Man, I wish I could go," Dylan said, as though he'd been invited. "I'm swamped."

"Me, too," Michelle said.

"When's he going to play on a Friday night next?" Dylan said. "We should all go together. I haven't seen Scott in forever."

Matthew didn't know that Dylan and Michelle were friends and found himself a little taken aback. He was glad, however, that it looked like he'd be alone tonight to watch the C-Beams.

"If you do end up going," Michelle said to Matthew, "then introduce yourself to Scott. I've mentioned you, I think."

"I'll see," Matthew said.

The band started at eight o'clock. Matthew, who normally ate around six, made himself wait until seven before walking down to the tavern. It was dark out when he left the house. He could hear wind high up in the trees that lined his street, but he couldn't feel it. It was the perfect temperature, neither too cold nor too warm, and Matthew felt a rare sense of happiness. He was out by himself in the night, alone with the knowledge that Scott Doyle (Matthew found his full name on the C-Beams' website) was a possible new victim. It was an exhilarating thought, and Matthew felt himself walking faster, the wind now buffeting against him, pulling his blazer open so that he had to fasten its two buttons. He told himself to walk slower, that tonight was simply a fact-finding mission, a chance to observe Michelle's boyfriend, to begin to make his decision. He needed to be composed, tranquil. A line went through his head, something he'd learned in college when he'd taken an elective in the Romantic poets: poetry was "emotion recollected in tranquility." He thought of that quote often, applying it to his own life. Tranquility was his goal, not just after he committed a murder, but before. It was what made it meaningful, and it was what made him impervious to detection.

At the tavern he sat at a small table in the front room, toward the back but with a good view of the stage. Although he was not a drinker (that was Richard's thing), he ordered a Guinness from the young waitress, plus the chicken potpie. When his drink arrived, he took a small sip, feeling as though he were wearing a disguise. He looked around the small room and toward the back bar, and noted all the men there with their pint glasses filled with their beer, just like him. Some were alone, and some with wives or girlfriends, but they all had that empty-eyed, stoop-shouldered look of men who'd just barely managed to get through their day and were now rewarding themselves with cheeseburgers and alcohol. Matthew didn't recognize anyone in the restaurant. No neighbors or former students. It would have been okay if he had—he was fine with small talk—but it was a much better feeling to be anonymous.

When he was halfway through his dinner, the three-piece band began to lug their instruments onto the stage. Matthew recognized Scott from the website. He was in his midtwenties, with short hair and a full reddish beard. He wore dark jeans and a purposefully ragged oxford shirt half tucked in. As he was adjusting his microphone stand, a woman who had just come in from outside ran up and gave him a hug. The rest of the band acknowledged her, nodding and smiling, and then she moved toward the bar. Even though it was early fall in New England, she wore a short black leather skirt and a sleeveless shirt. She had dirty-blond hair and wore bright pink lipstick. Was she a groupie? More important, did the C-Beams even have groupies? They were about to start, and the place was full, but that was mostly because of people finishing up their dinners. It seemed that a few people had come in to hear the music, but not many.

When the waitress cleared his plate, she asked, "You staying for the music?"

"I thought I might," Matthew said.

"You should. They're good."

"They've played here before?"

"Once, I think. But I've seen them play a couple times in Lowell. That's where I live."

Matthew ordered another beer. He planned to drink it slowly, while watching the band play. Was the wait-

ress another one of the C-Beams' groupies, another of
Scott's possible infidelities? She seemed excited that
they were here, but maybe she was just making small
talk with a customer. When she came back with the
beer, he almost asked her where exactly they played in
Lowell, but he didn't want to seem too interested, didn't
want to be memorable. After she placed his Guinness
on the wooden table, he watched her walk back to the
waitress station, her gait reminding him a little bit of
Mira's. Matthew heard Richard's plaintive voice in his
head—*Jesus, that ass*—and almost smiled. The waitress was pretty, but she couldn't have been much older
than twenty. Her eyes had the startled look of a fear-
ful deer, wide open and jittery. She probably *did* have a
crush on one of the C-Beams. He studied the band again.
The drummer was clean-shaven and pug-nosed and had
a slight beer paunch, and the bass player was lanky to
the point of emaciation, with one of those pronounced
Adam's apples that Matthew found disconcerting to
look at. If the waitress did have a crush on a member of
the band, it was probably on Michelle's boyfriend, with
his hipster beard and high cheekbones. Matthew tried
hard to discern if he was actually handsome, but found
it hard to do. All men looked alike to him. They either
had fox faces or pig faces. Scott was a fox face, while
the drummer and the bass player both had pig faces.

The band began, playing a decent version of "Not Fade
Away." The drummer was probably the most talented
instrumentalist, but Scott was the dynamic member of
the group, even though he sang with an annoying na-
sal twang. Matthew's waitress was watching Scott, and
the blonde in the short skirt, now holding what looked
like a vodka and cranberry, stood and kept time at the

edge of the stage, her eyes also on Scott. After "Not Fade Away" the band played two originals, then did a Johnny Cash cover. A few more people came in to hear the music, filling the tables that had been left empty by departing diners. It was obvious right away to Matthew that they were a much better cover band than an original band. His opinion didn't change as they continued their set. Their own songs were sludgy and unmemorable, and every time they played one, the energy in the room evaporated. But their covers—"Paperback Writer" and Springsteen's "Atlantic City"—were clearly their most popular songs, some of the fans cheering when they began to play them. By the time they were playing their encore—"Positively 4th Street"—the Owl's Head was nearly filled, and a number of people, mostly women, were dancing in front of the stage.

It was almost midnight, and Matthew, after paying his bill with cash, exited the bar just as they were finishing up playing. In the four hours he'd been there, the temperature outside had dropped at least fifteen degrees. It was a dark night, clusters of bright stars visible above the tree line. He walked home swiftly, trying to decide if he should go get a sweatshirt before getting into his car, but decided against it. Instead, he immediately got into his Fiat, turned on the heater, and drove back to the Owl's Head, pulling into a space on the darkest side of the parking lot. He turned the car off, killed the lights, and slid down a little in the bucket seat. He had a good view of the front of the tavern, where a small group of smokers had congregated, including Scott, recognizable from afar by his large reddish beard. Next to him, not surprisingly, was the blonde in the short skirt. Matthew watched her grind out her cigarette under her boot, then wrap her arms around herself, shivering. Scott seemed to be purposefully ignoring her, talking with the skinny bassist, then helping the drummer load pieces of his kit into the back of a beat-up van. The blonde lit another cigarette as more customers departed the bar, getting into their cars and driving away. The parking lot was emptying, and Matthew felt a little bit exposed, even though it was dark where he was. But he had come this far, and he wanted to see if Scott went straight home or if he went somewhere else first.

After the drums were loaded in the van, the drummer drove away. Scott kept talking with the bass player, both of them smoking, and eventually, the blonde, after giving Scott a lingering hug, took off. Her car was parked near where Matthew's was, and he watched her sit for a moment in the driver's seat, still gazing toward Scott at the front of the bar, before she drove out of the parking lot. When her car left, Scott watched it go, then said something to the bass player, and they both laughed. Shortly after, they hugged—one of those man hugs that involved smacking each other on the back—and parted ways to go to their separate cars. The bass player drove off right away, but Scott leaned up against his car, a Dodge Dart—"He's had it since high school," Michelle told him once—and checked his phone, the light from its screen illuminating his face. Then he got into his car, but instead of immediately taking off, he just sat in the driver's seat for about five minutes.

Matthew wasn't surprised when the waitress—the young one from Lowell—came out of the bar and walked briskly to Scott's car, getting into the passenger side.

The car started loudly and pulled out of the parking lot, its wheels scattering gravel.

CHAPTER 9

Hen sat in her car across the street from the Owl's Head Tavern and wondered what Matthew Dolamore, also sitting in his car in the bar's parking lot, was up to. Who was *he* watching?

It was Thursday night. She and Lloyd had made fish tacos for dinner, then watched two episodes of *Better Call Saul* before Lloyd said he was going to bed to read. Even though it was early, Hen decided to go to bed as well. She had the new Margaret Atwood, and while it had been months since she'd really gotten into a book, she was still trying.

The bedroom was cold. She'd cracked the window earlier in the day for Vinegar, who loved to sit in open windows, but the temperature had dropped and the room was frigid. She shut the window, just as Lloyd, oblivious to any temperature fluctuation, came into the room, holding a new paperback in his hand. Something science fiction–y. He had the dazed look he got when he was getting ready to get into bed. She imagined he was already falling asleep, which made sense, since once he got into bed, he'd be asleep about thirty seconds after he finished reading and turned off his lamp. Hen, on the other hand, would lie in bed for at least forty-five minutes, her mind turning the day over and over, slowly revving down enough so that she could edge her way into unconsciousness.

Tonight was no different. Before Hen had even gotten into bed, wearing flannel pajamas she had to dig out from one of the large bins under the bed, Lloyd was deeply asleep. Hen began to read her book, but her mind wouldn't allow her to absorb the words. It had been three days since Hen had confessed to Lloyd her suspicions of their neighbor. Since then, she had done nothing more. Well, that was not entirely true; she had spent more time online, looking for any information she could glean about Matthew Dolamore. There wasn't much, and there wasn't much new on Dustin Miller's homicide, either. But she hadn't, as yet, gone to the police with her suspicions. And Lloyd hadn't asked her if she had, clearly hoping the whole subject would be dropped.

Hen put the book away, not bothering to mark with a bookmark that she'd made it all the way to page two, and turned off her own lamp. She lay on her back, her eyes on the ceiling, wide-awake. She could hear the *tap, tap, tap* of Vinegar's nails along the wooden floor of the bedroom, coming to check if the window was still open. It wasn't, but he jumped on the windowsill anyway, and Hen turned her head to watch Vinegar's tail twitching from under the curtain. An image came to her—a potential piece of artwork—of a human-sized cat tucked into a bed and a small, naked girl asleep on a windowsill. She imagined that outside the window, crouched on the bare branch of a tree, was a small, naked boy with large catlike eyes. As always happened when Hen imagined an etching, the entire image was instantly in her mind, exactly as it would look and exactly as it should feel. She got out of bed, went downstairs to the living room, and sketched the idea, just as she'd seen it in her mind. It felt good; she hadn't had an idea for an original etching in months, at least since before they'd moved to West Dartford. She wasn't sure her idea was any good—it was just a little obvious, the transposition of a pet and an owner—but something about the rendering of the sketch was working for her. It creeped her out to look at it, in a good way, and she felt the familiar buzz, the aliveness in her chest, that she got when she created a piece of art. She captioned it: "The boy was back again the very next night." She'd always titled her artwork as though the images were illustrations for a nonexistent book, part of an ongoing story.

She put her sketchbook away, already looking forward to contemplating the drawing the next day with fresh eyes. The problem was that she was now fully awake. She considered getting back into bed, trying to read again, but knew it was useless. Her mind was buzzing.

She went back up to the bedroom, put on socks and slippers, and got a thick cardigan to put over her pajamas. Vinegar had moved to the bed, settling down by Lloyd's feet. He eyed Hen with suspicion.

Back downstairs, Hen put the kettle on to make some herbal tea. Waiting for the water to boil, she stood in the living room looking out at the night. There were stars in the sky, something she'd rarely seen in Cambridge, far too close to the bright lights of Boston. The Dolamores' house was almost completely dark except for some faint light coming through the curtains of the downstairs living room. She was just about to turn away when movement from the street caught her eye, and she turned her

head to see a man walking down the Dolamores' driveway. A motion sensor light went on above the front door
as the man passed, and Hen could tell it was Matthew.
She expected him to enter the house, but instead he
got into his car. Hen checked her watch. It was almost
midnight. Where could he be going? And where was
he coming from on foot? The words *follow him* jumped
into Hen's head. He was clearly up to something, and she
might be able to find out what it was. Without thinking,
she grabbed her own set of car keys from the hook by
the front door and went outside, speed walking toward
the Volkswagen as Matthew's taillights receded down
Sycamore Street toward the center of town.

She thought she'd lost him but then spotted brake
lights, a vehicle turning into the parking lot of the Owl's
Head. Hen slowed down. Instead of following him,
she backed into a driveway across the road, immediately killing the engine and dousing her lights. It was
a risk, but less of a risk, she thought, than following
Matthew into the parking lot. And from there she had
a good view. Matthew, after parking, had turned off
his lights, and she waited for him to emerge from his
car, but he didn't. There was activity in front of the bar,
even though the lights that illuminated the Owl's Head
sign had been turned off. She could see a small cluster of people standing around near the entrance, but she
was too far to see what they really looked like. It did
seem, however, that the few remaining people outside
of the tavern might be members of the band. That was
confirmed when she saw a drum kit being loaded into
the back of a van. But Hen was most interested in Matthew, now sitting in his car on the outskirts of the lot. It
seemed as though he had purposefully chosen the dark-

est spot in the lot. It was clear that he was there to watch someone, just as Hen was doing. But who? And where had he been coming from before he got his car, when he'd been on foot? It did occur to her that maybe he was coming from the Owl's Head—it wasn't far—and that he'd returned in his car so that he could follow someone.

The van pulled out of the parking lot, then a woman got into a car by herself and left. A lanky figure with what looked like a large beard got into a long and boxy car. Matthew stayed put. She could just make out the outline of his head in the darkened car. The lights in the tavern dimmed, and Hen watched as a woman with long hair came out the front door and walked toward the long car, opened the passenger-side door, and got in. The car pulled out of the lot and headed west. Ten seconds passed, and Matthew's headlights went on. He turned out of the parking lot, following them.

Hen started her own car, glad to get the heater working again, and began to follow Matthew. His taillights—slanted circles—looked like widely spaced eyes. They were on Acton Road, heading toward Middleham, a neighboring town that was mostly farmhouses and pine forests. Hen tried to hang back, but Matthew was going slow. Still, would he possibly notice he was being followed, especially since he was following someone himself? Following two people, actually, since Hen had seen the woman get in the passenger seat. She decided to risk it, almost laughing out loud at the absurdity of the situation, tailing her neighbor in the middle of the night. But now that she was actually doing this, she badly wanted to know what was going on. She started to speculate, then stopped herself and concentrated on her driving, on keeping an eye on Matthew's taillights. They turned off onto a winding side street that cut through wooded areas, so dark that Hen's headlights seemed to barely cut through the blackness. She started to worry that this particular road—she hadn't spotted the name—was too isolated and that Matthew really would realize he was being followed. She also started to worry that she was going to get lost; she hadn't brought her phone with her, and it had been years since she'd gone anywhere without using GPS. But she also desperately wanted to know what Matthew was up to.

After taking several hairpin turns, Hen drove over a crest, and suddenly the landscape opened up, with moonlit farmland on either side, and for a brief moment, she could see the taillights of both cars ahead of her. She slowed. Up ahead, the first car turned off the road, its lights illuminating what looked like an empty parking lot.

Matthew passed by, and so did Hen, slow enough to see a posted wooden sign that looked like it was from the Massachusetts parks department. The sign had a map on it, and she guessed that the turnoff was into a small parking area that probably led to a hiking trail. She was turning her head back to see if the car Matthew was following had stopped in the lot, and she nearly sideswiped Matthew's car. He had suddenly pulled up on the side of the road about a hundred yards down. She went around him, drove another hundred yards or so herself, and pulled into someone's driveway, cutting her engine and the lights again.

She sat for a moment in the car, putting her hand on her chest to feel her heart thumping beneath her pajama top. She shook her head and laughed out loud. What was she doing? She told herself she should turn the car around and drive back home. Who knew what was going on? It was probably some sordid love triangle; Matthew had been involved with some woman, *or* some man, and now he was checking up on them. But it didn't feel like that. It felt like he was stalking someone, just like he'd probably stalked Dustin Miller in Cambridge before killing him.

Knowing it was stupid, she opened her car door and stepped out into the cold night, quickly shutting the door behind her to douse the interior light. She was still for a moment, a sharp wind pressing her pajamas against her body. She heard a noise, then watched as a slow-moving mammal came around the corner of the dark ranch house. They stared at each other, neither moving. As her eyes adjusted to the dark night, she could make out the fleshy tail and white face of a possum. As she opened the door and got back into the car, it hissed at her. It was time to go home. It had been a stupid idea, thinking she should sneak through the night to see what was happening in the parking lot.

She pulled out of the driveway, turning back the way she had come. She put her high beams on once she'd passed Matthew's car, still parked on the side of the road. She slowed down as she approached the parking area. The road curved, and for a moment, the light from her headlights illuminated the parked car in the lot. She could clearly make out Matthew—it had to be Matthew—stooping down by the car, peering through its window at the inhabitants.

Hen kept driving, reaching into the cup holder to see if her phone was there, even though she'd already realized she left it at home. Should she call 911 when she got the chance? Was he planning on attacking whoever was in that car, or was he just spying on them? And if he was just spying, was it because he knew them, or was it just something he did? Was he a Peeping Tom?

Her mind was moving so rapidly that she went the wrong way when she got back onto Acton Road and had to do a three-point turn. For some reason, now that she was returning, she was the most nervous she'd been all night. Her chest ached, and she caught herself chewing at the side of her thumb, an old habit. She couldn't decide whether to call the police when she got home. Had she witnessed an attack about to happen? She didn't really think that was the case. But Matthew was definitely stalking someone, for whatever reason.

As she drove down Sycamore Street, she could make out the front porch lights, fully ablaze, at her house.

When she got nearer, she saw Lloyd, standing on the porch in his robe. She pulled into the driveway, lowering her window as he came over. He looked both relieved and angry.

"Where were you?"

"Sorry," Hen said. "I took a drive. I never thought you'd wake up."

"You left the kettle on."

"Oh, Jesus. I totally forgot."

"You're still in your pajamas."

"I know, I know. Let's go inside, it's freezing. I'm so, so sorry."

Back inside, she hugged Lloyd and apologized again. He told her he'd been about thirty seconds away from calling the police, that he really thought something terrible might have happened.

"I never would have left if I thought you'd wake up. I was wide-awake, and the stars outside were so pretty."

"This has nothing to do with our neighbor, does it?" Lloyd asked.

"No," Hen lied, not really sure why she was lying. "No, nothing. I was just driving around looking at the stars."

CHAPTER 10

All night Matthew flitted in and out of sleep, the image of what he'd seen in Scott Doyle's car exciting and enraging him.

He'd pulled his car over on the side of the road, just past the entrance for the Pocumtuck State Park, then walked back to a spot where he could see Scott's Dart parked under a large maple tree along the edge of the Pocumtuck lot. He'd almost turned back, but decided to take a risk, walking briskly down to the Dart to confirm what was happening. He just wanted to make sure it wasn't something else, although what could it be? A heartfelt conversation? Were they doing drugs together?

He crept up to the car, its windows closed and slightly fogged, but he could see through the back window. The waitress was on her knees, her head pressed awkwardly against the door farthest from Matthew, and Scott was behind her, his jeans down around his thighs. Matthew looked for all of three seconds, saw Scott's pale ass frantically pumping, the Dart rocking slightly. Bile rose in the back of Matthew's throat.

A car swept past on Bingham Street, its headlights briefly touching the car. Matthew crouched, then jogged back to his own car.

He wasn't surprised by what he'd seen. He would have been more surprised if Scott had gone straight home after his gig. It wasn't just that Scott was a typical predatory male who would obviously use whatever tiny amount of fame he got from his band to seduce anything in a skirt; it was also that Michelle was a victim, one of those women who believed in the goodness of the human race. She believed that her students cared about learning. She believed that the arc of the universe bent toward justice. And she believed that her fox-faced, untalented boyfriend would be true to her. Because of all these beliefs, Michelle was probably doomed, but Matthew did have an opportunity to do something about it.

If he could find a way—a flawless way—to murder Scott Doyle, then he would do it. He would rescue Michelle.

The next morning, before he went to work, Matthew FaceTimed with Mira.

"I woke up this morning," she said, "and couldn't remember where I was. It took me five minutes to figure it out."

"What time does your flight get in?"

"Late. I don't know. I think I should be back home by midnight, though."

"I'll stay up," Matthew said.

"Don't be silly. Go to bed, then when I get home I can immediately crawl under the covers with you."

"Okay," Matthew said. "I can't wait." He realized, saying the words, that it was true. As was always the case, he looked forward to Mira's leaving, and he looked forward to her returning.

At school that day he saw Michelle only once, when they walked past each other in the hall during the lunch hour. She clutched a thick sheaf of papers in a manila folder, and her face was flushed, as though she were in a hurry. But she stopped as soon as she saw Matthew.

"Did you go last night?" she asked.

"I actually did," he said. "The band's not bad."

She looked surprised. "No, they're good, right?"

"I didn't say that," Matthew said, and they both laughed. "No, I did think they were good. Scott has a nice voice."

Michelle lowered her voice and said, "Any women there throwing themselves at him?"

"Honestly, I didn't pay that much attention. I went for dinner, mainly, and stayed for a while to listen to the music, but . . ."

"I was just kidding. *Half kidding,* as you know."

"I didn't see anything."

"Well, that's good. He told me it was a good turnout, that people stayed late."

"Hey, different topic," Matthew said. "I haven't asked you about your father for a while. How's he doing?"

"Not great. I'm going home to visit on Columbus Day weekend, and I keep wondering if I should go earlier."

"What does your mom say?"

"My mom is delusional, unfortunately. She tells me he's going to be fine and that I shouldn't bother coming back at all."

Matthew couldn't remember what type of cancer Michelle's father had, just that it was serious. "You should go anyway," he said. "Make Scott go with you."

"Yeah, right," Michelle said. "I think he has a show that weekend, but even if he didn't I'm sure he'd find some other excuse."

Students had started to fill the hallway, and Matthew realized lunch was nearly over. He and Michelle ended their conversation, and as Matthew returned to his classroom with just enough time left to eat his egg salad sandwich, he congratulated himself for getting the information he'd wanted to get from Michelle. Columbus Day weekend. That afternoon he'd go online to find out where the C-Beams were playing.

CHAPTER 11

Hen had slept very little. She kept imagining what it was going to feel like when she checked the news the next morning to discover that a couple had been found murdered in their car in Middleham. Then she'd try to convince herself that that wasn't the case, and if, God forbid, it was, then at least she would know who'd done it. At least Matthew Dolamore wouldn't get away with it.

But the following morning there was nothing on any of the news sites she regularly checked. She did searches for "Middleham" and "murder" and nothing came up. She was relieved, of course, but told herself what she'd seen had been someone stalking someone else. Just because he hadn't committed a crime last night didn't mean he wasn't going to.

After Lloyd left for work, Hen called the Cambridge Police Department from her landline and asked to speak to whoever was in charge of the Dustin Miller homicide.

"Detective Martinez isn't in yet. Can I put you through to another detective?"

"I'd prefer to talk directly to him. Can I leave you my phone number?"

The detective called her back twenty minutes later.

"Can I help you?" he asked, and Hen thought he was probably eating breakfast while he spoke.

"I have information that might pertain to the death of Dustin Miller."

"Okay. Can I get your name?"

"It's Henrietta Mazur, but I'd like to be anonymous. Not to you, but I'd rather my name not be made public in any way."

"I will do my best, I promise you, Ms. Mazur."

"You can call me Henrietta, or Hen."

"What information do you have, Henrietta?"

She told him the story about going to dinner at her new neighbors' and seeing a fencing trophy on view, and how that triggered a memory of having read about Dustin Miller's unsolved murder. She told him she wouldn't have thought too much about it except that Dustin had attended Sussex Hall and that was where her neighbor Matthew Dolamore was a teacher.

"What makes you think that the trophy you saw didn't just belong to your neighbor?"

"Because I asked him if he fenced, and he said he didn't, that he just liked the trophy. I think he said he bought it at a yard sale."

"And you didn't believe him?"

"There's another thing. I went back to look at the trophy again, and it was gone."

"When did you go back?"

"The dinner party was last Saturday night and I went back on Monday. Mira Dolamore, the wife, was there, and she gave me another tour of her house—"

"What did you tell her?"

"What did I tell her about why I was there?"

"Yes."

"I told her I wanted another look at her house, at how she had decorated it. It wasn't entirely untrue. We have the same house, the same design, I mean. But I really wanted to see the trophy again. There was writing on the base that I hadn't been able to read the first time."

"But you saw *some* writing."

"I am almost positive that I saw the words 'Junior Olympics.'"

"Not completely positive."

"I'm positive. I saw them. I don't know why I said 'almost.'"

"That's okay," the detective said. "So you went back, both because you wanted to look at your neighbors' house again and because you wanted a second look at the trophy. Did you see it again?"

"No, it was gone. It had been moved."

"You're sure?"

Hen was pacing. It was what she did when she talked on the phone. "I'm positive. It was there on Saturday and it was gone on Monday morning. He moved it or got rid of it, and I'm pretty sure it was because he'd seen the way I noticed it."

"At the dinner party?"

"Yes. I guess I stared at it for a little bit and asked him about it, and he noticed. I could sense that he noticed."

The detective coughed, then she could hear him sipping a drink, then he apologized. "Can I ask you why you noticed the fencing trophy in the first place? It's not an incredibly uncommon object. Did you make the connection right away? How did you even know there was a fencing trophy taken from the scene of Dustin Miller's homicide?"

"You reported it, didn't you?"

"We did, yes, but that was a while ago. You just re-membered reading about it?"

Hen told him how she used to live in Cambridge and that she'd been interested in the crime. She left out that she'd lived right down the street from Dustin—she could hear Lloyd's voice saying that it would be a *huge coincidence* to live on the same street as a murder victim and then the same street as the murderer—and she left out her obsession with the crime, with Dustin, really.

"I think it was all in the back of my head," she said, now looking out the second-floor window in the upstairs guest room. "The fencing trophy. Sussex Hall. And then I put it all together."

"So why are you just calling me now? Why didn't you contact me on Monday or immediately after seeing the trophy on Saturday?"

Hen had already decided to not tell the police detective about what she'd seen the night before. She knew it would make her sound crazy, following her neighbor in her car at midnight. She could tell him later, if she had to. "I just didn't know if I was reading too much into it, but as the week went on I got more convinced. I also looked up some stories about the case and read about how Dustin Miller had been accused of rape when he was in high school. I thought it might all be connected."

"Uh-huh," the detective said, then asked, "When did you move from Cambridge to Dartford?"

"West Dartford. Just in July."

"And what do you do, Henrietta?"

"Hen. You can call me Hen."

"Okay, Hen. What do you do?"

She explained that she was a children's book illustra-tor. She expected some comment or question—*That's interesting,* or *What books do you illustrate?*—but the detective just told her that she'd been very helpful and could he call her back if he thought of more questions.

"Are you going to question him?" she asked.

She thought he might be vague about it, but he said, "I will. I'll drive out myself. Do you know if he's around today?"

"As far as I know he is. He teaches during the day, but I think he gets home around four in the afternoon."

"I'll come out then. I won't mention you."

"Thank you so much."

After the call ended, Hen stood for a moment, the phone still in her hand, trying to figure out if she'd done the right thing. Her body, relaxing somewhat, told her that she had, and she hung up the phone.

CHAPTER 12

As Matthew pulled into his driveway at just past four, he noticed the dark blue Ford parked along the street between his house and the new neighbors' house. *Police,* he said to himself, just by looking at the vehicle. And as he got out of the Fiat, a man in a suit got out of the parked car and began walking slowly toward him.

Matthew turned, and the policeman, tall and angular, said, "Matthew Dolamore?"

"Uh-huh," Matthew said, and let a quizzical expression pass over his face.

"I'm Detective Martinez, Cambridge Police." He flipped open a badge, and Matthew looked at it.

"Cambridge Police?" Matthew said.

"I'm on a wild-goose chase," he said, smiling. "Do you have a moment to answer a few questions?"

"Uh, sure. What about?"

"Do you mind if we go inside?"

Detective Martinez followed Matthew inside the house.

"I've never been out here to Dartford. It's nice," he said. "Cheaper than living in the city, I'd think?"

"I wouldn't know," Matthew said. "Do you want to sit? Can I get you anything?"

"No, I'm good."

Matthew put his leather briefcase down by the coffee table and sat on the edge of one of the chairs while Detective Martinez settled into the sofa, his legs so long that his knees were higher than his lap. He pulled out a spiral-bound notebook and said, "This shouldn't take long, Mr. Dolamore, but your name has come up in an investigation, and I need to ask you a few questions."

"What investigation?"

"You teach at Sussex Hall, correct?"

"Yes."

"Do you remember a student of yours named Dustin Miller? He graduated seven years ago."

"He was murdered," Matthew said.

The detective nodded. "Right. So you do remember him?"

"Not well. He took one class with me. I don't think I would have remembered him if he hadn't . . . if he hadn't been in the news. Are you still investigating his murder?"

"It's unsolved, so, yes, we are. Some new information led us to believe his death might have had something to do with the time he spent at Sussex Hall, and that's why I was hoping you might be able to shed some light on that time of his life."

"I really . . . I barely knew him, to tell the truth. He was not a memorable student."

"Why wasn't he memorable, Mr. Dolamore?"

"You can call me Matthew."

"Okay. I will. And you can call me Iggy."

Matthew, besides being bothered by the detective's

presence, was also bothered by the detective's face. He was neither a fox nor a pig. He was something new, with his round cranium and sunken eyes, his small chin. Was he an owl?

"What was the question?" Matthew asked.

"You said that Dustin Miller wasn't memorable. I was wondering why that was. Why wasn't he memorable?"

"Well," Matthew began, somehow unnerved by the question, "you remember your best students and you remember your worst. He was neither. Not particularly bright, but not a problem."

"What about friends? Do you remember what type of friends he had?"

Matthew frowned as he shook his head. "No."

"Did he play sports?"

"Most of the kids at Sussex Hall play sports. I don't pay that much attention, to tell the truth."

"So you don't know anything about what happened when Dustin Miller went to the Junior Olympics of fencing?"

Matthew pretended to think. It was fairly big news at the time, a lot of gossip among the teachers. "It does ring a bell. Something bad, right?"

"He was accused by a fellow student of sexual assault."

"Okay. Now I remember."

"Do you remember Courtney Cheigh?"

"Again, not well. I think she was in my freshman world history class, and she took a seminar with me her senior year. Ancient Rome."

"Did she complete that class senior year?"

"No, now that I think of it. She left early that year. She transferred to Lincoln-Sudbury High School." *I was sad to see her go when she left. She had the palest eye-lids, almost appearing translucent, and she was small with narrow shoulders. Shortly after she'd arrived at Sussex Hall, she'd developed large breasts that she worked very hard to cover. It was probably the reason she switched from field hockey to fencing, because of the uniform, how stiff the material was, how much it covered. But she'd gotten excellent at it and qualified with Dustin Miller and Brandon Hsu for the Junior Olympics after all three did well at the New England qualifiers. She'd actually come to me, excited, after finding out that she was taking the trip. She wanted to know about the history of St. Louis, if it was worth going up inside of the arch. Dustin raped her in her hotel room. He'd managed to bring alcohol on the trip, and they'd both gotten drunk. After Courtney left Sussex Hall—I was amazed and proud that she'd stayed as long as she did—I overheard Dustin and one of his friends trying to figure out who had the biggest tits in school now that she was gone.*

"So what can you tell me about the incident at the fencing tournament?"

"I know she filed a complaint, but I'm not sure she ever pressed charges. I remember hearing they'd gotten drunk together."

"The trip wasn't chaperoned?"

"I know that the fencing coach went—he always did—and maybe one parent, but Courtney had her own room."

"You remember more than you thought you did." The detective smiled slightly, but it didn't change his sorrowful eyes.

"I guess I do. It's one of those things you hope to forget about."

"Did you have an opinion about the incident?"

"I'm not sure I ever knew enough about it."

"But you must have had some opinion, having taught both students. If it was a he said, she said type of situation, then who would you have believed? This isn't an official question, by the way, I'm just interested in your opinion."

"Do you think that what happened at Sussex Hall had something to do with Dustin Miller's death?"

"Nope, not really. To be honest, we're just following leads, and the more information I can get on this situation, the better. Again, I'm not looking for an official statement, I'm really just hoping for an opinion."

"It was a long time ago," Matthew said, scratching at his chin, trying to look thoughtful. "I don't want to be quoted on this or anything, but the way I remember it was that Dustin was a good kid. They both got drunk, and maybe he should have been more careful, but she should have been more careful as well. It was just one of those things . . . it happens. I don't think it would have been worth ruining Dustin's life over what had happened."

The detective smiled again with his thin lips and studied Matthew for a moment. "Thank you. That's very helpful," he said. He put his hands on his knees, as though he was ready to stand.

"Is that all?" Matthew asked.

"That's all. Unless you can remember anything else?"

"Like I said, I don't remember him very well."

"But he was a good kid, you remember that?"

"Well, he wasn't a bad kid, that much I can remember."

The detective stood, rising easily from the sofa, and so did Matthew. They walked together to the door, Matthew wondering if Detective Martinez was going to ask to use a bathroom or look around the house. This had to be about the fencing trophy, right? This had to be because his new neighbor had called the cops on him. Matthew almost hoped that the detective would ask to look around and that he could show him into his study, but once they were through the front door, the detective was offering his hand to shake, and Matthew was shaking it.

"You came a long way for not very much," Matthew said.

"Well, you never know. And it's a beautiful day for a drive."

Matthew hadn't noticed the day, but it *was* beautiful—dry crisp air, deep blue sky. "It's nice," he said.

"I love this area. All these nice houses. Lot of kids in this neighborhood? Good schools?"

"Yeah, the public school is good," Matthew said. "That's what I hear."

Matthew stood in the doorway for a few minutes and watched the detective drive away.

CHAPTER 13

After making the phone call to the Cambridge police that morning, Hen paced the house some more, then got herself a second coffee and tried to sit with her sketchbook. She still hadn't sketched the two remaining illustrations for the new chapter book she was working on. The book was called *School for Lore Warriors: The Anti-Claus*. It was the first in a series—all children's books these days were in series—and it was about a military school for teenagers that taught them how to fight supernatural creatures. Most of her commissions these days involved the supernatural. It wasn't her favorite type of book to work on, because she often had to imagine what make-believe creatures looked like, and the authors were never happy. She'd much rather do illustrations for young adult suspense, like the ones she'd loved as a teenager. Lois Duncan. V. C. Andrews. But these types of books just weren't that popular these days.

When she opened her sketchbook she saw the picture she'd drawn the night before. A large cat in bed, and the young girl on the windowsill. She'd forgotten all about it, and it startled her, especially the eyes on the boy who perched on the limb of the tree. She loved the drawing, as much as she'd loved anything she'd drawn for years, and suddenly, with an almost physical pull, she wanted to go to her studio and begin the process of creating a print. She bolted upstairs and put on her clogs, plus a light sweater that, because of several small holes, had recently been demoted to a work sweater. Downstairs, she got her sketch pad and her keys and went outside. She felt guilty, knowing that she should be spending any work time fulfilling her contract for the chapter book, but told herself that once she was in her studio she'd find time to work on *Lore Warriors* as well. She walked to the end of Sycamore, turning right onto Crane Avenue, then down the hill to the Black Brick Studios, where she'd rented her space. It was in an old textile mill, built next to the Scituate River, four stories in brick that contained just over sixty studio spaces. Hen's was in the basement, one of the less desirable studios because it didn't have a view. But it did have a utility sink, which she needed, and it was large enough to hold both of her printing presses, moved at great cost from her previous studio space in Somerville.

She entered the studios through the back entrance, a poster on the door reminding her that Open Studios was coming up soon. Being present during open studio weekends was one of the aspects of being an artist that she dreaded. The artists' studio she'd belonged to in Somerville had required all the artists to be present during the annual event. The first five years she'd been there she made the mistake of treating the event like a gallery opening; she'd put on her good jeans and stand around talking awkwardly with the people walking through. But the last five years she'd treated the weekend as a working weekend, keeping herself busy pressing out prints while people came through. No one ever seemed to mind, and it made it easier for people to feel like they could browse her work without commenting on it. And if people did talk with her it was often about the technical aspects of what she did: how to engrave a plate, what chemicals she used, how long it took her. Hen was always happy to talk about her process; what she didn't like talking about was where her ideas came from.

All the lights in the basement were off, which meant she was alone down there. Hen entered her studio and went directly to her drafting table, where she re-sketched the cat drawing onto a piece of paper the same size as the plate, then began to prepare the copper, sanding down the sides, degreasing it, then applying wax. While she did this she played an Ani DiFranco CD on her ancient player. At home she listened to music through a streaming service, but she'd always had a CD player in her studio spaces, and all of her CDs—she hadn't bought a new one in at least five years—were from an earlier time in her life, many from before Lloyd. That clunky five-disc player (it also had a cassette player) was like her own personal time machine. She might be growing older, and she did children's illustrations now instead of her own art, but the music had stayed the same. She got so immersed in her work that she didn't notice when the Ani DiFranco CD changed to Neutral Milk Hotel—she'd already gotten her diamond-point scribe and was beginning the process of etching into the wax. She'd just begun when she heard a distant door slamming, and all the lights except for her table lamp went off.

She yelled, "Hey," then walked to her door. The lights

all flickered back on at once, and a man's voice yelled out, "Sorry. I thought no one was down here."

"No problem," she said, as the man, younger than his voice had suggested, came around the corner into her hallway. She recognized him from the only members' meeting she'd been to, but didn't remember his name.

"Hi, it's Hen," she said.

"Right, I remember. I'm Derek." He was unusually short, with a heavy brow, and she wondered, as she'd wondered during the meeting, if he was just short or if he had some condition related to minor dwarfism. "Getting ready for Open Studios?" he asked.

"No. Just working. On the morning of Open Studios I'll come in here at the crack of dawn and put up a bunch of prints." Hen tried to remember what kind of artist Derek was. His clothes were clean and that made her think that he was a photographer.

"And a bowl of candy?"

"I put out a giant tub of the pretzels with the peanut butter in them. One year I put out a bottle of tequila with salt and lime wedges to see if anyone would do a shot."

"Did they?"

"Of course they did. Free booze. My studio turned into a party. I'll never do it again."

Derek rocked from one foot to the other. Hen thought he was going to leave, but he said, "Do you have some free time? Can I see some of your work?"

"Sure," Hen said, and he followed her into the studio, where she opened a box that contained some of the prints she'd planned to show during Open Studios. They were mostly original illustrations done years earlier, but a few were favorites of hers from her book illustrations.

"Wow, these are great," Derek said.

"Thanks."

"And dark."

"Yes, I have what my mother used to call a vivid imagination."

After looking through all the prints, Derek eyed the larger of her two printing presses. "How much do the presses weigh?" he asked.

"Honestly, I have no idea, but too much. I've decided I have to like this studio because I am never moving again."

"You'll like it here. It's not too cultish. Artists are encouraged to be involved, but if you aren't, no one judges you . . . Oh, wow, is that new?"

Derek was looking at her recent sketch, the one she was calling "The boy was back again the very next night." He looked at it for a long time, and Hen realized that the boy on the branch looked more like a small man. Like a dwarf, really, and Hen worried a little that he might find it offensive.

"It's like looking at someone's dream," Derek said. "It actually sent a shiver down my spine."

"Me, too," Hen said, then added, "That's the type of art I like, when it freaks you out."

Before Derek left, Hen promised him she'd take a break during Open Studios and come look at his stuff. She still didn't know what his stuff was, exactly. When she was alone again, she finished etching on her plate, the CD player now playing the *Lost Highway* soundtrack. She slid the plate into the acid bath, then quickly began one of the sketches for *Lore Warriors*. It was a scene toward the beginning of the book, when the evil Santa Claus is emerging from the fireplace. She sketched an idea quickly, one in which just his foot was emerging, then did a version in which a clawlike hand was visible as well, plus just a sliver of the creature's face. It wasn't half bad. She'd gotten so engrossed in the drawing that she worried she'd left the plate in too long. But after removing the wax, adding ink, and doing a first run through the press, it turned out perfect, one of the best things she'd done in a while. She ran several more prints, then quickly sketched an idea for the second illustration she owed the publisher. Before she knew it, Ani DiFranco was singing again, the player having cycled through all five discs, and Hen realized she was starving. It had been a good day of work. She locked her studio door, shut down the lights after yelling out to see if anyone else was in a basement studio, and emerged back into the bright sunshine of the day.

CHAPTER 14

After the detective left, Matthew went back inside the house. He had planned on making mulligatawny soup, one of Mira's favorites, so that she would have something to eat if she was hungry when she got home. Instead, he rooted through the freezer for a frozen dinner and settled on some French bread pizza.

While he ate, he began the process of finding out everything he could about his neighbor. She, or maybe the husband, had obviously called the police. It was the fencing trophy, of course. Hen (who didn't really look like a hen; she was a fox, the exact opposite) was the one who'd spotted it, who somehow knew about its connection with Dustin Miller. And now she'd brought the police to him, something that had never happened to him in his entire life. It had gone okay, he thought, or as well as it possibly could have. He did wonder why the detective hadn't asked to look around or asked anything about the trophy. He assumed that was because it would have made it far too obvious that he'd been turned in by his neighbor. And, of course, Matthew could have refused, could have asked that a search warrant be provided. No, it was clear that it was nothing more than a fishing expedition. And with the trophy gone, the police would have nothing to connect him with Dustin Miller.

Matthew did a search using "Henrietta," "Lloyd," and "wedding" and instantly got a wedding page. Henrietta Mazur and Lloyd Harding were their full names. He almost did a search for "Henrietta Harding" but realized there was a much better chance that she hadn't changed her name and searched for "Henrietta Mazur" instead. Because of her illustrations, she was all over the internet. She had her own website, plus she was on Twitter and Facebook and Instagram. There were surprisingly few pictures of her, but there were multiple images of her work: dark, intricate etchings that Matthew found intriguing. Many were from children's books, but he found a Boston gallery that had thumbnail pictures of some of her original artwork, and Matthew studied them. He didn't know too much about art, but thought that they might be brilliant. Genius, almost. His favorite was an etching of a family eating dinner—mom and dad and three pretty girls. There was a large roast on the table, and all the family members were eating pieces of it greedily, some with juice dripping down their chins. Underneath the table, although it wasn't obvious at first look, one of the girls was missing a leg, severed just under the knee. It looked freshly bandaged. The title of the etching was "Christmas that year came and went most pleasantly."

Henrietta Mazur's art was so interesting that Matthew, for a time, forgot why he was researching her in the first place. He found himself studying several of her pieces and beginning to wonder how much a signed print would cost. He could already imagine one hanging in his office.

Before shutting down his computer, he did one more search, using "Henrietta Mazur" and looking to see if there were any news stories about her. There was one gallery announcement, from eight years ago, and then there was a story about a Henrietta Mazur who had been involved in an incident at Camden College about fifteen years earlier. Matthew almost skipped it, thinking it was another Henrietta Mazur, but the phrase "Ms. Mazur, an art major who had won several awards in high school for her dark and arresting sketches and paintings" made it clear that it was his neighbor. She had been charged with criminal assault for attacking a fellow student. Matthew read all the stories he could find. It wasn't entirely clear what had transpired, but the basics were that Henrietta had had some sort of breakdown and had become convinced that a fellow student was trying to kill her. She'd raised these concerns with both her college adviser and the local police, but then she'd attacked the other student herself, winding up in a psychiatric hospital and then court. Reading the articles, Matthew got the strange feeling that, even though it was clear the young Henrietta had had a break with reality, maybe she'd been right. One of the articles had a picture of the other girl in the case—Daphne Myers—and Matthew recognized something in Daphne's dead eyes, even through the pixelated image on the screen.

And now Henrietta Mazur was after him, sending cops his way, probably spying on him. It occurred to Matthew that Henrietta's criminal past could help him, if it came to it. He suddenly wasn't nervous. He felt strangely calm and just a little bit excited that his new neighbor seemed to suspect who he really was.

That evening Matthew's brother called.

"When's Mira getting back?" Richard asked.

"Later tonight."

"Too bad. I was going to come over again. I have something to show you."

The last time Richard had said those words, he'd shown Matthew a truly disturbing website.

"Why are you showing me this?" Matthew had asked.

"Relax. They're just actors. I'm showing you because can you imagine if Dad had been alive when the internet was around? He would've thrived on this stuff, don't you think?"

"Sounds like you're thriving on it yourself."

"This shit, not really. I'm just showing you because I was thinking of Dad. Remember how we used to think he was one of a kind, you know, a true original, like Dracula or Frankenstein."

"I don't really remember that."

"Well, I thought it. And now it's pretty clear that there's a whole shitload of men out there who think just like Dad. Enough to support a website like this. It's a strange world, Matthew."

Richard had been almost thoughtful that time. He'd drunk too much, though, and Matthew had caught him masturbating the next morning in the living room, the laptop open on his lap, a look of shame and happiness in his eyes.

"What is it you wanted to show me?" Matthew asked on the phone.

"I met someone."

"Oh, yeah. Has she met you yet?"

"Not in the flesh, but we've exchanged a few messages. I wanted to show you some of the pictures she posts."

"I'll pass, thanks."

"You don't know what you're missing. When's Mira leaving again?"

"Not for a while, Richard. You're going to be okay, aren't you?"

Richard laughed, but said he'd be fine, and that was the end of the conversation. Despite being disgusted by his brother, Matthew worried about him all the time. And it wasn't just worry about his brother; he worried about what he might do. He knew, more than anyone, just what the Dolamores were capable of.

When Mira returned that night Matthew was already in bed.

"Shh, keep sleeping," she said as she slid in next to him, looping a hand around his chest and squeezing him toward her.

"Welcome home," he said.

"Your heart's racing. You okay?"

"I'm just so happy to see you," he said, turning and kissing her on her neck. She was wearing a T-shirt with nothing on underneath, and he slid a hand between her legs. She shifted, opening her legs for him. Quickly, before the feeling went away, he slid on top of her, pressing his face into the pillow next to her neck. He thought of his neighbor, what she might sound like if he were doing the same thing to her, then quickly pushed the thought away.

"That was a surprise," Mira said, after he had rolled away from her, and they were in the same position as before, Mira up against his back, her hand around his chest.

"I've missed you," he said.

"I've missed you, too."

"It was a long trip," Matthew said.

Mira laughed. "Not really, but I'm glad you think it was."

"What are you doing Columbus Day weekend?" he asked.

"I don't know. Why?"

"Wanna go away for a night?" he asked. "Maybe up to that hotel in Portsmouth?"

"The one with the clam dip?"

He laughed. "Yes, the one with the good clam dip. You would remember that part."

"I remember the rest, too. Yes, I'd love it."

"I'll book it tomorrow," Matthew said.

Before they fell asleep, Mira said, "Your heart rate is back to normal."

CHAPTER 15

Detective Martinez called just as Lloyd, home from the office, was rooting through the refrigerator.

"Can you hold on a moment?" Hen said, then told Lloyd it was her agent and she needed to talk with him in her office. Hen raced up the stairs, wondering if it had been obvious that she was lying. Once in her tiny office—the place where she struggled with all forms of paperwork—she said into the phone, "Yes?"

"I wanted to let you know that I visited your neighbor and we talked."

"And?"

The detective paused, and Hen knew that he was about to report that nothing was going to be done. "And he's a person of interest, that's all I can say right now."

"Oh," Hen said. "You think he's guilty?"

Detective Martinez laughed. "No, I didn't say that. Frankly, the interview produced nothing, really, but he was aware of the situation between Dustin Miller and Courtney Cheigh, so you've provided some valuable information. I'm calling to thank you for the tip."

"It wasn't just a tip. He's guilty, you know."

"Even if he did have a fencing trophy, it could have—"

"It's not just that," Hen said, pushing her foot against

the office door to make sure it was completely closed. "I know he did it. I followed him the other night, and he was stalking someone else. Hunting him."

"When was this?" the detective said.

Hen told him the whole story, about following Matthew while he followed the couple in the car.

"What makes you think that that behavior had anything to do with what happened with Dustin Miller?" the detective asked after she'd finished her story.

"I think it proves he's some kind of serial killer, or at least a serial stalker. There's something wrong with him. He's creepy."

"Trust me when I tell you that there are many creepy people out there. But most of them are not murderers."

"I'm sure you're right," Hen said, "but some of them are murderers, right?"

There was a lengthy pause, and for a moment, Hen thought the detective had hung up. Then he said, "There are many reasons he could have been following someone, very few of which would have anything to do with Dustin Miller."

"Yes, I know. But it was suspicious."

Another pause, and then, "Can I ask you to do me a favor, Hen?"

"Sure," she said, knowing what it would be.

"Let us take it from here, okay? If your neighbor is guilty of murder, then we'll get him, but it's not going to be helpful to us if you're following him around. And it could be dangerous for you."

"Sure," Hen said. "I understand."

"You promise, then?"

Hen laughed. "I pinkie-swear promise."

"I'm serious," he said. "It's not just for your safety,

but it could compromise the investigation. You understand that, don't you?"

"I do," Hen said. She nearly added his name—it was Iggy, wasn't it?—but it just didn't feel right.

"Okay," the detective said. "Thanks. And feel free to call me anytime if you think of anything else. I'll keep you updated as well if anything comes up."

"Thanks," Hen said.

Back downstairs, Lloyd asked, "Who was on the phone?"

"I told you. My agent. My original contract for the *Lore* book called for eight illustrations plus the cover, and now it's up to twelve illustrations."

"Have you done them all?"

"Almost."

"Are they paying you more?"

"They are. It's more to do with the time commitment. I'm supposed to have started on book two already, and I haven't even read it. How was your day?"

"Pretty good," he said, his standard response.

She got herself a glass of wine and pulled out chicken breasts, plus a head of broccoli, for dinner.

"Have you thought any more about Columbus Day weekend?" Lloyd asked, and for a moment Hen panicked, trying to recall their previous conversation. Then she remembered.

"Rob's party," she said.

"Right."

"Um, probably not, Lloyd, if that's okay?" she said.

Rob was Lloyd's best friend from college. He lived just over the Massachusetts–New York state line, about two and a half hours away, and he had a bonfire party every Columbus Day weekend. Hen had been many times in the past. She'd even had fun a few of those times, but Rob was a professional pothead and Hen had quit smoking ten years earlier. She occasionally missed the way her brain exploded with new ideas when she smoked, but she certainly didn't miss the crushing paranoia. Or the stupid conversations.

"That's okay," Lloyd said.

"You'll spend the night, right?" Hen asked.

"Oh, yeah."

"I'll go next year."

"You don't have to. I know he's not your favorite person."

"I don't have anything against Rob. I just don't really have anything to say to him. And I miss Joanna."

Joanna had been Rob's longtime girlfriend, a funnier, smarter, more sarcastic version of Rob. Hen hadn't been surprised when she'd moved out of their drafty farmhouse and gotten her own place in the Pioneer Valley, but, still, she missed her presence. Without her there, Lloyd and Rob quickly morphed back to their college personalities, and Hen felt like she was standing just outside of their pocket of pot smoke and dumb jokes, looking in.

"We all miss Joanna," Lloyd said. "Do you need me to do anything?"

Hen slid the slightly rubbery broccoli his way and asked him to cut it up.

After dinner, while Lloyd watched the Red Sox game, Hen went to her laptop and looked up the website for the C-Beams again. She was now somewhat convinced that the lead singer for that band—they'd been playing at the Owl's Head on the night she followed Matthew—was the bearded man whom Matthew had been following. It would make perfect sense. He'd clearly been part of the band—she'd witnessed him helping the drummer load up his van—or, at the very least, associated with them. Hen was now assuming that Matthew had gone to the Owl's Head to watch the C-Beams play, and then he went home, got his car, and came back to follow the lead singer, one of the last to leave the bar. The question, of course, was why?

His name was Scott Doyle, and Hen tried to find out more about him. She wondered, for example, if he had some connection to Sussex Hall. Was he a previous student? Maybe Matthew saw himself as a vigilante, killing off his most immoral students long after they'd left school. But all she could find out about Scott was information pertaining to his band. He had a Twitter account, but all he ever posted there was either links to his songs or plugs for upcoming performances. The C-Beams' next show, coincidentally, was the Saturday night of Columbus Day weekend, the same night as Rob's bonfire party. It wasn't at the Owl's Head, but at a bar called the Rusty Scupper on the North Shore. Maybe she'd drive there that night, just peek in. It would give her something to do for the night she was alone. And if she got a chance to speak with Scott Doyle, then she could ask him if he'd gone to Sussex Hall or if he had any connection with Matthew Dolamore. Because if he did, she genuinely believed he was in trouble.

And what if Matthew was there himself? What if he saw her? Well, then, so what? It would be a coincidence. And maybe it would stop her neighbor from committing another murder.

"Get out of there!" Lloyd was yelling at the television. His groan immediately afterward told her that he'd just witnessed a long fly out instead of a home run.

CHAPTER 16

'␣ve had too much already, Matthew," Mira said.

"It's not like we have too far to go to our room," he said. "We could also get dessert, if you'd prefer?"

"Ugh, I couldn't eat another bite. One more drink, okay? But only if you have one."

Matthew ordered a Rusty Nail for Mira and a second Guinness for himself. They were in the bar of the Portsmouth Arms, a four-story boutique inn on a pretty cobblestone street in Portsmouth, New Hampshire. Columbus Day weekend had started with a cold, stinging rain coming off the Atlantic, but by four o'clock on Saturday the skies had cleared, and the sun had appeared briefly to paint the city in a mellow pink light. Matthew and Mira had taken a walk along the waterfront, then returned to the hotel for drinks and the restaurant's signature clam dip. They'd split the prime rib special, a bottle of wine primarily finished by Mira, and now she was sipping a Rusty Nail.

"What's in this? It's good," Mira asked, her voice slurry. She wasn't much of a drinker, although, oddly, she loved the taste of alcohol. Two drinks was her regular limit.

"Scotch and Drambuie." Matthew sipped at his beer

as well, planning on dumping it into the nearby hanging plant if he got a chance. He was going to drive down to New Essex tonight, and he needed to stay sober.

"Okay, now I'm done," Mira said, finishing her drink, ice clicking against her teeth.

"Me, too." Matthew slid both of the glasses toward the bartender and asked for the check. Mira didn't notice that his beer glass was more than half full.

In their hotel room, she pulled her jeans down around her ankles and sat heavily on the made-up bed. "The room's spinning," she said.

Matthew helped remove the rest of her clothes and tucked her in under the covers, making sure to pull the sheets loose at the bottom of the bed. He didn't think there really was a chance of Mira's waking up, but if anything was going to wake her, it would be so that she could kick her feet free from the covers.

Matthew opened the window a little—the radiator in the room was hissing and crackling, and it was far too hot—then went to his suitcase and pulled out the few things he thought he might need: the stun gun, the telescopic baton, the jackknife, his vinyl gloves, and the fleece cap that would cover all his hair. Just touching each object was making his heart race. *Slow down,* he told himself. *It might not happen tonight. It probably won't.* But he knew that if the opportunity arose, if he managed to be alone with Scott Doyle . . . he did a silent dance, crouching and pumping his fist repeatedly, just to expel some of his nervous energy. Then he breathed in through his nostrils and put his coat on.

Before leaving, he bent down to Mira and whispered in her ear. "I'm taking a walk, honey," he said. "Can't sleep." She responded with a throaty sound, more annoyance than a reply. He thought of waking her and telling her again, but decided he didn't need to do it. His only worry was that she'd need to pee, and that would force her out of bed. Should he leave a note just in case? The desk in the room had a pad of paper and a pen, both embossed with the name of the inn, and he scrawled a note to say he was on a walk and he'd be back soon. He put a water glass on top of the note, covering some of the words, so that he'd know, when he returned, whether she'd read it.

He left the hotel room, taking the back stairwell that led into the rear parking lot of the hotel. He stepped outside into the cold night and pulled his gloves on. There was no one visible in the parking lot, but in the distance he could hear the whoops of a group of people out on the street, going from one bar to another.

He got into his Fiat and began the drive to New Essex. On the way, he thought of Mira, safe in bed, in a locked hotel room. No one could hurt her, even if they wanted to. And then he thought of Michelle, visiting her dying father while her boyfriend fucked a waitress on the side. A wave of almost suffocating rage surged through Matthew. If you gave a man just the smallest amount of power—a handsome face, the ability to sing, a little money—the first thing he'd do is destroy a woman, or two if he could. He allowed himself to briefly think of his father, the way he shrank the world so that he was its dictator, and how his mother had no choice but to live under his rule. Matthew had no choice, either. Neither did Richard, for that matter.

The green sign indicating that his exit was two miles away flickered in his headlights. He rolled down his window and breathed the salt-tinged air into his lungs.

He'd memorized the directions to the Rusty Scupper, having left his phone back in the room.

He passed through two traffic lights, crossed a short bridge over the inlet, then turned right onto Seagrass Lane, the road that led to the bar. With the window rolled down, he could hear the distant thump of a bass line as he passed the Rusty Scupper's parking lot. The air now smelled like low tide, marshy and dank, plus Matthew caught the distinctive tang of marijuana drifting in from a group of four figures huddled around a pickup truck.

He drove another two hundred yards and parked in the back lot of a small insurance agency. He'd studied Google Maps and knew that there was a footpath that ran along New Essex River toward the back of the bar. It was easy to find—a small sign marked it as the New Essex River Walk—and Matthew casually walked down the wooden pathway toward the bar. As he walked, a fish broke the surface of the river, and something scuttled through the stunted brush. Once he was near the bar, all he could hear was the familiar sound of the C-Beams doing their cover of "Positively 4th Street." If the previous show was any indication, they were near the end of their set. Matthew looked at his watch. It was nearly twelve.

He walked into the parking lot, quickly scanning vehicles, looking for Scott's Dodge Dart. He spotted it parked toward the rear of the two-story brick bar, just underneath the back patio where patrons smoked. It was next to a van that Matthew recognized as belonging to the drummer of the band. His own car was in such a perfect location, parked in the dark shadows, that Matthew couldn't suppress the buzz that was telling him that tonight was actually going to work. Things were falling into place.

Glancing around to make sure that no one was within sight, Matthew flicked open his jackknife and punched a hole in the rear left tire of Scott's car. The knife stuck briefly, stale air already escaping in a ragged hiss. Matthew yanked it free, then walked back to the river walk. There was a bench that faced the river, but if he twisted his body he could see back toward the bar, with a view of the Dodge Dart. He waited. Only one person passed him, a middle-aged man smoking a filthy-smelling cigar. Matthew put his chin on his chest and pretended to be asleep, hoping that the cigar smoker wasn't a do-gooder who might check and see if he was okay. He didn't.

The live music from the Rusty Scupper had ceased, and Matthew watched as patrons spilled outside and weaved their way back to their cars. Everyone was talking loudly, snatches of inane conversation reaching Matthew on his bench. In between keeping an eye on the bar's exit, Matthew looked at the river, black under the starless sky. But despite the darkness, he could feel its swiftly moving current, the water pulled by the ebbing tide back toward the ocean. Lights went on in the second-floor windows of the Rusty Scupper, the few remaining customers being shamed into leaving. The parking lot was nearly empty now. A middle-aged couple stood by a truck arguing about who was going to drive home. A set of double doors at the back of the building swung open with a metallic clang, and Matthew recognized the two other members of the C-Beams trucking out their equipment, the drummer beginning to load the same van that Matthew had seen that night at the Owl's Head. The bass player was helping the drummer with his kit. Where was Scott? Probably surveying the remaining groupies in the bar for his next victim. It was actually good that he wasn't there. Matthew was hoping that his bandmates would leave first and that he would have to change his tire alone. He knew it was still a long shot that Scott would be by himself in the dark parking lot, but if he was, then Matthew was ready.

Another twenty minutes passed and the drummer and the bass player both left. Shortly afterward, Scott emerged from the rear entrance of the building, but he wasn't alone. There was a girl with him, and although she was dressed differently—a tight dress that could have been a T-shirt—it was clear that she was the waitress from the Owl's Head. Matthew wasn't surprised she was there, but he was disappointed. Scott slung his guitar case into the backseat of his car, then they both got in. The engine started, and the Dart reversed swiftly along the tarmac, then stopped just as swiftly. Scott jumped out of the car, examined his back tire. Matthew heard an audible "fuuuck" float his way, then the sound of another door slamming shut. The waitress was out of the car as well, now crouched beside Scott. He could hear their voices—his exasperated, hers querulous—but not the words. Scott opened his trunk and pulled out a spare, plus what was probably the jack. He crouched by the car again while the waitress stood two feet away, her arms across her middle. Even from a distance, Matthew could tell she was shivering. Scott, wearing a fleece-lined jean jacket, had begun to jack up the car.

The waitress said something—the words were still unclear—and Scott, still focused on his task, responded without turning his head. The waitress went back to the heavy double doors and banged on them. Five seconds passed, and the doors opened, the waitress sliding inside.

Matthew felt a surge of adrenaline. He realized that, until this moment, he hadn't really believed he'd get his chance. But here it was.

He stood, pulled his cap farther down his forehead and around his ears, and surveyed the parking lot. There were still a few cars, but no one was visible. He whipped the telescoping baton so that it snapped to its full length, twenty-one inches of solid steel. With the baton down by his leg and the stun gun, just a precaution, in his other hand, Matthew walked purposefully, but not too rapidly, toward the Dart, then came around it to stand behind Scott. The car was jacked up, and Scott was trying to twist the lug nut wrench. He hadn't noticed or heard Matthew, who was right behind him. For five seconds, Matthew just stood there, the steel in his hand, savoring the immense power he had over the insect crouched in front of him. Then he reared back and swung, bringing the baton down with as much force as possible across the top of Scott's head. Scott made a guttural sound in his throat, then dropped onto his side, unconscious.

Matthew knelt on one knee, lifted the baton again, and brought it down as hard as he could on the same spot he'd hit before. Instead of a solid thud, this time the sound was more like a splintering crack. Matthew stood quickly, prepared to jump back in case there was blood. He very much wished he had brought a plastic bag with him and his duct tape, although he didn't think he'd have time. Besides, Scott was most likely dead. That in itself was enough satisfaction. He wondered if he should hit him again, just to make sure, but was worried about overdoing it, about his baton sinking into brain matter. He would never be able to stomach that.

He did crouch one more time, collapsing the baton by pushing its tip against the pavement. He studied the body for any signs of life, telling himself if he heard the double doors open behind him to just bolt back down onto the river walk.

Satisfied that Scott was dead—felled by two powerful strokes—Matthew stood. About twenty feet away, a woman in a knitted hat stood in the middle of the parking lot and stared back at him. Their eyes briefly met.

CHAPTER 17

H en opened her mouth to say something to Matthew Dolamore, but no words came out. He looked right at her—she thought there was recognition in his eyes—then he turned and walked swiftly away. She lost him almost immediately in the dark shadows of the Rusty Scupper.

"Hey," she managed to yell, her voice sounding strange and helpless to her own ears, then she jogged toward the Dodge Dart and around the back. Scott Doyle lay on the pavement, curled as though he were asleep. She shook his shoulder, knowing he wasn't going to respond, but he rolled over, his eyes open and staring. He managed a few garbled words, sounding as though there was liquid in his throat.

She pulled her cell phone from her jeans and called 911.

SHE'D ACTUALLY ENJOYED THE C-Beams. It had been a while since she'd seen a genuine bar band, a band that actually wanted the bar patrons to dance. She'd arrived at the Rusty Scupper just after they'd started playing and found a place at the bar, in between two sets of couples. She'd ordered a dirty martini—probably not the best bar to get a martini in, but she was craving one—and spun her chair so that she could get a look at the band, playing what she thought was a Kinks cover. She looked around the bar, trying to see if Matthew was there, but she didn't spot him. She hadn't yet decided what to do if he did turn out to be there. Probably just watch him. Try to make sure he didn't see her. She was slightly disguised, wearing jeans, cowboy boots, and a flannel shirt. On her head was a knitted newsboy cap, something she'd bought several years ago but never wore.

The martini came, its surface dangerously close to the rim of the glass, and she dipped her head and took a sip of the salty, ice-cold drink. She felt somehow good in her disguise, completely anonymous. What would someone see, looking at her? She really did wonder, since she had no idea. She knew she was attractive, but she also knew that there was something off-putting about her, something cold that people reacted to. She lifted the glass and took a larger swallow. Across the U-shaped bar were two women, one in a Patriots jersey and the other with tight jeans, a shiny black shirt, and spiky hair. Hen caught one of them looking her way. At one point in her life, Hen had been intrigued by same-sex relationships. For no good reason, she sometimes believed that if she'd been a lesbian, her life would be more interesting than it was. She still thought it, even though she savored her uninteresting life.

The band was playing a song she didn't recognize, and she assumed it was their own song. The Rusty Scupper had a small stage and a small dance floor, but people were actually dancing, even to the original. It was an unusual sight; Hen had become so used to going to see Lloyd's favorite bands, mostly arty lo-fi bands that attracted men in jeans and black T-shirts and with the beginnings of a middle-aged gut who stood and appreciated the music, their arms crossed. Occasionally, some of them would bob their heads to the beat, but they never danced. Here, there were two couples dancing, plus a group of middle-aged women clearly out on a girls' night. And there was a lone woman on the periphery of the dance floor, wearing a gray-and-white-striped T-shirt dress and high black boots. She looked too young to be at the bar, but she held a bottle of Miller High Life down by her thigh, and Hen could see that she was mouthing the words of the song. She must be one of the band members' girlfriends, and Hen wondered if she was the one who got in the car with the lead singer that night at the Owl's Head. It seemed likely.

She finished her martini—far too fast—and ordered a vodka tonic, telling herself to nurse it. Periodically, she'd look around the room, scanning faces for Matthew. When she got up to go to the bathroom, she passed a separate room that had two pool tables and wandered through it, just to make sure he wasn't in there. A man asked her if she wanted to play pool, and she told him that she was just looking for someone.

"Oh, he'll show up for *you*," the man said. He wore a Lowell Spinners cap, and Hen wanted to tell him he shouldn't wear a hat indoors, but remembered that she was wearing one as well.

"It's a she."

"*Nice.*"

Back at the bar, she felt a little light-headed and asked if they were still serving food.

"Kitchen's closed, but we have potato chips."

Hen ordered a Diet Coke and two bags of salt and

vinegar chips. She thought of Vinegar, Lloyd's cat, back at home, most likely asleep on Lloyd's recliner in the living room. And then she thought of Lloyd, at Rob's bonfire party. He'd be very stoned and talking rapidly with Rob or another one of his college friends. What would they be talking about? Years ago, it would've been music, or Lloyd would be going on about the documentary he wanted to make, a music documentary that would profile a band without ever letting the audience hear one of their songs. Or something like that. Now, they'd probably be talking about politics, the ways in which they could fix the world.

"Want to join us for a drink?"

It was one-half of the lesbian pair—the one in the shiny shirt. She turned her head to indicate her butch friend in the Pats jersey.

"Sure," Hen said, and followed her around the *U* of the bar.

"What'll you have?" the woman asked, after introducing herself and her friend to Hen. The band was playing a revved-up rockabilly version of a Beatles song, and Hen couldn't quite hear their names. She thought they were Stephanie and Mallory, neither of which fit the women in front of her.

"Narragansett looks good," Hen said, and Stephanie/Mallory ordered three.

They hung out and chatted while the band finished their set—half the patrons stepped out onto the deck to smoke cigarettes—and then came back on, playing "November Rain," then a Bob Dylan song that Hen liked but couldn't remember the name of. Hen and her new friends danced through the encore in the crush of the dance floor. Everyone smelled of smoke and sweat, and

most everyone sang along—"You got a lotta neeerve"—
and Hen forgot all about the reason she was here in the
first place. She was having fun—unironic fun—and she
had new friends.

Back at the bar, in the relative quiet now that the band
was finished, Hen told the two women she'd driven to
the Rusty Scupper all the way from West Dartford.

"Why?"

"I saw this band at a bar near me, and I was all alone
tonight, so I thought I'd go somewhere new to see them.
Glad I did." She sucked the foam off the top of her new
can of beer.

"That's a long drive back," said Stephanie (it was
definitely Stephanie—Hen had heard the girl in the Pats
shirt call her that). "We're right down the street if you
wanna crash on our couch."

"Oh, no, no. I'm fine."

"We're not hitting on you."

"No, I know. I just . . . I should get back."

"We could call you an Uber."

Hen suddenly realized that they were trying to make
sure she didn't get in a car and drive. She put her can
of beer down and said, "I'll be fine, but maybe I'll skip
this beer."

The lights popped on, and Hen realized the bar
was closing. She looked around. The place was nearly
empty, and in the glare of the overhead lights, everything looked a little shabby. She spun to look at the
stage, and the band had packed up and gone. "What
time is it?" she asked.

In the parking lot, Hen said good-bye to the two
women, hugging each in succession. She bummed a
cigarette from Mallory, who lit it for her before they

took off. It had been many years since Hen had smoked; she took two deep drags, then felt dizzy and ground it out on the paved parking lot. She got into her car, trying to assess just how drunk she was. Maybe it would be foolish to drive. Instead, she closed her eyes for a moment, almost fell asleep, then opened them again. The inside of the car windows had fogged up, and she opened the door to let some air in. There were now only a few cars in the parking lot. She unfolded herself from the driver's seat and bounced on her toes for a moment in the chilly air. The Rusty Scupper, filled an hour ago with people and music and drinking and dancing, was now a dark, unremarkable two-story block of brick. In the shadows toward the back, a long, boxy car looked familiar. She took a few steps toward it, as though she were being pulled. She heard a muffled shout coming from its direction, and the car seemed to buck a little. A feeling of real fear surged through her body, sobering her up. She took another two steps forward, then saw a figure appear behind the Dart, standing almost perfectly still, then moving fast, dipping out of sight. There was a sound like a hard tennis serve, then another sound, the crack of a bat hitting a baseball. Her legs almost disappeared out from under her, but she moved two steps closer. The figure stood up behind the car. He was in the shadows—how did she know for certain that the figure was a man?—and wearing a tight black cap, but light from somewhere caught his eyes as he stared back at her. It was Matthew Dolamore. He turned and ran.

IMMEDIATELY AFTER SHE CALLED 911, doors loudly opened behind her, and a woman—more a girl, really—

emerged, looked confused for a moment, then ran to Scott Doyle, now on his back on the ground.

"I called 911," Hen said.

"Is he . . . what happened?"

"Someone was just here. I think they hit him with something."

The door opened again and two men emerged, both Latino. One was beginning to light a cigarette as the other came over to Hen's side. "He okay?"

"I don't know," Hen said. "I called 911."

Scott was still conscious, saying something to the girl in the tight dress—Hen now recognized her from the dance floor earlier.

The girl said, "You're going to be fine. Just lie still."

Scott said something back, and she said, "Outside the Rusty Scupper. In New Essex."

Hen moved a little closer to see if she could hear his words, just as a light went on above the double doors, flooding the parking lot with fluorescence. The other man had gone back inside, probably to turn on the lights. In the stark yellow glow, Hen could see the extent of the head injury, a dark, bloodied indentation and a sliver of white that was either skull or brain matter. She involuntarily lifted her hand to her mouth.

"What state?" Scott asked the crouching girl, sounding as though he were speaking through a wet towel.

"Massachusetts, Scott. It's where you live?"

"I wish it was Maine," he said, and Hen, even from five feet away, saw the life go out of him.

The girl began to howl and shake his shoulders, then Hen heard the sirens and caught the distant pulse of red lights.

The EMTs were the first to arrive, followed by two uniformed officers in a police cruiser, one of whom asked Hen if she was a witness.

"Yes," she said. "I'd like to make an official statement. I know who killed him."

CHAPTER 18

Matthew had been in the interrogation room for just over an hour when his lawyer, Sanjiv Malik, arrived, wearing a slightly rumpled suit and with a two-day beard.

"Sorry," he said to Matthew as he settled himself into an adjacent chair. "I didn't get Mira's message until an hour ago. How long have you been here?"

"We got back from Portsmouth about noon and the police were waiting there for me. What did she tell you?"

"Everything she knows, which isn't much. You were arrested?"

"I agreed to come in for questioning, and when I told them I was going to leave, then I was arrested. They say they have a witness who positively identified me at the scene of the crime. It's ludicrous. I was asleep with Mira all last night, and—"

"She's given an official statement. You won't be here long. They've just made a mistake, is all."

"I don't even know . . . Who was it again who got killed?"

Sanjiv looked at his notes. He was distantly related to Mira on her father's side, although Matthew always suspected that Mira had been introduced to him as a potential husband around the time that Matthew and she were dating.

"The lead singer of the band that had been performing at the Rusty Scupper that night. They were called the C-Beams."

"Right. They told me. I did know that band because they played at a place near me called the Owl's Head."

"Oh," Sanjiv said.

"I mean, I didn't know them, but they were playing there on a night when I had dinner. It's just a coincidence. The only reason I remember it is because someone I work with knows a member of the band."

"Which one?"

"I think it was the one who got killed, but I'm not sure. The police officer said his name was Scott."

"Scott Doyle."

"I think that's probably him, but I never knew his last name. Who says they saw me there?"

"I don't know yet, but I'll find out."

Matthew had barely slept the night before, lying in bed while he went over and over in his mind the events that had taken place outside of the bar. Hen had been about twenty feet from him. He could see her perfectly, but he was in the shadows and there was no way she could know for sure that it was him. Plus, he had an alibi, an incredibly strong one. Mira would say he was there by her side all night. He doubted very much that she would even mention that she'd been drinking. And any physical evidence was now gone. He'd driven back to Portsmouth via back roads and pulled over at an abandoned gas station on the edge of a salt marsh. He'd thrown the baton, wiped clean of prints, out into the water, and he'd buried the jackknife and the stun gun, plus his hat and gloves and shoes, underneath a broken piece of asphalt where there had once been a parking lot. After that, he'd returned to his hotel room—no one had seen him—and he'd showered and gotten into bed, not even bothering to wake Mira.

The hardest part of the day had been trying to act surprised when they'd returned to their house on Sycamore Street and been confronted by two detectives with a search warrant for the premises.

"Matthew, can you think of anyone . . . Is there anyone you know who might want to mess with you?" Sanjiv asked.

It was a question that hadn't been asked yet by either of the two detectives.

Matthew took a breath. "Actually, I think there is someone," he said, and then proceeded to tell all about his neighbor and how he believed she had already sent a police detective from Cambridge to his house to investigate an old crime.

"Why do you think it's her?" he asked.

"Well, it's embarrassing, but I googled her, just because I was curious, new neighbor and all, and she has a history of accusing people of crimes they didn't commit. So, it's a possibility—ridiculous, I know—but for some reason I thought of her right away this afternoon when the police were there."

"What's her name?"

"Henrietta Mazur," Matthew said.

"You need to tell the police everything you just told me. Exactly as you told it, okay?"

Matthew said, "Okay."

HE WAS RELEASED JUST before five o'clock. Mira drove him home, and as they passed Henrietta's house, windows dark in the encroaching dusk, he craned his neck to see if he could see any signs of life.

"What are you looking at?" Mira asked.

"I want to see if our neighbors are home."

"Why?"

"I think that Hen was the witness who said I was at that bar last night."

"What?"

Back inside their home, after drinking a much-needed Diet Pepsi, Matthew told Mira about his suspicions.

"She came here," Mira said.

"What do you mean?"

"I never told you because it was the day I flew out to Charlotte, but she dropped by the house and asked if she could have a tour again. Look at all the rooms."

"What did you say?"

"What do you mean what did I say? I said sure. I was excited to see her."

"So she went through all of our rooms?"

"Don't get mad at me. It wasn't like I left her alone in here. We walked through the rooms together just like we did at the dinner party."

"Did she want to see my room?"

"What, our bedroom?"

"No. My office."

"We measured the size of your desk because she told me she was thinking of getting one. It never even occurred to me . . ."

"I know. I'm not blaming you. I'm just still freaked out. I think she's insane, Mira. I think she's decided I'm a murderer and now she's out to get me. She probably planted some kind of evidence here."

Mira frowned. "I believe you, but I just don't get it. Why you?"

"I think she made a connection between me and Dustin Miller. He was a former student from school who got killed a couple of years ago."

"While at Sussex?"

"No, no. Many years later. I honestly don't know that much about it, but the case is still open. And a police officer from Cambridge came out and talked with me about it."

"When? Why didn't you tell me?"

"I didn't want to worry you. And you were away on your trip to Charlotte. It was nothing. At least I thought it was nothing."

"And you think that Hen sent the cop to you?"

"I know she did." Matthew didn't want to mention the fencing trophy, knowing that it would look strange that he'd gotten rid of it. "I don't think it's personal. I think it's just . . . a problem she has. Like a compulsion. She sees murderers where there aren't any."

"Well, not really, Matthew. There's a real murderer. Someone killed that singer last night."

"Right. I guess she just latches on to someone and begins to think that person's guilty."

"But why was she there? I mean, she witnessed the crime. That doesn't sound odd to you?"

Mira got up and went to the window that faced their neighbors' house. She moved the curtain two inches to one side.

"Lights on?" Matthew asked.

"Nope."

"What were you saying?"

Mira turned. "Maybe she had something to do with it. I mean, are they looking at her? She was there. You weren't. Maybe she's framing you for a crime."

"That doesn't make any sense."

"Why not? She thinks you've killed someone and gotten away with it, so she kills someone else and says she saw you do it."

"It's ridiculous. But if that's what happened then the police will figure it out."

"Can you show me that article, the one about her in college?"

THAT NIGHT, IN BED, Matthew listened to his wife's breathing as it slowed and began to purr a little. He thought she was finally asleep when she said, "What time do you think the police detectives will be at work in the morning?"

"I have no idea."

"I'm calling as soon as I get up. You never know, they might get there early."

Five minutes later, she asked, "Are you sure the door is bolted from the inside?"

"I am," he said, "but I can check again if you'd like."

"No, I believe you. What a bitch," Mira said, as though they'd been in the middle of discussing their neighbor. It was not a word Matthew had ever heard his wife use.

"Let's not totally jump to conclusions, either. Maybe it's just a big misunderstanding. Maybe she really did think she saw me there."

"I'd think that, too, but that article. What she did to that girl in college."

"I know," Matthew said. *And now she's wrecked everything. I had two lives before I met Henrietta Mazur, both of them simple, with their own comforts and rewards. And from out of nowhere she's come along and turned those two lives into one. One complicated mess of a life. I never thought I'd lie in bed and listen to Mira talk about murders, but here I am. I want to call Hen a bitch as well, but that is what my father would've called her. She's not a bitch, but she is too smart for her own good. I feel like I'm on a small boat in the middle of a huge storm. I need to ride the waves and wait for it all to blow over.*

Before she finally fell asleep, Mira said, "I love you, Bear," a name she hadn't used for at least a year. He immediately curled up next to her, making himself small, moving his leg across her thighs.

"Love you, too," he said, burrowing his face into her neck.

"Shh," she said as he tried to squeeze closer to her, as though he were freezing and she were his only source of warmth. "Shh, it's going to be all right."

"You promise?" he said, his voice whispery.

"I promise, Bear, I promise."

CHAPTER 19

M ira opened her eyes at dawn. She knew she'd slept, although her body and her mind didn't feel rested. She swung herself off the bed, moving carefully so as not to wake Matthew, still curled up on his side.

She put on a robe and went downstairs, making coffee, then chugging a glass of water. She was still so thirsty, a remnant of the hangover she'd suffered the previous day, after drinking far too much at the Portsmouth Arms. Her stomach was queasy and there was a pulsing ache in her temples, almost like one of her migraines, but she knew it was from alcohol and stress. She went into the living room, thought about lying down on the couch, but decided to try to meditate instead. That was something her father did, ten minutes of meditation every morning before he drank his coffee. He swore by it, and she trusted him because, other than the meditation, her father was maybe the most pragmatic non-new-age-y person she knew. She got her yoga mat and sat cross-legged on the floor, focusing on her breathing and staring at a patch of early-morning light that lay in a rhombus across the hardwood floor. It almost worked, but she couldn't shut out the bizarre events of yesterday, especially learning that it was Hen, their new neighbor, who had claimed to have witnessed Matthew at the scene of a murder. It was ludicrous—the whole thing was ludicrous—but Mira was trying to make sense of it. Hen *had* told her that she suffered from depression, mentioning how she didn't want any children because she didn't want to pass along her brain. Maybe she was just unhinged, and, for whatever reason, she had decided—this was what Matthew believed, anyway—that Matthew was some kind of serial killer. It was just that . . . Hen *seemed* sane. And she seemed nice, even though Mira now knew that Hen had come over after the dinner party only in order to look for evidence, or maybe even to plant evidence. Suddenly she was scared. How far would this woman go? She thought back to after they had all met at the neighborhood party, how much she'd already decided that she liked her arty new neighbor with the pixie hair and the interesting jewelry, how she told Matthew that she really wanted to have them over for dinner.

"They're total strangers," he'd said.

"Strangers are just friends we haven't met yet, you know that, Matthew," she said, laughing. She didn't really want to have *that* discussion—that argument, really—about friends. For a few years Mira had wanted more friends and Matthew, if anything, wanted fewer.

"Do what you want," he'd said.

And she had done what she wanted, and look what had happened. She had a psychotic neighbor now, out to get her husband.

But there actually was a murder on Saturday night. Some man died.

Mira did some stretches. There was too much to think about, and her mind was getting rattled. *Calm down,* she told herself. *Think about yesterday. Try and put it in perspective.*

So, with her toes gripped by her fingers, she thought about the previous day. There was her hangover, of course, the worst she'd had in years, the worst she'd had maybe ever. Why had she drunk so much?

Your husband made you do it.

Matthew had encouraged her, that much was true. Matthew, who drank about two alcoholic beverages a year, if that. They'd been in that pretty bar at the inn, all dark wood and flickering candlelight, and the wine had tasted amazing, and then she'd had some sweet-tasting Scotch drink that had tasted just as good. She remembered thinking: *He's trying to get me drunk, Matthew's trying to get me drunk.* She'd wondered why and told herself that maybe it had to do with a sex thing, that maybe he wanted to try out something in the bedroom, a thought that wasn't entirely objectionable, but not exactly enticing, either. The last time he'd gotten a little bit kinky—this was over a year ago—he'd asked her to keep her black stockings on while they had sex. That part had been fine—it actually did feel pretty sexy—and it had been equally fine when he'd flipped her over onto her stomach and finished from behind. What hadn't been fine—what had been fairly awful—was that afterward, when she'd turned to look at him, he'd looked back at her with an expression of complete disgust on his face, very brief but it was definitely there. Then he'd flushed bright red and couldn't meet her eye.

"That was fun," she'd said, hoping to salvage the situation, but he was already heading to the bathroom to shower.

It had definitely occurred to her, even before he

plied her with clam dip and alcohol, that maybe he'd suggested the Portsmouth Arms getaway in order to try something else new in the bedroom. With that in mind, Mira had purposefully not brought black stockings on this trip. She never wanted to see that almost hateful look on his face again.

As it turned out, as soon as they got back to their room she'd sat down on the edge of the bed and the whole room had listed to one side like a boat in bad weather. She remembered Matthew gently tucking her under the covers, and her wondering if she'd ever get to sleep with the room churning the way it was, but that was all she remembered about that night.

The next day she'd woken early, as she had this morning, and gone to the bathroom and taken four ibuprofens, washing them down with three glasses of the tinny hotel tap water. Her stomach roiled, but she was able to fall asleep again. When she next woke up, Matthew, already dressed, hair damp from a shower, was carrying a tray of room service breakfast across the room. He'd ordered her a tomato and cheese omelet, her favorite, and after a tenuous first bite, she'd gulped down the rest with three slices of buttered toast and decided that she was going to survive.

When they'd gotten back from Portsmouth early that afternoon, they'd found the detectives waiting for them, one in the unmarked car and one leaning against its side. *We've been robbed,* Mira thought, as Matthew said, "Huh," in his quiet voice.

But they hadn't been robbed. Matthew had agreed to go into the station for questioning, even though Mira kept pressing them to say more about what it was about. "It's okay," he said. "I haven't done anything wrong, so we have nothing to worry about." He sounded like her pragmatist father, although her father's pragmatism would have led him to say the opposite. Being innocent was no guarantee of safety.

"Should I call Sanjiv?" she'd asked, as he'd gotten into the vehicle with the two detectives.

"Don't bother him," he'd said, but she'd called their lawyer anyway, and she was glad she did. After he'd agreed to go to the police station, another detective had arrived at the house, this time to question Mira, asking her about her husband's whereabouts the previous evening.

"He was with me all night," she said. "Why are you asking?"

"Was he away from you at any point during the evening?" This detective seemed impossibly young, a light-skinned black man in a too-loose suit, as though he'd recently lost a lot of weight.

"No. We spent the whole night together at an inn in Portsmouth. Whatever it is you think he did, he didn't do it."

Mira went to the police station, where, after she'd waited close to two hours, Sanjiv finally emerged with Matthew, looking very calm for someone who'd been accused of murder, as it turned out. He told her all about their neighbor Hen, that she had accused him of a crime, and that there was nothing to worry about because the police didn't believe her. She had a history of this sort of thing.

Still, why'd he get you so drunk?

Mira pushed the thought away. She knew where it would lead, and she wasn't going to think about all that. Not right now with too many other things going on. There were things about her husband—about Matthew—that made him different. How could he not be with the childhood he'd had, the family he'd been part of? Considering what they'd been like, he was unbelievably normal, really, just a regular guy with a solid job who had always been good to her. More than good. He'd been her savior. He'd saved her from a lifetime of abuse at the hands of Jay Saravan.

How exactly did he save you, Mira?

She shut the voice out, telling herself he'd saved her only by being there when Jay died, being there to sweep up all the pieces and put her back together. That was all there was to it.

What if that wasn't all there was?

Then he still saved me, Mira thought. *He still saved me, and—*

A truck rumbled by on Sycamore Street. Mira stood and went to the window. All the yards were hazy with early morning mist.

"You're up early." It was Matthew, at the foot of the stairs, dressed already but in his stocking feet, otherwise she'd have heard him come down.

"I woke up and couldn't fall back to sleep," Mira said after turning toward him.

"Yesterday was a little crazy," he said.

"A little?"

"Smells like you made coffee?"

"Yes, and I made a full pot. I figured we might need it."

Mira followed Matthew into the kitchen, and before she lost her nerve, she asked him the question she'd wanted to ask the night before. "Was there something about the fencing trophy, the night that Hen and her husband came to dinner?"

"What do you mean?"

"That night, when I was giving the tour, Hen acted strange when she saw the fencing trophy. I thought it might have something to do with what happened to the student from Sussex Hall who got murdered?"

"Apparently," Matthew said, stretching the word a little, "Dustin Miller was accused of raping another Sussex Hall student while they were on a trip to a fencing tournament. That's how she made the connection, I guess."

"What connection?"

"I guess that's how she first decided that I'd had something to do with Dustin Miller's death. Maybe she saw the trophy and that triggered her memory of the story, and then she somehow connected me to it. I don't really know how her brain works."

"Maybe she thought that the trophy belonged to Dustin Miller, that you took it when you killed him?"

"I wouldn't be surprised at all."

"But you got rid of that trophy?" Mira asked, trying to sound casual.

Matthew had finished adding cream and sugar to his coffee and took a sip. "I did."

"Why?" Mira asked.

Matthew took a deep breath. "The thing is . . . the thing is, I never really wanted our neighbors to come over for dinner—"

"Why didn't you—"

"It wasn't that big a deal, I just . . . you know me. I'm happy with our lives the way they are now. And they came over, and it was totally fine, but then I knew that something strange had happened when Hen was in the office. I saw how she looked at the trophy. I mean, we all saw it, right? She looked like she was about to faint. I had no idea why she reacted that way, but I noticed it and it bugged me. I guess I never even wanted them to look inside my office. I consider it a sacred space, in a way. So, the next day, when I was getting rid of a bunch of stuff, I decided to get rid of the trophy as well. It was just a whim."

"Where'd you put it?" Mira asked.

Matthew looked up at the ceiling, as though thinking, and said that he put it in the dumpster at Sussex Hall. "That was the day I brought back a bunch of old textbooks, and I just grabbed a few old things from here to get rid of as well. You don't think I—"

"No, it just occurred to me that it's something you might get questioned about. If Hen thinks the fencing trophy belonged to Dustin Miller, then the police could get a search warrant, and—"

"That won't happen. I don't think they're going to trust anything she says at all. She's done this sort of thing before."

"I just feel so helpless. There she is, right next to us, and she can say anything she wants about us. It's horrible. Maybe we should get some sort of restraining order."

"It wouldn't stop her from saying things."

"No, I know. But maybe it would stop her from coming onto our property, from approaching us. I don't know if it would help, but it couldn't hurt."

"Okay," Matthew said. "Who knows, maybe they'll just leave and things can go back to normal."

"Let's hope," Mira said.

"Yes, let's hope," Matthew echoed, as he opened the refrigerator door to return the cream to its shelf.

CHAPTER 20

"You let him go?" Hen said, trying to keep the anger out of her voice.

"He has an alibi." The name of this detective was Shaheen, a woman somewhere in her thirties with thin lips and humorless eyes.

"I'm telling you, it was him," Hen said. She'd gone over the details of the previous night at least seven times. She'd also given details about the night she followed Matthew back to the Owl's Head, the night he'd been stalking his next victim. She'd decided to tell the truth about everything, even though she knew it made her seem slightly crazy.

"You're one hundred percent sure it was him?"

"I am. We looked right at each other."

"It was pretty dark out behind the bar. Other witnesses said it was hard to make anything out."

"It was dark, but not dark enough that I couldn't see his eyes. What other witnesses, by the way?"

"Not witnesses to the crime, but other people we've interviewed who were at the back of the bar last night. The other members of the C-Beams. Gillian Donovan."

Hen had learned that Gillian Donovan was the girl in the tight dress, Scott Doyle's girlfriend.

"There was moonlight," Hen said.

The door to the conference room swung open. Hen had been interviewed in three different rooms. First, in an interrogation room with a camera filming her, then later in Detective Whitney's office. He seemed to be the lead detective on the case, although he also seemed too old to still be working. He had very little hair on his head and a pure white goatee. In every conversation with Hen, she thought he seemed exhausted.

And now she was in a conference room that looked like it hadn't been used for several months. Hen had peered into a mug that had been left on the wooden conference table and seen a black circle of petrified coffee covered with small white dots of mold.

"I'd like to change the subject, briefly, Mrs. Mazur, and ask you about something else."

"Okay," she said.

"What can you tell me about your freshman year at Camden College?"

Hen wasn't surprised to hear the question—she'd been expecting it—but the words still made her feel like she'd been punched in the chest.

"You're referring to my being arrested for assault?"

"Yes."

"I'm bipolar, and I had my first manic episode my freshman year at Camden College. I was not myself."

"But you accused a fellow student of attempted murder, didn't you?"

"I did, yes."

"And then you attacked that student yourself?"

"Like I said, I wasn't well at the time. That incident has absolutely nothing to do with what's happening now."

"But . . . you still are bipolar, yes?"

Hen told herself to make sure her words were calm and measured. "I am—I always will be—but my meds are working. I'm not having a manic episode. I'm not imagining anything about Matthew Dolamore."

The detective put her hand flat on the table, about an inch from where Hen's hand was. "I believe you, Mrs. Mazur, but I also need to look at every possibility."

"I get it. But it's different this time. It's entirely different."

"But if you were experiencing an episode of bipolar psychosis right now, you wouldn't necessarily know it," the detective said, leaning back a little in her chair. "That's one of the hallmarks of being divorced from reality, right?"

Hen thought that the detective had either done some research right before engaging in this conversation or had some personal experience with someone with mental illness.

"Sure," Hen said, and decided to not say anything else. She was aware that the more she protested, the worse it sounded.

They sat in silence for a moment, and then Detective Shaheen stood up. "Thank you, Mrs. Mazur," she said. "Your husband's here, by the way."

Hen hadn't called Lloyd to let him know what had happened until just after noon. She wanted to give him a morning of peace after what was probably a very late bonfire party. And she was worried about his reaction, worried that, like the police, he'd think she was having some kind of mental breakdown.

It didn't help that when she followed Detective Sheehan out to the Dartford Police Department waiting room, the look on Lloyd's face was one of concern, almost pity.

"How are you?" he asked after they hugged. He was wearing the clothes he'd probably been wearing the night before at the party and smelled of stale sweat and too much deodorant.

"I'm fine, Lloyd, but we're living next to a fucking murderer."

"Let's talk about it in the car, okay?"

Even though she was tired of telling the story, she recounted every detail to Lloyd, starting in the car and finishing at home. He listened patiently, hardly speaking. She thought he looked tired from his trip, dark circles under his eyes, and his skin an unhealthy pallor. When she was done, she asked, "Do you believe me? And tell the truth."

He paused, and she almost hoped he'd say he didn't believe her. She thought she'd rather be doubted than condescended to.

"Apparently, he has a solid alibi. He wasn't there."

"You think I'm making it up?"

"No, I think you think you saw him, but it was someone else."

"Explain to me how it's possible that the person I think might get killed by our neighbor gets killed by someone else. What are the chances?"

"I'm not following you."

"I saw Matthew stalking this guy—this Scott Doyle. I'm sorry I didn't tell you about it at the time, but I knew how worried you'd be. And that's why I went last night to see his band. I wanted to see if Matthew was there as well."

"The police said you were intoxicated."

"Yes, I kind of was. I admit that. But, still, think for a moment. What are the chances that Scott Doyle just happens to get killed by someone else, by someone other than our neighbor?"

"But . . . according to the police, he was."

Hen clenched her teeth and took a large sip of water. "Do you think I'm manic?"

"I guess I do, Hen, I'm sorry. You're acting like you did last time. You're obsessive."

"So I *seem* manic to you?"

Lloyd thought for a moment. "No, actually, you don't. You seem fine, but your actions . . . I don't know what to think. I'm worried, Hen."

By the time they'd finally gotten into bed, Hen had agreed to move up her annual appointment with her psychopharmacologist in order to check her blood levels, and Lloyd agreed to consider the possibility that Hen was 100 percent right about everything.

"What would you do if you totally believed me?"

"What do you mean, what would I do?"

"Would you confront Matthew Dolamore? Would you decide to move out of this house?"

"I guess I'd lay low and hope the police got to the truth."

"Mira must know everything."

"Who?"

"The wife, Mira. She must know, otherwise she wouldn't have given him an alibi."

"You can't get involved. You've told the police everything you know. Just leave it at that."

After Lloyd fell asleep, Hen slipped quietly out of the bed and went downstairs. She knew that her chance of sleeping that night was close to zero. She considered taking a sleeping pill but decided against it. She wanted to stay sharp.

In the living room, she peered across at the Dolamore house. Hen heard the tapping footsteps as Vinegar came around the corner, then stopped, sat, and stared at Hen. Hen stared back, directly into the cat's round eyes. Sometimes she thought Vinegar looked more like an owl than a cat. Wind buffeted the house, and Vinegar turned toward the rattling window. Hen moved to the couch, stretched out, and stared at the ceiling. *Do nothing,* she told herself. *Keep telling the truth when asked, but do nothing. Otherwise, it will make things worse.*

Around dawn she pulled a blanket tight around her body, curled onto her side, and fell asleep.

She was woken by the doorbell. In her dream it was a bell at the top of a tower that Hen had climbed. Wind was picking at the tower's brickwork, bricks scattering like leaves from a tree. Dustin Miller was at the top of the tower as well; he was speaking but the words were picked away by the wind. Hen reached toward him. *I forgot how beautiful you are,* she thought, and the bell rang again, and Hen was suddenly awake, then standing. Lloyd was coming down the stairs, looking as though the doorbell had woken him as well.

"Who is it?" he asked Hen as she went to the door.

It was two police officers, both uniformed: one who looked like a college football player, the other a pretty woman in her thirties with icy-blond hair and a gap between her front teeth. The policewoman asked Hen if she had a moment to talk.

"Okay," she said, not moving from the door.

"Inside?"

"Sure."

They all sat in the living room. Hen had raced upstairs to change into jeans and a sweater. When she got
back, she could smell coffee beginning to brew and took
a seat across from the two officers.

"This is a courtesy call, more than anything," the
policewoman, who gave her name as Officer Rowland,
said. "I wanted to let you know that Matthew and Mira
Dolamore have filed an official complaint of harassment
against you this morning, and they will be seeking a
protective order."

"Harassment?" Hen said, and Lloyd put a hand on
her leg and shushed her.

"What does that mean, a protective order? Is that a
restraining order?" Lloyd asked.

"It's essentially the same thing. As far as we know,
they will not be asking for you to vacate your premises,
but they are asking you to stop any contact. To not go
near their premises—"

"We live right next door," Hen said.

"—and to not spy on them or follow them."

"Is this an official request?" Lloyd asked.

"As Officer Rowland explained," the policeman (Hen
didn't catch his name) said, "this is a courtesy call. Ide-
ally, this issue would be solved without having to resort
to issuing a protective order. We are hoping you'll agree
to comply with their request. I've personally found that
most disputes between neighbors can be resolved peace-
fully."

Hen slid to the front of the sofa, and Lloyd took his
hand off her leg. "It's not a dispute between neighbors.
I witnessed Matthew Dolamore commit a murder. I'm
not going to change my story because of a restraining
order."

The policeman put both his hands, palms out, toward Hen. "I understand completely. We're not here to discuss the homicide case. We are just here to inform you that your neighbors have begun the process of applying for a protective order."

"Okay. Okay," Lloyd said. "How long will that take? For the order?"

"A judge usually has twenty-four hours to review the paperwork, but it's often approved before the end of that period. It could be served as early as today."

"That's fine. Thanks for giving us a heads-up."

"As of this morning, the Dolamores had not officially filed all the necessary paperwork. We are hoping that this conversation—"

"Fuck that," Hen said. "Let them file it. I don't give a shit."

Lloyd moved his hand toward Hen's back, and she stood up.

"Thank you, Officers, for doing your job."

After they had left, Lloyd said, "Jesus, Hen."

"What? I said what I meant. They can get all the restraining orders they want, but it doesn't change what I saw."

"Let's have some coffee and talk about this some more."

"I don't want to talk about this anymore. I know you don't believe me. I don't know how to change your mind on that."

"I believe you. I just think that you probably made some kind of mistake. Will you admit that that's a possibility?"

"No, I will not admit that that's a possibility. I'll admit that everything I saw up until Saturday night was my opinion. Maybe the fencing trophy didn't belong to Dustin Miller. Maybe Matthew Dolamore had some other reason for following people around in the middle of the night. But I saw him at the scene of the crime. With my own eyes."

"You were drunk."

"I wasn't that drunk."

"That's not what I heard."

"Where'd you hear that?"

"I talked to one of the detectives. Yesterday, before we drove home. He told me that you were extremely intoxicated."

"I wasn't. I'd been drinking, but . . ."

"They interviewed the bartender. You had at least five drinks, including a martini."

"I don't know if I had five, exactly."

"You know that with your meds it's like having ten drinks. Did you even eat dinner that night?"

"I don't know. Look, don't yell at me. I was drunk, but I know what I saw. Did you tell them about my meds?"

"Who? The police? They asked if you drank a lot, and I said no. I said that because of your meds you were usually very careful not to have more than two drinks."

"Great."

"I'm on your side, Hen. I'm worried about you."

"Don't you need to get to work?"

"It's Columbus Day."

"Oh, right."

"I do have work to do, but I can do it from here. I don't want you to be alone."

Hen caught herself clenching her teeth together, then stopped. "I was going to go to the studio today. I can't be here all day. Not with . . . not with him next door."

"Okay. You should go to the studio. That makes sense."

Hen drank some coffee and tried to eat some toast, but even the feel of food in her mouth made her want to vomit. She changed again and told Lloyd, now on his computer in the living room, that she was going to the studio.

"Can you do me a favor?" he asked.

"Okay," she said.

"Promise me you're only going to the studio. Promise you won't do anything foolish."

"I promise," she said, and went out the front door, not even looking at the Dolamores' house as she got into her car.

CHAPTER 21

Even though Matthew and Mira were told that police had visited and spoken with Henrietta Mazur, they still decided to go ahead with the order. The judge granted it at three that afternoon, and they were told that a process server would deliver the order directly to Henrietta either that evening or, at the very latest, the next morning.

"It won't prevent her from continuing to say that she saw you at the scene of the crime," Detective Shaheen told Matthew over the phone.

"I know. I just don't want her following me. I don't want her in my house. I don't want her talking to my wife. The last time this happened she attacked someone."

"I know. We'll do everything possible to make sure that doesn't happen again."

Mira went to the bedroom with a migraine, barricading herself in, shades drawn. Her headaches were not frequent, but when she got them—always from anxiety, Matthew thought, even though she disagreed—they'd wipe her out for a day. Matthew (his stomach not great) ate cereal for dinner. He realized that since Saturday night he hadn't had a moment to really recollect what it had felt like to bring that piece of metal down on Scott Doyle's skull, to feel the crack that meant his life was going to spill out of him and away. The glory of that singular moment had been immediately ruined by Henrietta, appearing like a ghost in the parking lot, her eyes meeting his. He tried to separate the two events, to acknowledge that it was possible to do something both divine and reckless at the same time. And yet, somehow he'd gotten away with it. It was what he'd thought might happen. Henrietta Mazur was an unreliable witness. Worse than unreliable. A false witness. A mentally ill woman unable to tell fantasy from reality. In some ways, it had worked out perfectly.

As the evening passed—Matthew feverishly reading everything he could find online about the homicide of Scott Doyle—he found himself thinking about Henrietta more than he was thinking about the killing. He kept coming back to that frozen moment, the two of them looking at each other, a current of electricity between them—as Scott lay at Matthew's feet. It reminded him of something . . . it reminded him of his mother, really, and he wasn't sure he wanted to think about that. But he let himself do it, just this once. That stare—that blank, knowing stare—was something Natalia Dolamore had mastered toward the end of her life. He pictured it now, the look on her face clearing the dinner dishes, picking hers up from the floor . . . one of those nights when his father had made her eat on all fours down on the kitchen linoleum, her food mushed together in a dog dish. She'd done it, of course, because she knew the consequences of not doing it, but her face had remained a frozen mask, impervious to the humiliation. Her face was the face of a witness, observing what was happening to her. Not living it, but watching it.

That was how Henrietta had looked. She was the face of a witness also, and Matthew couldn't help but feel that in that moment she saw everything. Not just what was happening, but everything that had happened to Matthew since he'd been old enough to remember. She saw the monstrosity of his father, the fragility and grace of his mother. She saw his brother, Richard, twisted into a monster himself. She saw the door that had opened inside of Matthew as he watched someone die for the first time; she witnessed him stepping into a world of color that he'd never even imagined before. She saw Jay Saravan, passed out in the front seat of his car, its interior filling with exhaust. She saw Dustin Miller, dead in his chair, and Matthew taking the fencing trophy from the top of his bureau. She even saw how badly he needed that trophy, that desire to claim it as his own. And she saw the foolish compulsion to publicly display the trophy in his office.

She'd have told the police all about that as well. The trophy she'd seen when she'd come over for dinner. He was safe, though. The trophy was gone. If they asked him about it, he would just have to tell them what he'd told Mira earlier that morning, that he'd gotten rid of it—that it had come from a yard sale and his office was too cluttered and how he'd put it in a dumpster. It would sound suspicious, but what could they do? The trophy was buried way back in the supply closet at Sussex Hall, wiped of prints, pushed behind the spare chairs and old cutlery. If the police decided to search for the trophy, would they possibly even look there? They could look through his house and maybe through his classroom, but not there, could they?

His stomach tightened. Maybe they would look for it there, and maybe they'd find it. He thought about going to the school at that very moment and retrieving the box, bringing it somewhere it would never be found. But that idea made his stomach knot up even more. Not now, he told himself. It was too risky.

He went back to his computer, refreshing his searches, seeing if there was anything new about Scott Doyle. One of the stories referred to Scott as a promising musician, a "future rock star." *Well, at least I gave him that,* Matthew thought. He went from a wannabe fronting a cover band to a future rock star in one weekend. None of the stories referred to Michelle Brine. He thought it was a little strange, but it wasn't like they were living together; she was just his girlfriend, and God knows how many of those there were. He wondered if she even knew and considered the possibility that she didn't. She'd been visiting her dying father. Would the police even know she existed? She'd have tried to call him, of course, on Sunday, to ask him how his show went. How much would she have worried when she hadn't heard from him? She'd be back now, of course, giving herself time to start to prep for the week ahead. Maybe he should call her, tell her he'd heard what had happened. There was no need to mention that he'd been picked up as a possible suspect. No charges had been filed, and his name had stayed out of the reports.

He rang her cell phone.

"I was going to call *you*," she said, answering the phone. He could tell from her voice that she knew what had happened.

"I'm so sorry," Matthew said. "I just heard the news. What happened?"

She took a ragged breath. It was clear that she'd been crying.

"I kept trying to call him on Sunday, just to find out how the show went, and he wasn't picking up. It's funny, because I knew that something awful had happened. I felt it. And then Jeremy called me and told me. I was driving back from my parents'—"

"Who's Jeremy?"

"I'm sorry. I'm not making any sense. Jeremy was in Scott's band. He was the drummer. He called me and told me that Scott was dead, and I almost said, 'I know.' That's how inevitable it felt. I don't know . . . Maybe I'm crazy."

"You're not crazy. You're just in shock, probably."

"The thing is, we broke up, right before I left on Friday. You'd have been so proud of me. I asked him one more time if he wanted to come with me to visit my dad—that he was doing so much worse—and he said he couldn't because of the gig and how important it was. So I suggested he drive out with me on Friday night and just visit briefly, and he could take my car back on Saturday afternoon, and I'd take a train, and he actually said that he needed to be in a good headspace for his performance, and I just told him to fuck off . . . well, not quite, I told him I thought we should break up, and he fought me . . . a little bit, anyway, but then we did it. We broke up."

Matthew thought she sounded proud for a moment, almost as though she'd forgotten that Scott was now dead, but then she made a sudden exhalation, almost a groan, and she was crying.

"Maybe . . ." she started to say, then didn't continue.

"Do you know what happened? Was it a robbery?"

She took two deep sniffs and said, her voice relatively normal again, "It was after the show. He had a flat tire, and while he was fixing it someone hit him on the head. I went to the station. They wanted to know if he had any enemies, and if he was faithful to me, and why we'd broken up."

"You told them that you'd had a fight and broken up on Friday?" Matthew asked.

"Yeah, I told them everything. It's not like I'm a suspect. I was in Pittsfield all weekend."

"So how do you feel?"

"God, I don't know. Name an emotion and I have it. I was actually happy this weekend that I'd finally shed myself of Scott. I mean, I wasn't happy, exactly, because my father is so much worse than my mother's been saying, but I felt relieved. And now I don't know what to feel. Am I supposed to grieve for him? I'm just so confused."

"You should take the week off work."

"God, no. That's the last thing I want to do. If I have to spend any more time alone here in my apartment I'm going to go crazy. Hey, I don't know if I should ask this or not, but I don't really care. Are you free? Can you come over, or is that a strange thing to ask?"

Matthew rapidly considered his options. If he was going to tell Michelle that he'd been accused of the murder by his unhinged neighbor, now would be the time. On the other hand, she hadn't heard yet, and she might never hear. Clearly, the police hadn't even bothered to show her a photograph of him. It was a very good sign that they didn't take Henrietta Mazur at all seriously. He decided not to tell her. If she found out later, he'd just say that he didn't want to upset her further.

"Actually, Mira is sick right now," he said.

"Oh no, I'm sorry."

"It's nothing serious, but she gets migraines, and they just knock her out."

"No, no. Totally. Forget I asked."

"If you do wind up going into school tomorrow, let's get together after classes. Maybe get coffee and talk."

"Sure," she said.

"And call me back later, okay, if you need someone to talk with. Don't hesitate."

After they ended the call, he knew she wouldn't call back. He sat for a moment, his mind flipping through images of what it would be like to go over to Michelle's place—she lived in one of those apartment developments built to look vaguely Tudor-ish and with a name like Courtly Estates or something. How would it feel to comfort a woman whose boyfriend (*ex*-boyfriend) he'd hunted and killed? And how would it feel when he told her he had to leave, and she pulled him into a hug, pressed her lips against his? He went so far as to allow himself a moment to imagine her sliding back onto her bed, lifting her hips so he could pull her jeans down her long trembling legs. He shuddered a little at the image and thought of Mira in her cocoon of darkness. He had never cheated on her, and he never would. Cheating was what his father did. That wasn't what he did.

And besides, as tempting as it was to visit Michelle, released forever from the physical manifestation of Scott Doyle, Matthew found that he was still thinking of Henrietta Mazur. What would it be like to visit her? What would she say to him if he knocked on her door?

It wouldn't be her, though; it would most likely be her husband, Lloyd, who'd probably punch him in the face. Still, he couldn't stop thinking about her and how much he wanted to know what she was thinking. He knew this much: she'd been thinking about him, too. Nonstop. And sometime within the next twenty-four hours she'd be getting the protective order that barred her from interacting with him and Mira. Would they leave the neighborhood? He doubted it. He also doubted that she would stop interfering with his business. It gave him a perverse thrill that he couldn't quite understand.

CHAPTER 22

After receiving the protective order from a burly, disinterested process server on Tuesday morning, Hen called Lloyd at work to let him know it had happened.

"Shit, it's real," he said.

"Yep."

"How do you feel?"

"I don't know," Hen said. "Like I've been validated, a little bit."

"But you're not going to do anything more, right?"

"What do you mean? Like break into their house?"

"Uh-huh."

"No. I'm done. I've had my say. I'll get my blood levels checked to see if my meds are working. I'll keep my head down. I'm fine, Lloyd. I'm not manic."

"I believe you." It had taken all of Hen's persuasion to get Lloyd to go into the office that Tuesday. She had promised him that she was feeling okay and also that she'd call him every two hours to check in.

"I will say this, though. If nothing happens in this case . . . if Matthew isn't arrested, then maybe we should think about moving. He is a murderer."

"Okay," Lloyd said, and she could hear the muffle of

the phone as he put his hand over it and spoke briefly to someone in his office. "Yes, I agree. That's fine."

"I'll call you in a little bit."

She went to the large window that looked out onto Sycamore Street. She'd pulled the curtains on all the windows that faced their neighbor. Since she'd confirmed for herself that Matthew was a murderer, and was also sure that he knew she knew, she wondered why she didn't feel more scared. Wouldn't he come for her at some point? But she didn't think that would happen. One of the reasons was that if something bad happened to her, the police would obviously immediately suspect Matthew, the man she'd accused. But it wasn't just that. It was also that she didn't think she was his type. He killed men. She didn't know why, but that's what he did.

One of the neighborhood moms walked by. She was wearing yoga pants and carried small weights in her hands. She turned and glanced toward the house, and Hen took a step back from the window into the shadows. Did the woman know anything? Hen didn't think so; neither Matthew's name nor hers had been mentioned in any of the reports about the homicide in New Essex. Still, she wondered.

It was a beautiful day out, the sky a hard blue, and the maple tree across the street fully red now, only a few of its leaves having fallen. Hen loved weather in all its forms, but something about the big months of change—October and April—made her ache with a sadness that she couldn't quite articulate. She thought of her parents, just back to upstate New York from a three-week river cruise on the Rhine. Her father would be obsessing about the yard, the number of leaves already fallen, and her mother would be planning their next trip to Europe.

Hen decided to call them later, after taking a walk down to her studio space. Open Studios was this weekend, and she had a lot of work to do.

That week, as the weather stayed perfect, each day cloudless and crisp, Hen got into a solid routine, walking every day to the studio after breakfast, working all morning on the remaining prints for the *Lore Warriors* book, getting lunch at the small riverside café just down the street from the studios, then spending the afternoon preparing for the weekend. She cleaned her space, selected fifteen prints—including her most recent, the cat in bed with the girl on the windowsill—to display on the wall. She even drove to Walmart to buy one of those giant plastic buckets of pretzel nubs filled with peanut butter. It was her favorite junk food, and she only ever allowed herself to buy them on open studio weekends, putting out a bowl for the visitors, but, really, it was her small reward for the misery of having strangers stroll through her workspace, judging her.

It was a good week, strangely enough, despite how often she found herself thinking of Matthew Dolamore and what she'd seen him do. In the evenings, Lloyd and she cooked dinner together. The Red Sox had bowed out in the first round of the playoffs, sending Lloyd into a silent sulk for twenty-four hours, but now they were free to catch up on the last season of *Game of Thrones*.

She kept all the curtains that faced the Dolamore house pulled closed. Lloyd had no doubt noticed, but he hadn't mentioned it.

On Saturday morning Lloyd walked with Hen to Black Brick Studios to see what she'd done with the space. Open Studios was noon to five both weekend days, and the place was bustling, as it had been all week. Lloyd drank coffee and looked at the prints she'd selected to hang on the wall. Hen knew that most of them were familiar to him—her "greatest hits" that she always trotted out for shows—but he hadn't seen her newest work, and he stared at it for a while before asking, "Have I seen this one before?"

"I just did it."

"I like it," he said. "Creepy. What's it about?"

It was a question she hated, and a question that Lloyd should have known she hated, but sometimes he couldn't help himself. He loved her artwork, at least he always said he did, but also felt a need to analyze it to death.

"It's about Matthew Dolamore," she said.

Lloyd swung around, concerned, and she bugged her eyes out at him and said, "Kidding. I don't know what it's about. It just popped into my head."

He stuck around for most of the morning, eating pretzels until she told him to stop.

"What are you putting out with these?" he asked. "To drink?"

"I have apple cider."

"Ooh, you should warm it up, put some spices in it. It would make it smell nice in here."

Hen thought that was a good idea. She had a hot plate in her studio and sent Lloyd to get a pot and buy some cider spices. She was glad to get rid of him. She knew he'd leave as soon as people started walking through her space, but she wanted a little time alone. She prepped about eight copper plates that she could run through her press that afternoon. She found it so much better to stay busy, hating the act of standing around watching strangers look at her art. Lloyd returned right before noon.

He had their yellow Dutch oven, a packet of spices, and even a pint of Maker's Mark.

"You think I should spike the cider?" Hen said, laughing.

"I thought it might be good to have it, just in case."

He put the cider on low, and soon her studio was filled with the smell of apples and cloves. Lloyd and she each had a mugful, spiked with bourbon, and she felt a sudden, overwhelming sense of well-being, that things would turn out all right. When the first visitors arrived—a middle-aged couple, the man glum and uninterested, and the woman with a streak of purple in her hair, wearing two handmade brooches on her coat—Lloyd took off.

It was a busy afternoon. The nice weather brought out a ton of people, and the cider was gone by three in the afternoon, nothing left but a dark slurry on the bottom of the pot. Hen had underpriced her prints and wound up selling about fifteen of them. She was used to doing open studio events, having done them for years in Somerville, but it was a slightly different crowd out in the suburbs. They asked more questions and spent more money. At five o'clock she was exhausted. She called Lloyd and he came to pick her up. He'd spent the afternoon making chili, he said, and watching a little college football. He smelled like he'd had many beers as well, and Hen was glad he was only driving a mile back to the house.

The weather changed on Sunday, the morning overcast with swollen clouds and the air humid. Hen took the car herself, not wanting to get caught in the rain if she walked. It was a long day. By noon, the sky had opened up, and there was a steady, drenching down-pour. Hen, in her basement studio, couldn't see it, but the few people who dropped by told her how miserable it was outside as they dripped on her floor.

Because of the rain, and because the Patriots were playing an afternoon game, there were significantly fewer visitors. Other artists dropped by, willing to leave their studios to venture out, and Hen did a quick walk around the basement level, popping in to see Derek, one of the few artists whose name she remembered.

"Hi, Hen," he said as she entered.

"How's your Open Studios been?" she asked.

"Today's quiet. Yesterday was nuts."

She looked at his photographs, fairly interesting, all black and white, mostly of buildings—town centers, shopping malls, a cluster of suburban homes—but often photographed at a tilt so that the sky dominated. She wondered if the perspective in the shots had anything to do with his own shortness and almost considered asking him, but stopped herself. It was the type of question she herself hated. What does this art have to do with you? She knew hers was an unpopular opinion in a culture obsessed with individuality, but sometimes the artist and the art were separate entities.

Instead, she asked, "Sold many?"

"One, yesterday."

Impulsively, Hen told him she wanted to buy her favorite photograph of the bunch, a beautiful, silvery shot of a pile of pumpkins at what looked to be some fall festival. A child crouched near the pumpkins, running a stick along the bare ground. The sky above was inter-laced with clouds.

"You don't have to do that," Derek said.

"I know I don't have to. I love this shot. It'll give me inspiration for the next book I'm illustrating."

She ran to her studio, got her credit card, and came back and purchased the pre-framed print. As soon as she had it in her hands, she actually loved it. She thought she could hang it above the low bookshelf in the living room.

At four thirty she began to clean up, pretty sure that there would be no more visitors. She poured herself some bourbon in a water glass and played the soundtrack from *The Painted Veil* on her CD player. As she was washing her hands in the big industrial sink, she sensed someone enter her studio. She turned, hands wet. Matthew Dolamore was five feet away from her, his hands pushed down into his jeans pockets. His jacket was pocked with rain.

Hen's body went cold, and her eyes flitted toward the door. Matthew took a step backward.

"I'm not here to hurt you," he said.

"Then why are you here?" Hen was amazed at how calm her words sounded.

He half shrugged, then said, "I want to talk. And I wanted to see your art." His eyes now moved around the space, his hands still tucked into his jeans, and Hen realized he was nervous. She took a step forward.

"I'd prefer that you leave," she said. "As you're aware, you have filed a protective order against me, and I don't want to violate it."

"You were spying on me."

"For good reason," Hen said.

"Look . . ." Matthew said, but stopped speaking.

"I actually do want you to leave," Hen said. "Right now."

"You don't want to talk? That's all I'm here for. I'm not here to hurt you or threaten you."

"Or kill me," Hen said.

He smiled, and Hen thought he looked like a child caught saying something dirty at the playground. "No, I would never kill you," he said.

"But you killed Scott Doyle. And you killed Dustin Miller."

Matthew looked back over his shoulder to see if anyone else was near, then said, "Yes. I did."

Hen was scared again. It must have shown on her, because Matthew pulled his hands from his pockets and held them up. "I would never in a million years hurt you. I promise."

"What do you want from me?" Hen asked.

Matthew smiled again, almost sheepishly. "I don't know yet," he said. "I suppose I want you to know the truth."

suspect my brother is not what he seems. Not that I blame him. Anyone who got through our childhood gets to do what he wants.

We are owed, he and I.

I'VE HAD SOME OF the same urges, I will admit, but I'm proud to say that I don't act on them. The world is safe with me in it, even though I do like to have fun sometimes. Not quite the same fun that I suspect my father used to have. He came home once from one of his business trips and I followed him into the bedroom while he unpacked his suitcase. Mom stayed downstairs. She was cooking a pot roast, his favorite, and she wanted to make sure it didn't burn. He'd been away for at least a week (it felt like longer to me, but everything feels longer when you're a little kid), and I watched him pull clothes from his suitcase, dress shirts mainly, plus underwear and socks. He dropped them on the floor for Mom to pick up later, but then he pulled out a pair of ladies' underwear, beige and lacy, worn thin in places. He held it up for me to see, smiling with his mouth open enough that I could see all his fillings, then laid it carefully down on top of the nubby bedspread, about halfway down. Then he pulled out a bra and laid it about two feet above the underpants so that the thick, pointy cones of the bra stuck up. I was just old enough to imagine what had been underneath that bra, and I remember getting aroused standing there. One of the cups was darker than the other, and I peered inside. Dark blood, more brown than red, smeared the inside of the bra.

My father watched me, then raised and lowered his eyebrows and said, "She didn't want to take it off, but I convinced her."

"Are they Mommy's?" I asked, even though I was pretty sure they weren't.

My father laughed at that, his head thrown back. "Your mommy couldn't fill out that bra, trust me," he said. "But I brought them back as a gift for her, to let her know I've been thinking about her while I was gone. Oh, got something for you, too, little man."

That was the real reason I'd followed my father to his bedroom. I'd been hoping for a gift—he almost always brought me something, even if it was just little bottles filled with shampoo and lotion—and he fumbled around in one of the pockets of his suitcase, then pulled out a pack of cards and threw them toward me. "From my good friend Bill," he said. "Those are some special cards. Don't let Mommy see that you have them."

I pulled the dog-eared cards from the box they came in. On the backs were naked ladies, showing all their parts including their bushy triangles.

"Just keep those to yourself, okay? You show them to the other boys in school and one of them will decide to steal them from you. Just put them away in your room."

I don't remember the rest of that night, or what my mom did when she found the bloody underwear on her side of the bed. I remember thinking it was a trick, like when my dad pretended to pull his finger off his hand, or when we'd go out to the quarry and he'd pretend he was about to throw me over the edge. But I still have the cards, even more dog-eared now than they were before. The girl on the eight of spades is my favorite—she's on all fours, looking back over her shoulder, and I think it's just a shadow, but it looks like she has a dark, fist-sized bruise on her left buttock.

I HAVE THE SAME dream, again and again. I'm visiting a house somewhere deep in the woods. I've wandered upstairs to where I shouldn't be. There is a long, dark hallway, lined with doors to many bedrooms, most of them rotting and unused. At the end of the hall is a dark figure watching me, waiting to see where I'll go. The feeling when I see him is always the same. I need to know who he is. But when I move closer to him, he ducks into one of the rooms, and I can't find him. I am scared of what is in these rooms, but I need to open the doors. I need to find him.

THREE DAYS AGO I went to downtown Winslow on a pretty day, knowing they'd be out in force, herds of Winslow College students in their tiny dresses and their field hockey uniforms. I got a Thai steak salad from Winslow Market and snagged a table on the sidewalk. Just as I was finishing my salad—the steak overcooked and rubbery—I spotted her. She was all alone—maybe a little too old to be a student, but still in her twenties. She was in black yoga pants, neon-orange sneakers, and a T-shirt that actually said THE FUTURE IS FEMALE on it. She was coming from the café across the street—Latte

Da, it was called—and walking purposefully toward the center of town. I dumped my salad, began to follow her up the incline, but turned back as soon as I saw her unlock her Prius, parked on a slant on Main Street. My own car was a couple hundred yards back, and I turned and walked as fast as I could without breaking into a run. When I pulled onto Main Street she was gone, but at the top of the hill I spotted the green Prius turning left on River Street. I followed her, two cars back. She'd gone only about a mile when she pulled into a new apartment complex on the Waltham River, four stories of brick, each apartment with its own deck. I parked in a visitor's spot and watched her walk across the parking lot, head down, looking at her phone, a large leather purse bumping against her pistoning hip.

I got on my phone, went to my fake account on Instagram, and punched in #latteda, not really expecting to get a hit, but not entirely surprised when the most recent post, a close-up of some latte foam swirled into a heart, was by a haleyfpetersen. Her pictures, mostly selfies, confirmed it was the blonde I'd just followed back to her apartment. She called herself an activist, writer, and yoga instructor. The hashtags on the picture she'd just posted half a minute ago included #shoplocal, #girlboss, #yogalife, #thefutureisfemale, and #thehappynow.

The parking spots at the complex were numbered, and I walked over to where her car was parked. Spot 17.

And like that, I owned her. Her name. Her personal photos. Where she lived and what she drove. I knew that, without a doubt, I could murder her in the next twenty-four hours and never get caught. She'd go from a living girl, pretty enough to have two thousand followers on Instagram, to a dead girl, pretty enough to make the national news.

I drove home, thinking about the specifics of how I would do it. The thoughts were enough for now. I felt better than I'd felt that morning. But somehow it had been too easy, way too easy, and I thought, as I often did, about upping the game, about actually going through with it.

WHEREVER MY BROTHER GOES, death follows. Has anyone else noticed this? That kid from his class in college, Jay something, some piece of shit with a dark fuzzy mustache who brought a BMW with him freshman year and killed himself in it the following year. It was the first time I suspected. When I asked Matthew about it, he said that Jay deserved to die, but that he had nothing to do with it.

Likely story.

ON HOT SUMMER DAYS Mom would take us to a pond two towns over. We'd paddle around in the roped-off area, the bottom rocky and weedy, while she sat in the lawn chair she'd brought with her, reading magazines and smoking mentholated cigarettes, the minty smell of them floating out over the water.

Sometimes a man with a hairy chest would come and sit near her. They never talked, but when Mom would go to the restroom—"Stay where you are, Mommy'll be right back"—he'd follow her there.

"Is that man your friend?" Matthew once asked from the backseat of the station wagon when we were heading home.

"What man?"

"I saw you in the woods together."

She was quiet for what seemed like a long time. I took a bite from my Fudgsicle and my teeth went numb. "If you tell your father about him he'll kill me. Do you understand that?"

Matthew said that he did.

IN THE OTHER DREAM I have I am driving alone at night, down a dark road, my headlights carving out a cone of white light. Up ahead a man runs. It is the same man from the house with all the rooms. I'm pretty sure of it. And no matter how fast I go, he keeps running away from me, just out of reach of my headlights.

I TOLD MY BROTHER that I'd seen Henrietta Mazur on her front porch. It's true, but it's not the only time I've seen her. Sometimes I come to Matthew's house when I'm not invited. I park a few blocks away and walk over. I know that Mira—uppity bitch that she is—doesn't want to see me, but I like to see her sometimes, or see my brother with her, the way he helps her cook dinner and rubs her feet at the end of the day.

He's pretending, I think.

And now I get to see Henrietta Mazur as well.

I've seen her through the sliding glass doors at the back of her house. Henrietta in the kitchen, bopping along to some music I can't hear. Once I saw her there in just a short oxford button-up and a pair of black panties. She had to stand on her toes to reach anything, and the shirt would ride up, showing off two perfect ass cheeks, just barely contained by some shiny fabric.

She's small, with dark hair that's cut a little short for

my taste, and moves like a dancer. I imagine she's flexible, that if you got hold of her ankles you could push her legs all the way back to either side of her head. I've been to her website and seen her etchings—sick, twisted stuff—and I can only imagine what goes on in her head. Sometimes I picture her with thick black pubic hair like the women on the playing cards, and sometimes I imagine she's completely shaved. That's what the girls these days do, right? Keep themselves shaved down there all the time, because they never know when some man will come along and pull those little panties off.

THERE WAS A MURDER up in New Essex outside of some bar. The singer from the band got his skull caved in. I didn't think much of it until I saw the name of the band. The C-Beams.

Wasn't Matthew telling me about some band he checked out at the bar near his house, said he knew the girlfriend of the lead singer and how he was cheating on her and she had no idea? It rings a bell. I don't get over to Matthew's house very often these days even though Mira is always away (I sometimes wonder what *she* gets up to on all those business trips), and sometimes I drink too much and forget what we talk about. I always think that maybe Matthew will insist I sleep on the couch some night, after I've had too much, but he never does. Just sends me on my way.

Brotherly love.

HALEY PETERSEN ADVERTISES A yoga class on her Instagram. She's teaching it in her own apartment on a Saturday morning, and I almost think I'll go. The thought of talking with her face-to-face when I already know so much about her gets me very excited. I've studied all her Instagram photos (she loves to show off her body any way she can, especially doing yoga poses in lacy underpants) and read all her Twitter posts (she was depressed over the winter; she went to Lisbon in the spring) and reviewed her website (she writes terrible poetry that makes me think she's been abused).

Imagine being in her apartment—everything is white if her Instagram is telling the truth—and being able to smell the sweat on her body. What if I was the only one who showed up? The thought is too much, so I go to Craigslist and look at the Women Seeking Men section for Boston MetroWest, nearly writing an email to HuNgRy for BaD DaDDy in Billerica. I've seen her posts before (no pictures, of course), but I just can't bring myself to write her. I don't know if I trust myself.

MY FATHER FOUND OUT about my mother and the man at the swimming pond. I know because he made her wear her bathing suit around the house for weeks. She'd wear that suit when she ate her meals on the kitchen floor. Matthew says she used to eat on all fours like a dog, but I don't remember it that way. Matthew doesn't remember the time she returned to her old seat at the kitchen table when Dad was out of the room on a long phone call. She didn't hear him come back into the kitchen, and he smacked her face down onto her dinner plate, shattering it. I saw the whole thing. I never knew Dad could move so fast. Afterward, Mom just sat there, her head tilted forward, blood from her nose spilling all across the porcelain tabletop with the yellow flowers. Matthew doesn't remember it because he's phobic about blood, but I remember it well. Mom never tried to stop the bleeding, never put her handkerchief to her face, and I remember thinking that she hoped the blood would just keep coming out of her, that it would never stop.

I KEEP READING ARTICLES about the death of Scott Doyle. In the last one I read it mentioned that he'd been dating a teacher from Sussex Hall, where Matthew works. And now I really do wonder if he had anything to do with Scott Doyle's death. The teacher's name is Michelle Brine, and she doesn't have Facebook, Instagram, or Twitter, but there's a picture of her on a LinkedIn page. A thin face and thin brown hair, and the kind of lips that have no color whatsoever, just the color of her flesh, but she has a long, slender neck, and it would be just like my brother to think he was saving her from the big bad wolf. She looks like she needs saving.

So I don't go to yoga and meet Haley Petersen and I don't send an email to the HuNgRy girl from Billerica, and I decide to devote all my energy and resources to finding out what I can about Michelle Brine. She's more of a challenge, a girl like that, someone who doesn't put herself out there. Someone who doesn't think anyone is looking.

I could just ask my brother about her, but I don't think I'll do that. He'll get defensive, the way he does.

Besides, he hasn't called me in a while even though I know Mira is away again. Maybe I'll drop in. He can't hide from me forever.

PART 2

FROM THE LIVING
TO THE DEAD

CHAPTER 23

suppose I want you to know the truth," Matthew said, his heart beating in his chest louder than it had when he'd killed Scott Doyle.

Hen's forehead creased, and then she laughed. "Please leave," she said again.

"Okay," Matthew said, taking two steps backward so that he was standing just inside the open door of her basement studio. "If you change your mind, I just want to talk with you sometime."

She kept her eyes on him. He realized that stepping back had been the right move.

"Why'd you kill Scott Doyle?" she asked.

Matthew shrugged. "He was a creep. He deserved it. I know his girlfriend and she's a good person. He wasn't." *It wasn't just what he did; it was that he was so pleased with himself. I killed him because he was a smug, arrogant fox face, and I would do it again.*

Now Hen really laughed. "What makes you think I won't go straight to the police after this conversation?"

"Go ahead. I'll deny it."

"You're in a public space. Someone will have seen you come in here."

"I won't deny I came here. I'll tell them I came to

have a reasonable conversation with you, to ask why you've decided to persecute me, to ask you to please respect the protective order. I'll say that's all we talked about. Who are they going to believe?"

He watched her think about it. "I still don't understand why you're here."

"When you're like me . . . when you have needs like mine . . ." His heart was beating fast again, like he was on a date that wasn't going well. "You realize I can't talk with anyone, not even a therapist—"

"I am not your fucking therapist."

"God, no. I wasn't suggesting. I'm just trying to explain the special nature of our relationship. I can tell you anything, and you can't do anything about it. It could go both ways, too. That girl in college that you attacked. Was she really after you?"

"Daphne Myers? No, she wasn't. I was mentally unwell and paranoid. Look, I'm so happy that you think we have some kind of *special* relationship, but we don't. I know who you are, and the police will know soon, too. Now leave before I call them."

Matthew saw her glance over to a cloth bag that probably contained her cell phone.

"Okay," he said. "But if you change your mind, I think it will be worth it to you. You will never be in any danger. I don't kill women. I would never hurt you. Even if I was threatened by you."

Matthew turned and left, walking straight down the low-lit, whitewashed corridor, then up the metal stairs and back into the dark afternoon. It had stopped raining, but the rutted parking lot of the studio was filled with rippling puddles, and the trees were still dripping rain and shedding wet leaves. Matthew took a deep breath of the cool, damp air, and it was almost as if he were drinking it in. His mouth was dry, and his back was tight. He got into his car, pulled out of the parking lot, and turned toward Dartford Center. He'd told Mira that he was going to the library to pick up a book he'd reserved, which was true. He asked her if she'd like to come along for the ride and was relieved when she said she'd rather stay home and get ready for her next trip. She was going to Wichita for a regional conference that would last the week.

As he'd been getting ready to leave, she'd said, "It's Open Studios this weekend, you know."

"Do you wish we'd gone?"

"We couldn't have, could we? Not with her there." Mira had taken to referring to Hen as "her" or sometimes "that woman."

"We could have gone and just avoided her studio."

"I know, but she could have been walking around, or Lloyd might've been there. I just couldn't . . ."

"I get it. I didn't want to go, either."

It was starting to rain again when Matthew pulled up alongside the library, parking under the horse chestnut tree on Munroe Street. Outside of the car, he briefly paused to look along the ground for fallen chestnuts. He pushed his foot down on one of the spiny pods, half split already, and a chestnut, hard and shiny, rolled free. He picked it up and slid it into his jeans pocket.

In the library he retrieved the book he'd reserved, *The Haunted Wood,* about Soviet espionage in Cold War America, then took it to one of the padded leather chairs in the reading room. He wanted to sit for a moment and think about his conversation with Hen, go over every word. It had actually gone better than he'd expected. He'd imagined showing up in her studio and Hen panicking, bolting from the room, going straight to the police. She'd been nervous when she'd seen him, but not too nervous. He knew that down deep she believed she was safe with him, and he hoped that that feeling would allow her to get to know him. The thought thrilled him in a way he hadn't felt for years.

He only hoped that she wouldn't tell her husband about the encounter, although she probably would. He could picture Lloyd storming over to the house, demanding that he leave his wife alone. Well, if that happened, he'd just give up on the idea of getting to know Hen. But it wasn't going to change anything with the police. They were never going to believe her, not with her history, and especially not now that he'd learned how drunk she'd been the night of the killing. Detective Whitney had told him that—"she was feeling no pain that night, so who knows what she even saw"—and the words had further convinced Matthew that he was safe, that he'd gotten away with it again, even with an eyewitness on the scene.

He riffled the pages of the book in his lap, then pictured Lloyd storming across to the house, shouting threats, and realized that he should be there if it happened, that it wasn't fair to Mira if she were there alone.

He drove home, coasting through stop signs, and entered the house to find Mira supine on the couch, watching an episode of *The Bachelorette*.

"You caught me," she said guiltily.

"Keep watching. I'm going to start reading my book in the office."

"How is it out there?"

"Cold and rainy. I don't recommend going outside."

"I wasn't planning on it," Mira said.

In his office, with the door shut, he considered telling Mira in advance that he'd gone to see Hen. The only reason to do that would be as a preemptive strike, just in case Hen *did* file a complaint with the police or Lloyd *did* come banging on the door. But he decided to risk it. For some reason, he didn't think Hen was going to tell anyone. He actually thought she just might take him up on his offer. He'd seen her artwork, knew how her mind worked. She had a morbid curiosity. He was offering her so much. He was offering himself to her.

Instead of looking at his new book, Matthew went on the internet. He looked again at some of Hen's art, and then, because he hadn't done it yet, he looked up Hen's husband, Lloyd Harding. There wasn't much about him online. His name was listed on his company's website. There was a LinkedIn profile. He did, however, find an old blog that hadn't been updated for five years. It was called *Documenting Lloyd* and was a list of short, mostly snarky reviews of documentary features. On the About page, Lloyd referred to himself as an aspiring documentary filmmaker. Matthew wondered what had happened to that dream. He didn't like Lloyd, hadn't liked him the night he'd been over for dinner. He seemed soft and lazy and could barely hide his boredom at having to sit through dinner at his neighbors' house. Matthew had also thought that he hadn't been remotely complimentary enough of Mira's cooking. Hen said several times how much she loved the food, while her husband merely shook his head minutely in agreement, made an affirmative grunting sound. Matthew remembered looking across the table at Lloyd and imagining how he'd look with plastic wrap across his face.

Matthew made a decision to find out what he could about Lloyd Harding. There was probably nothing, but you never could tell.

After dinner that night—Mira's amazing lentil soup—Matthew finally relaxed, realizing that if either the police or Lloyd were going to come knocking on the door, they'd have done it already. Hen hadn't told anyone about his visit. That didn't mean that she would agree to meet with him, but at least it meant she was keeping it to herself.

They had a secret, the two of them, and there was no better way to start a friendship than with a secret.

MATTHEW DIDN'T HEAR FROM Hen that evening or the next day. Mira left early Monday morning to catch her flight, and Matthew went to school.

Michelle, after taking a week off from teaching, was returning to Sussex Hall. There was an early-morning all-staff meeting before she arrived, during which Donald Hoogheem, the head of the history department, told everyone that Michelle had indicated that she'd prefer to not talk about the death of her boyfriend. She'd rather spend her time catching up on the work she'd missed.

Matthew assumed he was exempt from that particular request, especially since he and Michelle had already talked on the phone. He wasn't surprised when Michelle came by his classroom at the end of the day, closing the door behind her after she entered.

"What are people saying?" she asked.

"Nothing, really. Donald got us all together this morning before you got here and told us not to bring it up with you."

Michelle rapidly shook her head, said, "Arrgh, I don't

know if that was the right choice. I just didn't want to have to explain to everyone that we weren't going out anymore, that I know nothing about what happened to him, that—"

"What did happen to him? Have they made an arrest?"

"I haven't heard anything. They did question me, but it was for all of about fifteen minutes, just asking me about our relationship and if he had any enemies . . . I told you this already, didn't I?"

"You did, but that's okay."

"Well, that's the last I heard from them. My guess is he pissed off some guy at the bar by hitting on his girlfriend."

"He was a bad guy, you know that," Matthew said, trying to make her feel better.

Instead, she frowned, then her lower lip trembled and she started to cry. Matthew went to her, guided her to a chair, and they both sat.

When she could finally talk, she said, "I know that he was bad for me, but I'm not sure that means he was a bad man."

"People are defined by their actions. What they do is who they are."

"I know. I'm glad he's not going to be in my life, but I'm still upset about what happened to him. He was so young."

Matthew knew when to be quiet, and he didn't say anything. After a moment, Michelle took a deep breath and said, "I think my students know what happened to me. No one—not even Ben Gimbel—gave me a hard time."

"Silver lining," Matthew said, and Michelle smiled.

"The other thing is that suddenly I have *nothing* to do in my life." Michelle sat up straight. "When I was with Scott, then either I was with him, or else he was away and I was obsessing about him, wondering if he was cheating on me. And for the twenty-four hours after we'd broken up, before I heard he was dead, I was just as obsessed, wondering whether I did the right thing, if he missed me, if he was already with someone else. But now . . . now I have nothing. It's a huge hole."

"You'll meet someone else," Matthew said.

"Will I?"

"Eventually."

She laughed, loudly this time. "The way you said that did not sound too convincing. I do have a stalker, though. That's something."

"What do you mean?"

"I got an email last night from some guy saying how sorry he was about my loss, and how he saw a picture of me and was thinking of me. How creepy is that?"

"Who was the guy?"

"I don't know. Some guy. Richard, he said his name was."

Matthew's chest tightened, and he tried not to show it on his face. "Did you write him back?"

"God, no. I ignored it."

"Did you tell the police about it?"

"Why?"

"I don't know. Maybe he had something to do with what happened to Scott."

"I don't think so. I mean, I think he just read an article, and saw my name, and then googled me, and—"

"How'd he get your email?"

"It was my Sussex Hall email. If you google my name, it comes up that I work here. You okay, Matthew?"

"Yes, sorry. I was just worrying, that's all, that this guy would email you out of the blue."

"I'm a famous victim." Michelle laughed. "The creepy men will all come calling. Maybe one of them will be husband material."

"Well, don't write him back."

"I won't," she said, then added, "My protector," and blushed.

MATTHEW CONTACTED HIS BROTHER that night. He thought about asking him over sometime that week since Mira was away, but as soon as he heard his voice, he came out and asked him. "You didn't by any chance write an email to Michelle Brine, did you?"

"Who?" Richard said.

"Michelle Brine. I work with her. She told me she got a creepy email from a Richard."

"I have no idea who you're talking about."

"Okay," Matthew said. Richard sounded convincing, but he always sounded convincing.

"Who is she? Another of your girlfriends that you hide from Mira?"

"No."

"Why is she telling you about the emails she gets?"

"She's a friend from work. Not a girlfriend. You know I'm faithful to Mira."

"You're not really, you know, Matthew. Just because you don't fuck these women you become friends with doesn't mean you're faithful. Let me guess: this Michelle tells you all about her personal life, and sometimes you give her a hug, and sometimes it goes on a little too long—"

"I'm not in the mood, Richard."

"Fine. Fuck you, and fuck Michelle Brine as well. Someone ought to do it."

Matthew lay in bed that night wondering if talking with Richard had been a mistake.

CHAPTER 24

Hen kept thinking about Matthew Dolamore.

She hadn't yet told Lloyd about his visit to her during Open Studios. She *couldn't* tell Lloyd, not really, because telling him was a lose-lose situation. He'd either confront Matthew himself—and what would that accomplish?—or make Hen go to the police and tell them everything, and that would only make Hen look more unhinged. Matthew was right about that— anything she said about him now would look like a lie. And that was the other reason she wasn't telling Lloyd about the encounter. Because what if her own husband didn't believe her? What if he thought she was making the whole thing up? He'd want to hospitalize her, wouldn't he? Change her meds, at least. That's what she might consider if the positions were reversed.

And because she couldn't tell anyone about what had happened, she kept thinking about Matthew. He was the one person who now believed her. The thought was funny, in a grotesque sort of way. She and he were the only two people who knew the entire truth. Matthew would never tell anyone, because if he did he'd spend the rest of his life in prison. And she couldn't tell anyone, because no one would believe her, because everyone would decide she was having another manic episode.

Maybe I should meet with him.

That same thought kept crossing her mind, even though the very idea of it terrified her. *Maybe I should hear what he has to say.*

In her mind she kept playing it out. She was thinking that it would have to be in a semipublic place, a place where he couldn't hurt her. They could meet at the Burlington Mall, grab a couple of Cinnabons, and stroll past the storefronts, Matthew telling her about his life as a psychotic killer. She supposed they could also meet closer to home, go grab a drink some afternoon at the Owl's Head Tavern, get a cozy table. The problem with that scenario was that it would look like they were having an affair. Another neighbor might see them. She supposed they could go to another bar altogether, something in another town.

You could go to his house. Sit in his office. He kept one souvenir—the fencing trophy—so maybe he kept more. It could be like show-and-tell.

The truth was that Hen mostly believed Matthew when he told her that he would never hurt her. She didn't know why, exactly, but she did. When he came to her at her studio it wasn't to threaten her or scare her. He seemed to genuinely want someone to talk with. And if that was true, then wasn't the right thing, the moral thing, to do to listen to his story? He might give something away, tell her a detail that would allow her to go to the police. She might also be able to help him, get him to realize that he needed to turn himself in. The more she thought about this line of reasoning, the more

she became convinced that it really was her moral duty
to sit and talk with Matthew Dolamore. There was no
other option. She knew that he was dangerous, but there
was no way to convince the police (*or her goddamn
husband*) of that fact.

In the afternoon she returned to the studio, taking the
car because the rain that had begun on Sunday had crept
into Monday as a steady, cold drizzle. It was quiet on the
basement level, and Hen was glad that the exterior door
was locked, unlike yesterday. Back in the studio, she
tidied up, trying hard not to think too much about Matthew's visit the day before. She'd hoped to be able to get
a little bit of work done—put down some preliminary
sketches based on the outline she'd received for the next
Lore Warriors book, tentatively titled *The School for
Lore Warriors: Scary Godmothers*—but she found herself still thinking about meeting with Matthew, wondering if there was more to it than just trying to do a good
deed, trying to stop a criminal. Was there a part of her
that was a little bit interested in hearing the details of
what he'd done? She was, after all, being offered something that most people were never offered: A look inside
someone's mind. A look inside a monster's mind. Of
course anybody would be interested. It was why people
watched true-crime shows and read books about serial
killers. It was why people liked her artwork. She was
well aware that the more disturbing her etchings, the
more interest they received.

She was about to leave the studio when Lloyd texted
her: *Slow day. Coming home early.*

Hen knew that it probably wasn't that slow—nothing
at his company was slow—and that he was more likely

coming home early because he was worried about her. She wrote back, *See you soon,* and then added a smiling emoji face.

She left the studio, locking up behind her, and got back in the car. If Lloyd was leaving the city now, he wouldn't be home for another hour, give or take. Hen was still thinking about where to meet Matthew. It would have to be a public place. She remembered passing by what looked like a well-lit sports bar two towns over in Wickford. It was along Route 117. She'd passed it a few times because it was on the way to the best art supply store in the area. It wasn't far—a fifteen-minute drive—and Hen left the studio and headed toward 117.

It actually took her closer to twenty minutes, but that was because rush-hour traffic was beginning to pile up. The bar was called the Winner's Circle and was one of four businesses located in a single-story strip mall right after you crossed into Wickford. The windows advertised keno and the Massachusetts Lottery and forty-cent wings during all Patriots games. Hen parked next to a pickup truck with a Bruins bumper sticker and got out of her car. She really just wanted to look at the bar's interior, to see how dark it was, to see if anyone was there. She wondered if she could go in and pretend she was looking for someone, but didn't really want to draw attention to herself. Instead, she pushed through the door, then pulled herself up on one of the vinyl-covered stools along the bar. She was pleased that she wasn't the only customer, even on a Monday afternoon. There was one man at the other end of the bar, drinking a bottle of Coors Light and keeping his eye on one of the multiple televisions that were all showing what looked like a talk show devoted to sports. And there was a youngish couple in one of the booths along the other side of the bar. Between them was a pile of nachos the size of a bowling ball.

The bartender, a stringy blonde in black jeans and a white tank top, came down the bar, and Hen ordered a Shock Top, the only beer pull she could read from where she was sitting.

"Orange in that?"

"Sorry?"

"Orange slice. In your beer."

"No, thanks."

The beer came. Hen paid in cash, left a tip, and the bartender returned to the other end of the bar and began scrolling through her phone. Hen took a long sip of her beer, then looked around. The place was fine for a meeting with Matthew. The booths had high backs, and Hen assumed they'd be able to have a conversation without being overheard. It wasn't overly lit, but it was wallpapered in television screens, so it also wasn't that dark. And Hen assumed that no one she knew—not that she knew many people—would be hanging around the Winner's Circle in the afternoon.

She assumed that afternoons would work for meeting with Matthew. He was a schoolteacher, so he got out early. And there was simply no way that she could sneak out again at night. Lloyd would never forgive her.

She drank the rest of the beer, a light buzz settling into her body, relaxing her muscles, then checked the time. She'd have to leave now if she wanted to beat Lloyd home.

THE FOLLOWING DAY HEN didn't go back to the studio. It was sunny again after two days of rain, and the leaves that had held on to the trees were more vibrant than ever. All of Sycamore Street shimmered with color. After lunch, she pulled her winter clothes from the plastic storage containers they'd been in since the previous winter in Cambridge. She found her warmest sweater, a wool turtleneck in a color Lloyd liked to call "fungus" and she thought of as a muted orange, plus a fleece-lined cap, and went out onto the porch with a big mug of tea and her sketchbook. The sun was already low in the sky, just over the tops of the roofs across the street, but it kept the porch relatively warm. She moved her chair to the sunniest portion, put her feet up on the bench they'd been using as a table, and kept her eye on the road.

It was almost dark when Matthew's Fiat came down Sycamore and pulled into the driveway. Hen froze. She'd been so keyed up waiting to see when her neighbor returned home that she hadn't entirely decided what to do when he did.

He parked halfway down the driveway and got out of his car. Hen stood, forcing herself to push through the screen door, then walk down the three steps so that she was on the edge of her own driveway, looking across at Matthew.

He turned to her and Hen walked toward him, her head down a little, not wanting to make eye contact until they were talking. He waited for her, a leather briefcase in his left hand.

"Let's meet," she said, when she was close enough.

"Okay," he said. "Now?"

Hen hadn't been prepared for that and quickly shook her head. "No, let's meet tomorrow. There's a bar in

Wickford called the Winner's Circle. On 117. Do you know it?"

He shook his head. "No, but I can find it. Why do you want to meet in a bar?"

"I'm not meeting with you alone," Hen said.

"Right," he said, as though he just remembered why they were having this meeting in the first place.

"When can you get there?"

"I can get there by three thirty."

"That works. Three thirty. There are booths to the left when you walk in."

"Okay," he said, nodding.

Hen turned and walked back to her house before he could see how badly she was shaking.

CHAPTER 25

Matthew parked in front of the used sports equipment store that was next to the Winner's Circle. He didn't see Hen's Golf in the parking lot and wondered if he'd beaten her here or, maybe, she'd changed her mind.

He turned the engine off and got out of the car. It was a bright, blustery day, the parking lot littered with fallen leaves that skittered in the wind.

He pushed through the front door of the Winner's Circle. There were two middle-aged women at the bar and no one in the booths. Football highlights played on all the televisions. He walked up to the bar, trying to seem casual, and asked for a ginger ale with a lime wedge. He paid and brought the drink back with him to the booth in the far corner, and sat so that he could watch the doors.

One of the women from the bar slid off her stool and went to the jukebox, inserting a bill, then punching several numbers. The first song to come on was a hard rock ballad he recognized, although he couldn't remember the name of the band that performed it. He thought the song was called "Every Rose Has Its Thorn," and the chorus confirmed that he was right. The woman who chose the song kept peeking over at Matthew as it played, maybe looking for validation. He glanced down at his drink. The wedge of lime that floated on top of the ginger ale was dotted with dark brown spots.

The outside door opened, and Hen entered, ushering in with her a brisk gust of wind that Matthew could feel all the way at the back of the bar. He began to stand up to greet her, but she went straight to the bar without meeting his eye, so he stayed put. She brought her draft beer over to the booth and slid in across from him. She was wearing the same sweater she'd worn the previous day when she'd invited him to this bar. A thick, rust-colored turtleneck that had started to pill a little.

"Hello," she said.

"I'm going to have to pat you down, you realize that?" Those were the words he'd been planning on saying first. He was surprised that she looked surprised.

"Oh," she said.

"Otherwise, we can't have this conversation. You understand that, don't you?"

"You're looking for a wire?" she said, and made a quizzical expression. "I'm not wearing one."

"I believe you, but I have to check."

"Okay, how?"

"I'll just slide in next to you for a minute. It will look like we're hugging hello."

"I don't know," Hen said.

"It's up to you, of course, but I need to know for sure."

"Okay," she said.

Matthew slid out of his side of the booth. The woman who'd picked the music was now back at the bar with her friend. "Under My Thumb" by the Rolling Stones was playing. He slid in next to Hen and said, "Sorry about this," as he ran his hands along the sides of her bulky sweater.

"What are you wearing under the sweater?" he asked.

"A flannel shirt."

He put his hands under the sweater, thinking she'd object, but she lifted her arms, and he ran his hands along the soft flannel, up and down her sides, then along her back and briefly over her stomach. He felt nothing but her rib cage and the rapid movement of her lungs. Under the sweater she was wearing tight jeans, and he ran his hands down her legs as professionally as he could. He could feel the edges of her cell phone in her front pocket.

"Can I check your phone, make sure you're not recording?"

"Okay," she said, and showed him her phone, turning it on with her thumbprint, flicking through the different apps. Matthew didn't exactly know what he was looking for, but he didn't see anything suspicious. He hadn't thought that she'd come wired, but he couldn't be sure.

"Thank you," he said, and returned to his side of the booth. He attempted a joke, saying, "Now that the awkward part is out of the way . . ."

She frowned at him. "Don't try and be funny," she said. "It doesn't really suit you."

"Yeah, I know."

"You found the bar all right?" she asked.

"At least I'm not attempting small talk," he said.

She smiled at this. "Right. Tell me why you killed Scott Doyle."

"I thought you'd be more interested in Dustin Miller."

"I think I already know why you murdered him. He'd raped someone, right, when he was at Sussex Hall?"

Matthew sipped at his drink, a little thrown off by Hen's wording. "It wasn't just a 'someone,'" he said. "Her name was Courtney Cheigh."

"I didn't know that. I mean I didn't know her name."

"She was one of those students that stay after class and ask you more questions about what you've been teaching. She probably did it because she was too shy to ask the questions in class, but, still, she had a genuine intellectual curiosity."

"Is she . . . dead?"

"Oh, no. Sorry. I think I always refer to my students in the past tense. No, she's fine, as far as I know. She didn't come back to the five-year reunion, but one of her friends said she's in law school down in D.C. and doing well. I like to think she'll become a prosecutor and go after men like Dustin Miller."

"She won't have to go after *him,* though. You took care of that."

"Yes, I did. Right before he died I said Courtney's name to him so that he would know why he was dying." Saying those words out loud felt immensely satisfying, and Matthew worked to not let it show on his face. To not smile.

"And you think he knew in that moment. You think that he wasn't just utterly terrified."

Matthew leaned forward a little. "If all he felt was utter terror, then I still did my job. He was a bad man. He was going to make many, many women miserable."

"But wasn't there a possibility that he would change? That maybe what happened with the student at your school, as horrible as it was, was just a one-time thing? Maybe he would have gone on to get married, raise children, become an okay person."

"First of all, what he did to Courtney was enough. For that he deserved to die. You know, I overheard him make a joke about her after she left school. He and his friend were talking about which girl had the biggest breasts now that Courtney was gone. They didn't use the word *breast,* of course. No, trust me. He was a bad person. Personalities don't change. Do you remember the night you came over for dinner with your husband? You asked me about teaching, and I said something about how wonderful it is to watch kids grow up before my eyes, the changes that take place between freshman year and senior year?"

"I remember that."

"It's only partly true. I watch these kids mature, watch them go from awkward adolescence into adulthood, but what I never see is their personalities change. They are who they are. If they are kind their freshman year—even if they make mistakes or get in trouble—then they are kind senior year. It goes the other way as well. I knew that Dustin Miller was going to be an abuser of women his whole life, before I even heard what he'd done to Courtney in St. Louis. It was just in him. It was the same way with my father—he preyed on the weak." Matthew felt his voice rising, and he took a breath, told himself to talk at a lower volume. "Nothing would ever change that fact. He was what he was."

"And you changed him? You changed Dustin Miller?"

"Yes, I did. I changed him from the living to the dead."

"That's, uh, a pretty big change. Lots of people probably think like you do, but not many people act on it."

"I'm not like many people."

She hadn't touched her beer since sitting down, but she looked at it now and took a small swallow. "Do you think you can stop?"

"Stop killing people?"

"Yes."

"Is that why you're here, because you think you can stop me?"

"I'm here because you asked me to meet with you, because you said you wanted to tell the truth to someone. I assumed that maybe you wanted to unburden yourself of some guilt, maybe find a way to stop what you're doing."

"I can see why you'd think that, but that wasn't why I wanted to talk with you. I thought, maybe, that you'd understand what it is that I do. I've seen your artwork, and I thought—"

"You think you're some kind of artist as well."

"No. I don't. I don't think that, but I do know that when I kill someone—when I do it well enough—that what I feel afterward is close to the way I feel when I look at a piece of perfect art."

"Why is that?"

"You must know the feeling. When you create something—like that picture you drew of the teenage girl looking in the mirror and seeing herself with the . . . with the . . ."

"With the deer horns."

"Yes. When you first drew that—or engraved it, or whatever you do—how did you feel? It didn't exist until you drew it, right? You brought it into the world out of nothing. That's what I do but in reverse. I take a living, breathing person, and I subtract him from the earth. When I'm done with him, he is entirely changed—the most changed a person can be—and that's a monumental thing. You have to understand that."

"I understand that it's a monumental thing, but I don't understand what's good about it."

"You wouldn't go back in time to kill Hitler if you had a chance?"

"I'm not sure that really applies here."

"All right, then, would you go back and kill Ted Bundy if you had a chance?"

"You're saying that Dustin Miller would have become a serial killer? Or Scott Doyle? How could you possibly know that?"

"I'm saying that they were going to spread unhappiness—that they were going to make life miserable for people. By subtracting them from the world, I've added to the world's happiness."

Hen looked skeptical, and Matthew decided to stop talking for a moment, even though he was just getting going and felt like he had a lot to say. Hen didn't speak, either, so Matthew said, "Can you at least admit that I might be right?"

"That you might have been right in killing them? No, I can't admit that. You don't have the right to make that decision. It's not up to you. That's not the way it works. Look," Hen said, shifting in her seat. "I think coming here was a mistake. I don't know what I was looking for exactly. I think you need to get professional help. I think you need to stop doing what you're doing. You're not an artist; you're just a criminal. I watched Scott Doyle die, do you know that?"

"You mean that you saw him when he was dead."

"No, he wasn't dead when I got there. I saw him die."

"What was it like?" Matthew said.

"It was fucking awful. He was confused, and scared, and his brain was coming out of his head."

Hearing the words, Matthew's stomach turned over. He'd worried about that, worried that he'd broken through the skull the final time he hit Scott Doyle. He shook the feeling off and said, "Then he had two seconds of fear and confusion. Michelle Brine has felt a lot more than that."

"Who's Michelle Brine?"

Matthew stopped himself from saying more. He'd told himself before meeting with Hen that he needed to be careful about providing any information that she could use to prove that her side of the story was true. He wasn't sure Michelle fit into that category, but he wanted to be careful.

"She doesn't matter," he finally said, then quickly added, "I am very sorry that you had to witness what you witnessed. I never would have done it if I'd known that would happen. You do understand that, don't you?"

"Not really."

"You're not a bad person. I would never hurt you."

"What if you suddenly decided that I was a bad person? Wouldn't that change things?"

"I would still never hurt you. I would never hurt a woman."

Hen spontaneously smiled, her brow creasing. For a moment Matthew thought she was going to laugh at him. "You don't think there'd be a woman bad enough for you to want to kill?"

"No, there wouldn't be. Of course not. I know what you're thinking, that I've got some savior complex, that I'm going to save all the innocent females of the world from the big bad wolves. I'm not an idiot. I know that's part of it. My dad was a monster and my mother was his victim, and that's why I think the way I do. I've psycho-analyzed myself far more and far deeper than you or anyone else could. I know what I am."

"But—"

"But the truth is that men hurt women far more than women will ever hurt men. It's just a fact. And . . . and I would never hurt you not just because you're a woman, but also because you're a decent human being. I know that."

"So, if you believe that, if you believe I'm a decent human being, then maybe you'll listen to me. I think you should turn yourself in, confess to the police. Tell them what you told me."

"Why would I do that?"

"Don't you want to stop what you're doing? Isn't that why you're here, talking with me? You must feel guilt."

"I don't feel guilt. I'm here talking with you because I thought you might understand."

"I don't. I don't understand. I'm sorry. I think you've developed a bogus moral code, a story you tell yourself so that you can do what it is that you like to do. You like to kill people. It's obvious."

"I do," he said. "I like to kill people." A shiver went over Matthew's skin, a ripple starting at his back and going up to the base of his skull. It felt so good to say the words. "I would never pretend that it isn't part of it. I'm not delusional."

Hen sighed. "I think I should go."

"Don't you like it when you've created a piece of art? Something disturbing. Doesn't it give you a perverse thrill?"

"It's entirely different. My art doesn't hurt people. It's just art."

"It's not *just* art, really, though, is it? It's revealing a part of yourself."

Hen rapidly shook her head. "All it's revealing is my imagination, something entirely removed from reality. I can separate the two, and you can't. That's the difference between us."

"Okay," Matthew said. "Think about what I've said, though. You'd probably like killing, if you ever tried it."

"I wouldn't, trust me."

"Are you going to tell the police what I said today?"

"I haven't decided yet."

"They won't believe you."

"I know that, but I think you're going to get caught. And when they do catch you, I'll go to them and tell them everything."

"Does your husband know we're meeting here today?"

"I'll probably tell him about it," Hen said, and Matthew thought it was the first time she'd lied since sitting down across from him.

"He doesn't deserve you," Matthew said, and then witnessed a look of concern pass across Hen's features. "No, don't worry. I have no designs on Lloyd, but, still, he doesn't deserve you."

"You don't even know him."

"He came to my house for dinner. I watched him, and I could tell that he has no real moral compass. Whenever Mira left the dining room or came back in, he watched the way she moved. He probably imagined having sex with her."

"Jesus. All right, I should go." Hen slid along the booth.

"Can I ask you one thing? When you first got involved with him, was he with someone else?"

"That's none of your business."

"Clearly, he was. People don't change, Hen. He's cheating on you, but you probably already knew that."

CHAPTER 26

Hen had felt an array of emotions since sitting down at the Winner's Circle with Matthew Dolamore, but suddenly she felt real anger. All that bullshit philosophy about her artwork, and now it seemed like he was accusing (threatening?) Lloyd.

She stood. "Fuck you, Matthew," she said. "You're not anyone's savior, trust me on that."

"I'm not saying I'm a savior, just that your husband is probably not what he seems."

"What does that have to do with you?"

"Nothing," Matthew said. "I'm sorry I brought it up."

She left the bar, not realizing how dark it had been in there until she punched her way back out into the light of late afternoon. Wind was whipping leaves and trash around the parking lot. She got into her car and pulled out onto 117. The song she'd been listening to when she parked in front of the bar—"Shiver" by Lucy Rose— started up again. She slid the volume down, wanting a moment to digest the conversation she'd just had. Going over Matthew's words in her mind, she kept wondering if he'd given her anything, any piece of information, that would be worth bringing to the police. She knew they wouldn't believe her outright if she told them everything he'd said, but what if she had some solid evidence? But no, the more she thought about it, he just talked about his philosophical reasons for killing. If only she had figured out a way to record him—she'd definitely thought about it—then this would all be over. He wanted to talk. And it was clear that he also wanted to impress Hen, to intrigue her, maybe even to make her see life the way he saw it. And what was that shit about Lloyd? She thought back to the night they'd all had dinner together, tried to remember if she'd noticed Lloyd checking Mira out. She had no recollection of that. She did know that he looked at other women, which was 100 percent fine with her. She was more comfortable with his telling her that he was attracted to other women than she'd be if he told her he wasn't. Still, why was Matthew so confident that Lloyd was a cheater?

A horn blared behind her, and she realized she'd been sitting at a green light. She moved forward, catching up with the slow-moving traffic. It wasn't quite five yet, but the roads were busy. She pulled out her phone to see if Lloyd had sent her a message that he was leaving yet, and saw that he'd actually sent a text saying that he was working late and she would be on her own for dinner.

She thought, *Obviously cheating,* then laughed out loud in the car. She didn't like the way her laugh sounded, almost as if she were out of breath.

Back at home, she was greeted at the door by Vinegar mewling loudly. He led her to the basement and his empty food bowl, and she filled it, apologizing.

In the kitchen, she looked into the refrigerator for a while, trying to decide if she wanted another beer. She was trembling slightly, even though she'd felt relatively calm at the bar. But she'd been sitting across from someone who was insane, someone who was suddenly very interested in her life. All the beers in the fridge were Lloyd's overly hoppy IPAs. There was a small bottle of cranberry juice, and she made herself a drink over a lot of ice with the bottle of vodka they kept in the freezer. She took a long sip, then focused on her breathing. Her mind was jumping. She kept trying to think about what Matthew had said about Dustin Miller and Scott Doyle, but found herself thinking about Lloyd instead. If he was cheating on her, she supposed that it would be relatively easy. He worked in Boston, and she was stuck out here in the suburbs. He did occasionally work late, as he was tonight, but he always came back eager to tell Hen about the new campaign his firm was working on. If he was lying, then he was a very good liar. And Hen didn't think Lloyd was a good liar. So, if he *was* cheating, then when was he doing it? His last chance would have been at Rob's annual bonfire party, and she was pretty sure that the only people who showed up to that were other guys from his college, maybe the occasional girlfriend or wife. And it was hardly a sexy event, just a bunch of dudes getting high and playing with fire.

Hen put her drink down on the kitchen counter and went toward the stairs. The thought of that party had triggered a sudden memory in her from the day after Scott Doyle's murder. Lloyd at the police station, taking her in his arms. He'd come directly from Rob's house that day. She remembered the smell of him. The stale sweat, which was not a surprise. But there'd been something else, something she'd barely noticed because of everything else that was going on. He didn't smell like smoke. She'd been to Rob's bonfire parties many times, and the next day, and sometimes the day after that, you reeked of woodsmoke. It got into your clothes and into your hair. It got into your nostrils and stayed there.

In their bedroom, Hen looked at the overflowing laundry basket, two weeks' worth of clothes that both Lloyd and she had been ignoring. She started to paw through it, spreading the clothes across the unmade bed until she found what she was looking for—the outfit Lloyd had been wearing on his weekend away. His nicest jeans and a checked shirt with a frayed collar. She pressed her face into the shirt and breathed in deeply. There was no trace of smoke at all. Just to make sure, she pulled out all of Lloyd's clothes from the laundry basket and smelled them. Nothing.

Back downstairs, she picked up her cell phone and scrolled through her contacts, finding Rob Boyd, surprised she still had his number on her phone. Her thumb hovered over the Call button. What exactly was she going to say? She couldn't just out and out ask if Lloyd had showed up at the bonfire, because if Rob said no, she could almost guarantee that he'd alert Lloyd to the call right away. She racked her brain, coming up with a reason to call, and hit the button before she changed her mind.

"Hen?" came Rob's voice almost immediately.

"Hey, Rob," she said.

"Everything okay?"

"Yeah, yeah. Totally fine. I have kind of a random question for you."

"Okay?" His voice sounded like it was coming from a hollow room. Hen guessed he was driving.

"I'm doing a cover illustration for a new book, or hoping to, anyway. It's about witches and they want a bonfire on the cover."

"Cool," Rob said.

"I looked online for photos of bonfires and didn't find anything . . . I was wondering—"

"Yeah, I actually have some awesome shots. Want me to send you some?"

"Yes, that would be amazing. Very, very helpful."

"Not a prob."

"How *are* you? It's been a while."

"I'm all right. Getting old. Missed you guys at this year's party."

Hen felt an actual physical sensation move through the center of her body. "Oh, sorry about that . . . We just moved into this new house, and—"

"Yeah, Lloyd already gave me all your lame excuses. I didn't buy it from him and I'm not buying it from you."

"Who was there?"

Rob began to list names, most of which meant nothing to Hen. She pretended to listen, but all she really wanted to do was to get off the phone and absorb the information she'd just received. Lloyd hadn't gone to Rob's party, which meant that he'd gone on some romantic weekend away with whomever he was now involved with—there was no other possibility, was there?

Rob was finishing up his list. ". . . and Justin, of course, who never misses it."

"Hey, sorry again. Next year for sure."

"I'll believe it when I see it. Oh, fuck . . . Red light, lady." Hen heard the bleat of a horn, then Rob continued: "Look, I gotta go. I'll send you some sweet bonfire pictures."

"Thanks so much, Rob."

Hen dropped her hand to the top of her thigh, the phone gripped loosely, and just sat for five minutes.

Lloyd wasn't just having a fling; he was orchestrating weekends away. The thought was somehow so alien to her, as strange as hearing that Lloyd had once been a woman or that he was secretly employed by the CIA. She felt hurt, but she also just felt baffled, blindsided by this new information. Part of her bafflement was that she never really thought of Lloyd as someone who hid things, as someone with enough cunning, enough intelligence, really, to get away with a major affair. Suddenly, more than anything, she wanted to know more. She wanted to know everything.

Lloyd's laptop was charging on the kitchen counter, and Hen went and grabbed it. It was password protected, but Hen knew almost all of Lloyd's passwords. And unless it was the password for their bank account or credit card account, Lloyd almost always used ASDFJKL; (Hen had given him a hard time once about how easy that would be to figure out, but he'd kept it anyway). The password worked, and Hen went first to Lloyd's internet history. He'd cleared it the night before, and the only sites he'd visited that morning had been a Red Sox blog that she knew he commented on and his email account. She quickly scanned his emails, looking for anything from a woman she didn't know, but also looking for correspondence with Rob Boyd. She didn't find anything in his inbox, but when she went to his Sent folder, she did find an email exchange with Rob in which Lloyd had said that they couldn't come to the bonfire that year ("still got a shitload of unpacking to do") and that they'd definitely make it the next year.

Hen went further back, looking at all the emails Lloyd sent, most of them to his parents or to his brother in North Carolina. Going back over a year, though, she found an email conversation that he'd had with Joanna Grimlund, Rob's ex-girlfriend who still lived in Massachusetts.

The first email was from Lloyd to Joanna: "Hey, I had a really great time over the weekend." This was from a year ago, also in October. Hen had skipped that bonfire party.

According to the time stamp, Joanna had responded to Lloyd about five minutes later: "Me, too. Too bad Rob has to be there at his own parties. Otherwise they'd be perfect. Just kidding! J."

The next email came from Lloyd the following day and was five words: "Can you call me today?"

There was no response, or if there had been, it had been deleted. Whatever had begun that weekend had obviously continued without the benefit of email.

Hen opened up a new message box in her husband's email account and put Joanna's address in, then wrote, "We need to end this." She hovered the cursor over the Send button but didn't press it, even though the thought of it made a strange little giggle rise in the back of her throat. She deleted the unsent message, quit the browser, and shut the laptop. Lloyd would be home soon, and she needed to decide what to do with the information she had. If she accused him as soon as he came in the door, told him she knew he hadn't been to Rob's party over the weekend, then it would all spill out. Unless he somehow tried to make up an excuse, he would tell her everything. He was having an affair with Joanna Grimlund. He was probably in love with her, and he was probably going to leave Hen. In fact, he'd probably be thrilled that Hen would be the one who brought it up. It would end the torment.

Hen was pacing, and she found herself standing in the living room, looking out the window toward her neighbors' house. At least now she wasn't thinking about everything that Matthew had told her. That had somehow been eclipsed by the information that Lloyd had been lying to her for an entire year. Why hadn't he just left?

The phone in her jeans buzzed and she looked at Lloyd's text, saying that he was on his way home.

She put the phone back in her pocket and suddenly knew that she wasn't going to confront him tonight. It felt important, somehow, that she hold on to the information she had about him for a while, that she spend some time knowing more than he did.

And when he eventually entered the house, sullen and quiet, and gave Hen a perfunctory kiss on the top of the head and went straight to the refrigerator for a beer, Hen watched him, and it felt like she was watching a stranger.

CHAPTER 27

Matthew got home just before dusk. The inside of the house was dark, but he didn't turn on any lights. He went to his office and thought about the conversation with Hen. It had gone so much better than he'd ever imagined. He'd told her things about himself that he'd never told anyone, and she'd stayed in her seat, listening, her dark brown eyes looking right at him. Every word he'd said had lifted a weight from him, and now he felt as light as he'd felt in years and years.

He replayed the conversation to himself many, many times, his breathing getting shallow. Maybe he shouldn't have brought up Lloyd to her so soon—she'd been out of there as soon as he did—but he needed her to know that she wasn't immune from what men did to women, that Lloyd was as full of lustful thoughts as anyone. He wasn't sure, of course, that he was cheating, but it was a definite possibility. He was a man, after all, and that's what men did.

The name he really wished he hadn't mentioned was Michelle's. Why had he said that thing about her suffering at the hands of Scott Doyle? He did want to be entirely truthful with Hen—wasn't that the plan?— but that didn't mean he needed to tell her everything right away. No, the reason he shouldn't have mentioned Michelle was that Hen could look her up if she wanted to, go talk with her. Not that it would lead to anything, but the thought made him feel queasy, the way he felt knowing that his brother had probably sent Michelle an email. Jesus, he'd forgotten all about that. All the good feelings he had from his conversation with Hen suddenly drained from his body.

To make himself feel better, he called Michelle on his cell phone just to make sure she was okay.

"Hey, Matthew. Strange. I was just going to call you."

"Yeah, why?"

"Look, I just talked with Donald, and I'm going to take the rest of this semester off. He said he can get a permanent sub and that he'd hold the job for me if I wanted to come back in January."

"Seriously?"

"It's just that . . . with everything going on, with what happened with Scott and with what's happening with my father, I just don't think I have the time and energy to focus on work. I'm going to go home and live with my parents for a while—God, just saying those words out loud . . . No, it's the right thing to do. I feel good about it."

"Well, that's what matters the most."

"I feel good about it."

"Then I think you're doing the right thing."

"You do? It makes me happy to hear that."

"I do, just so long as you eventually come back. If not in January, then hopefully next year. You're a good history teacher."

"Okay, now I'm going to cry," Michelle said.

"When are you going to leave?"

"I'm driving to my parents' house tomorrow morning."

"What?"

"Yeah, I know. Donald already has a sub—it's the same woman who stepped in when Mandy was on maternity leave, you remember her?"

Matthew pictured a semiretired public school teacher, silver hair and purple dresses. "Yeah, I do. Your students will be okay."

"They will, won't they?"

"I can't believe we didn't get a chance to say goodbye."

"Want to come over tonight?" Michelle asked, the words coming out rushed, almost as though they'd been planned.

"Um," Matthew said, hesitating.

"I know it's last minute, but Mira's still away, right? It would be great to see you."

"I'm busy," Matthew said, "but sure. When would be a good time to drop by?"

"Now? Or anytime. I'll probably be up all night packing and getting organized. Come by anytime."

After eating a bowl of cereal—it was all his stomach could really handle—and FaceTiming with Mira, Matthew drove to Country Squire Estates, a sprawl of cheap apartment buildings with fake beams crisscrossed on the exterior siding. The sign at the entrance was forest green, COUNTRY SQUIRE spelled out in a faux medieval script. Matthew parked in the visitors' lot next to the swimming pool, which was covered with a tarp for the season. The tarp, filled with brown rainwater and fallen leaves, sagged in the middle, and Matthew suddenly had second thoughts about what he was doing. He knew that

Michelle harbored romantic fantasies about him and that coming here to say good-bye would only encourage her. Still, he did value her as a colleague and maybe also a friend. He wanted to say good-bye. Unable to decide what to do, he asked himself: *What is best for Michelle? What is best for Mira?* He decided to return home.

Back in his house, the lights still turned out, he watched out the window for signs of his neighbor. Her living room lights were on, and he occasionally saw a shadow cross the sheer curtains of the side window. He couldn't believe that there was another human being so close to him who now knew all his secrets. Not all of his secrets, of course, but she knew who he was. He pressed a hand to the windowpane and felt an ache of longing, something he hadn't felt for many years. He was startled out of his trance by Richard, calling him.

"It's late," Matthew said.

"Is it?"

"You know it is. If Mira was here you'd have woken her up."

"I know she's away," he said.

"Why are you calling, Richard?"

"I just wanted to talk," he said, his words slurring a little. Matthew assumed he'd been drinking. "Do you think Mom knew about us?"

"How drunk are you?"

"No, I'm serious. Do you think that Mom knew?"

"Do I think that Mom knew what?"

"That we're like Dad, that we think like him and *act* like him." The way that Richard put emphasis on the word *act* made Matthew suddenly very nervous.

"You've done something," he said.

"I don't want to talk about what I've done or haven't done. I want to talk about Mom. Remember Sally Respel in high school? Remember what we did to her?"

"*We* didn't do anything to her. You did it."

"It was you she was in love with. It was you who seduced her."

Matthew hadn't thought of Sally Respel in years. She'd been in the tennis club with Matthew, a year younger than he was, too tall and with a shiny face. Matthew had spent an afternoon helping her with her backhand, and after that, she'd been smitten with him, calling him every afternoon, always running into him in the hallway between classes, laughing explosively at everything he said. When she'd finally gotten up the courage to ask him to her junior prom, Matthew had gone to her house to let her down gently. They sat together on the swings of her childhood jungle gym, and he explained to her that he was interested in someone else ("She's from another town, the daughter of my parents' friends," he lied) and that he'd just like to be Sally's friend. She'd cried, but not for too long, and Matthew knew, even then, that he'd done her a favor by giving her a dramatic moment to remember. The two of them on the swing set, discussing love like adults.

He should never have told Richard about Sally, but he did, mostly because Richard, at that age, was already brimming with his own perverted fantasies, always trying them out on Matthew, and Matthew just wanted him to shut up for a while.

On the night of the junior prom, Richard called Sally up on her bedroom phone—she'd decided to stay home—and, disguising his voice by whispering, pretended that he was Matthew and said he'd changed his mind. Could he come over later, sneak in through her bedroom window? He was dying to kiss her.

Matthew never knew exactly how much Richard had done to Sally in the dark bedroom before she figured out she was with Matthew's brother and not with Matthew, but it was enough. Her terrified screams woke up her parents, who chased Richard away. The next day Sally's mother went directly to Matthew and Richard's mom, wanting to clear up the situation without getting the authorities involved. Richard had gotten off easy; all he ended up having to do was to promise he would never go near Sally again.

"I sometimes wonder what Mom thought about me after that happened," Richard said. "I wonder if she knew then what I was."

"Honestly," Matthew said, "I don't think Mom gave it a second thought. She had her own troubles, you know. I don't think what you did to Sally meant anything to her."

"What *we* did to Sally."

"You can say that all you want, but it doesn't change the facts."

"You were the same then as you are now. You love nothing more than to make women fall in love with you and then to let them down. It's your kick. Why was it worse for me giving Sally what she actually wanted?"

"Because she didn't want *you,* Richard, because no one has ever wanted you. She wanted me. What you did was disgusting." Matthew's stomach was beginning to hurt, and he really wished he hadn't picked up the phone.

"Hey, I didn't call you to get into an argument."

"Why did you call?"

"Do you think I could come and stay the night?" Richard's voice was suddenly smaller, almost pleading.

"Why?"

"I'll sleep on the sofa in the office. Mira will never know I was over, I promise. Look, you can go to sleep now, and I'll just let myself in. You'll never know I was there." His voice still sounded funny to Matthew, reminding him of how Richard had sounded as a messed-up, frightened kid.

Matthew sighed. "Just for tonight, okay?"

Richard was true to his word, and Matthew didn't see him until the next morning. Richard had made the coffee and was sitting at the kitchen table, head cocked slightly, one leg jittering up and down and the other spread out along the cork floor. He looked like their father. "Wakey, wakey, eggs and bakey," he said, arrogant and loud.

"Sleep well?" Matthew asked.

"Like a baby," Richard said. "I always sleep well on that sofa. Sleeping in my house is like sleeping inside of a skull. Just a bunch of stuff rattling around."

"Well, don't get used to it here."

Richard held up the palms of his hands. "Trust me, I know. You've made your feelings well known on the subject."

"Thanks for the coffee, Richard."

"Not a problem. I'll get out of your hair, but I do have a little gift for you, something you'll appreciate."

Matthew, filling his coffee cup, didn't like his brother's tone. He turned toward him. "What have you done?"

"Nothing that you haven't done many times. Trust me. I've got to go. There's an envelope in your office."

After Richard left, Matthew stayed frozen in place for a minute, the coffee bitter in his mouth, his stomach a hard ball. He put the coffee down and, steeling himself, went into his office. There was a single white envelope propped up on the mantel against the replica Rosetta stone. Matthew went to it, felt that there was something hard inside, and ran his finger under the seal, ripping the envelope open. Inside was a set of two keys attached to a key ring. Also attached to the ring was a pink *M* made from plastic. Matthew felt the coffee rise at the back of his throat, and he closed his eyes, breathed in through his nostrils until the feeling passed. He recognized the key ring. It had belonged to Michelle Brine.

CHAPTER 28

Back in her enormous hotel room, Mira shucked off her flats, sat on the edge of the queen-sized bed, and rubbed her feet. As part of her most recent promotion, she had to attend only two trade shows a year instead of four or five. It was a mixed blessing; standing all day at a booth doing software demonstrations was hard work, but now that she did fewer of these events, she found her feet hurt so much more. She assumed she was out of practice, but maybe she was just getting older.

Her phone buzzed. It was John McAleer, texting to see what her dinner plans were. Years earlier, John had worked at her company. They'd been sent together to Clark County School District, and after two long days of presentations they'd gone out to dinner at Le Cirque in the Bellagio. Afterward, they'd had one more drink, at his insistence, back at the bar in their hotel. She'd expected him to make a pass—it wouldn't be the first time she'd been hit on during a business trip—but she hadn't expected him to tell her that he'd fallen in love with her, that his own marriage had collapsed after half a year, and that he was the loneliest man in the world. He'd actually cried, prompting Mira to almost suggest shifting the conversation to one of their hotel rooms, which could have been disastrous. Instead, she told him they could continue the conversation in the morning and she left the bar, going straight to her hotel room. Over breakfast the next morning he'd apologized profusely, but ended by saying that his feelings stayed the same. He was in love with her and that would never change, but he wouldn't bring it up again, and he would start looking for a new job. He was true to his word. He never mentioned it again, and six months later he left Mira's company for a job at one of the big textbook companies. Three months after that she heard he got a divorce.

And now he was here in Wichita, having swung by to see Mira on the exhibitors floor. He'd gained weight and lost some hair, and he greeted her with a lot of friendly chitchat. "I was wondering if you'd still be working here," he said, laughing.

She thought the drop-by would be the extent of it, but now she was staring at a text from him. It sounded innocent—*Mira, great seeing ya. A bunch of us are doing bbq, and wanted to see if you had plans. No biggie if you're busy*—but she did wonder if he'd been planning this encounter, knowing she'd be working the booth, contriving to "casually" walk by and ask her out to a group dinner. She remembered his words—"I will always be in love with you"—made herself wait five minutes, then texted back, *Thanks, John, for the invite. I've just ordered room service. Exhausted!*

She scooched back on the bed, grabbed the remote from the side table, and turned the television on. Maybe she just attracted obsessive men, she thought. She was thinking of Jay Saravan (she'd been thinking about him a lot lately, because of everything that was happening with Matthew). He'd been her first serious boyfriend; they'd met at freshman orientation during her first week at the University of New Hampshire. On just their second date, Jay had told her he loved her. It had been a shock, but not necessarily an unwelcome one. For one, he was incredibly handsome; he'd reminded her of a real-life version of the cartoon Aladdin she'd been obsessed with for much of her childhood. He had wide shoulders and a slender frame and perfect hair, with a dark lock that fell across his forehead. Like her, his parents were originally from Pakistan, but unlike her, he'd been raised somewhat religiously—he fasted during Ramadan and celebrated Eid—and had actually been to Pakistan. They'd had a whirlwind courtship and stayed attached at the hip all through freshman year. Mira had found him a little bit possessive and demanding, but his assertiveness was thrilling, and he was unswervingly romantic.

And then it all went terribly wrong during sophomore year. Jay convinced Mira to move to her own off-campus apartment, and once she was there, he began to insist that she end the few friendships she'd made her freshman year. She was allowed to attend classes, but not to attend any social events. He started telling her what to wear and what to eat. When she suggested that maybe they should take a break—that maybe they were too young to be in so serious a relationship—he'd twisted her arm so hard he'd broken the skin. After that, she'd learned to be careful about what she said, but he still had outbursts, mostly centered on the clothes she wore to her classes. His anger would start with almost innocent remarks—"What size is that skirt?"—and would usually end with him squeezing her arm (sometimes her face), yelling at her that she was a slut and a whore.

Mira knew that her downstairs neighbor—she lived in the converted attic of a three-story house—heard what was happening. She knew because Matthew Dolamore was always attentive and chatty when she ran into him on her own, but he never acknowledged her if Jay was there. He must have known that if he'd said hi to her when she was with Jay then Mira would suffer for it. He was protecting her, in his small way, but the gesture seemed enormous to Mira. Once, to thank him, and knowing that it was an enormous risk, she invited him to her room for tea while Jay was away at a squash meet. They talked about everything except relationships. He was somewhat stiff, but one of those incredible listeners. Even as she told him the most banal stories, she felt his eyes on her, his entire attention on her.

After the afternoon tea date he'd asked her—only once—if she wanted to come to his apartment for coffee. She declined, saying that her boyfriend was back in town and it wouldn't be appropriate, hoping that he'd understand that nothing could change between them, that if he saw her with Jay he'd still have to pretend that he didn't know her. He clearly got the message, because the next time Mira and Jay passed Matthew—they were returning from the grocery store, and Matthew, backpack slung over one shoulder, was heading out—he entirely ignored Mira, only briefly nodding at Jay.

Despite this, Jay asked, "What do you know about that guy downstairs?" later that evening, after Mira had put away all the groceries.

"My neighbor?" she asked.

"Yeah. The one we passed tonight, the one you've obviously been thinking about."

"I don't even know him, Jay," she said. "I've never talked to him."

It got steadily worse, the conversation finally ending with Jay pushing Mira's head against the headboard of the bed, digging his fingers into her scalp while he screamed at her. She considered just telling him then and there that she'd had Matthew up to her apartment for tea, just to get it over with. He'd kill her, of course, but then it would be over. And if he didn't kill her, would he leave her? Unlikely, but it was a possibility.

But before she could get up the nerve to confess to him, he finally left. Mira lay on the bed, weeping for a while, then listening to the house, wondering if Matthew had heard that evening's entertainment. He'd clearly been going out to the library when they saw him earlier. Was he back now?

The only good thing about the fight was that Jay would be nice to her for a few days, at least. He'd be contrite, unless, of course, he ever found out that she really did have a relationship (of sorts) with her downstairs neighbor. *No,* she told herself, *he must never know. It isn't to protect me, but to protect Matthew.*

One week later—a week during which Jay *had* been contrite (even buying her white roses)—a police officer arrived at Mira's door on a Wednesday morning, asked her if she was Jay Saravan's girlfriend, then reported that Jay was dead. He'd been found in his BMW—his most prized possession after Mira—parked a few miles away down a dead-end street. He'd committed suicide by attaching a pipe from his exhaust pipe in through his window. He hadn't left a note.

During the next few weeks, a surreal period in which she was treated as a grieving girlfriend but felt like a fortunate survivor, Mira didn't see Matthew once. It didn't matter. Down deep she knew that her downstairs neighbor had something to do with the death of Jay Saravan. It wasn't just that he was the only one who had witnessed the true nature of their relationship, or that she knew for a fact that an egotist like Jay would never have taken his own life; it was that a few days before Jay's death she'd looked out her bedroom window and seen Matthew and Jay talking in the parking lot. Jay was showing off his car, and Matthew was enthusiastically asking questions. Mira understood now that that was how Matthew had worked it. He'd shown interest in Jay's BMW, then on the night of Jay's death, he must have caught him as he was leaving the apartment, maybe said something like, "Hey, wanna go for a ride in your car?" Jay would have said yes, and then somehow Matthew overpowered him, set it up to look like a suicide.

Still, when she next saw Matthew, after Thanksgiving break, he'd approached her with such a look of concern that she began to doubt herself. Could that soft-spoken history major have actually planned a murder and then gotten away with it? She began to change her mind. Maybe Jay, beneath his narcissism and his ego, had actually been so ashamed of his abusive behavior that he did kill himself. It was what she told herself to keep her going, especially after she and Matthew became an item, dating for the remainder of their college years, then getting married soon after graduation.

And now, all these years later, she was thinking about it again, wondering if Matthew really had killed Jay Saravan.

Of course he did. You knew it as soon as it happened.

It wasn't the first time in their marriage that she'd had doubts about her husband. For all his normalcy, Matthew had had a twisted childhood. He didn't talk about it much, but when he did, Mira realized just how much listening to Jay abuse her in the apartment above him must have triggered thoughts about his own parents.

And there were other sides to Matthew's personality. Most of the time he was just a regular all-American guy, a dedicated teacher, a trustworthy husband, but sometimes he was childlike and needy. And sometimes he was distant, scarily so, looking at Mira almost objectively, sizing her up.

And sometimes he does that right before or right after we have sex.

But all marriages must be a little bit like that. How well could you really know another person?

Still, she wondered: What if Matthew really had murdered Jay, and what if he'd enjoyed it so much that he'd continued to kill? Their neighbor Hen believed that Matthew had killed a former Sussex Hall student named Dustin Miller. Mira actually remembered the case; it had been all over the local news. An unsolved homicide of an affluent young man in a nice neighborhood in Cambridge. She'd brought it up to Matthew as soon as she learned that Dustin had been one of his students, and he'd told her he barely remembered him; maybe he'd even said he didn't know him, she couldn't exactly recall. Over the last week—since Hen's accusations—she'd been reading up about the Dustin Miller homicide, still unsolved, and one of the things that had come out was that Dustin had been accused of sexual assault during his time at Sussex Hall. That was news to her, and she couldn't help thinking that if that were the case, then wouldn't Matthew have remembered him? It would have been a huge deal.

Hating herself for doing it, Mira had looked up the exact date that Dustin Miller had died. It had been in the spring, two and a half years ago. She checked her work calendar; she'd been in Kansas City that entire week. It didn't really mean anything, considering how much time she spent traveling, but she would have been a whole lot happier to discover that she wasn't away during that particular week.

And now: Scott Doyle. She hadn't been traveling then, had she?

No. Just passed out because your husband kept ply-ing you with drinks.

And it turned out that Matthew did have a connec-tion with Scott Doyle, although a very remote one. He was the ex-boyfriend of Michelle Brine, a fellow history teacher at Sussex Hall. Had she told Matthew some-thing about her boyfriend, something bad?

He only kills men. He kills men who mistreat women.

Mira allowed herself a moment to consider that it was all true. Matthew killed Jay because he was abusing her. Then he killed Dustin Miller because Dustin was a rapist who had gotten away with it. And, finally, Mat-thew killed Scott Doyle because there must have been something rotten about him as well. Michelle, his fellow teacher, must have confided in him.

Mira realized she was grinding her teeth and made herself stop. She got off the bed and went to the window and stared out into the dusky evening, a sprawl of office buildings intersected by a grid of city streets. Most of the buildings were dark, some completely abandoned, and most of the car lights she could see were red, commuters fleeing downtown Wichita for bedroom communities.

What do I do? she thought. *If I really believe it's a possibility that Matthew is a killer, then what do I do?*

Would she turn him in?

He saved you.

He wasn't exactly a serial killer. He was a vigilante. And maybe (*please, please, let it be maybe*) he was neither of those things. Maybe Hen Mazur from next door was the crazy one, persecuting him, getting into her head, making her doubt her own marriage.

Mira heard the phone buzz on her bed and went back to look at it, expecting a message from Matthew. But it was John McAleer, texting her back: *No problemo. Totally understand, but I'll still check in later, see if I can convince you to get one drink.* After the message he'd put one of those smiling, winking emoji faces. Suddenly she realized that John was determined to see her during this trip, and she was a little nervous. Also a little annoyed. She decided to just not text him back, not give him any encouragement at all. Men were creeps. Like all women, she'd known this for a long time. Apparently her husband knew this as well. Maybe she should call him up, tell him she was having a problem with a pesky colleague here in Wichita. See if John McAleer wound up dead in a week. She actually giggled out loud at the thought, the laughter making her chest hurt worse than it already was.

She wasn't hungry, but she opened up the room service menu anyway. If she didn't eat now, she'd wake up starving in the middle of the night.

CHAPTER 29

"Where'd you sleep last night?" Lloyd asked.

Hen was in the kitchen, waiting for the coffee maker to beep, a mug in her hand.

"Oh, sorry. I slept on the couch."

"Were you up all night sketching?"

"No, I wasn't. I slept. I promise."

"I missed you," Lloyd said, and sat down at the kitchen table, pouring himself a bowl of Honey Nut Cheerios.

Hen took a sip of her coffee, then said, "I realized last night that I never even asked you about Rob's party. It was a little hectic when you got back."

"Yeah, I'll say. It was fine. Same old, same old."

"Who was there?"

"The usual crowd, plus or minus a few people. Todd and Steve, of course. Evan was there, and Chrissy, and then there were some new people. A couple of neighbors I hadn't seen before."

As he spoke, milk dribbled down his chin, and he wiped at it with the back of his hand.

"Rob seeing anyone new?"

"If he was, she wasn't there. No, I don't think so."

"Has he had any girlfriends since Joanna?"

"Since Joanna?" Lloyd looked toward the ceiling, and Hen tried to see if he was giving anything away. "I don't think so. It's not exactly like he lives in an area filled with available single women."

"Are they still in touch?"

"Is who still in touch?"

"Rob and Joanna."

"Why? You hoping they get back together?" Lloyd said, smiling, milk still on his chin.

"Sometimes. You know I don't really mind Rob, but she was his better half. At least for me she was."

"You know that I saw her pretty recently?"

"Who, Joanna?"

"Yeah, I ran into her in Boston. The company she works for is downtown. She still lives in Northampton, though."

"What does she do?"

"I'm not sure I remember. She told me. Something to do with public health research, I think."

Hen was watching Lloyd carefully. He was lying to her—although it was entirely likely that he might not remember the specifics of Joanna's job even if he *was* fucking her—and he was doing a good job. It was why she had decided to question him, wanting to see what he looked like when he was lying. Did he look guilty at all? Nervous? He actually didn't, and that fact made Hen's throat ache and swell, as though she were about to cry. She opened the refrigerator, pulled out a grapefruit.

"You want half of this?" she asked Lloyd, her voice sounding normal.

"No, I'm late, actually. I gotta run."

With a sharp knife, she sliced the grapefruit in half and carefully separated the fruit segments from their membranes. By the time she'd finished, Lloyd had kissed her on the side of her mouth and left for the day. Hen went to the bathroom and knelt down in front of the toilet bowl, convinced that she was going to be sick, but nothing came up.

She went to the living room couch. She'd lied to Lloyd as well that morning by telling him she'd slept the night before. She hadn't. She lay down now, too tired to even want to think about the ramifications of Lloyd's affair. She wasn't cold, but she pulled the blanket off the top of the sofa and onto her, then curled into the fetal position, cocooning herself in a small, dark bundle. She closed her eyes, thinking she wasn't tired enough to sleep, and the next thing she knew she was waking up, sweaty and confused, not having any idea what day or time it was. She pushed the blanket away from her face. Vinegar was perched on the sofa above her, purring rapidly.

"Hi, you," she said, and he purred even louder, their eyes locked.

She pushed the blanket entirely off her and looked at her watch. It was just past noon, and all the memories of the last twenty-four hours rushed in. But instead of feeling upset and sorrowful, she felt suddenly detached, as though the five hours of dreamless sleep had knocked all the emotions out of her. She stayed curled up on the couch, even though she had to pee, and thought about Lloyd, wondering if he'd fallen in love with Joanna or if it was just about the sex. Or was it something else altogether? She suddenly wanted to know, not out of a desire for revenge or self-pity, but because she loved Lloyd and wanted to know what was going on with him. She'd had her own close call, one that she'd decided Lloyd would never know about, but maybe she'd tell him now if he confessed to her what was happening with Joanna. One of the things she'd loved about Lloyd when they first met was his brutal honesty. When they'd become involved— when *she* was the other woman—he'd told her once that his goal was to have a new relationship with a different woman every year, to always be falling in love, then falling out of love, then falling in love again.

"Sounds awful," Hen had said.

"I know, right?" he'd said back. "I think I'm addicted to the misery of love. I need that drama in my life. Basically, I'm an asshole."

"I'm not sure it makes you an asshole, exactly. More like an idiot."

"Right," he'd agreed, and laughed. "More like an idiot."

She had actually been attracted to that side of Lloyd, the one who promised to make her life more exciting, more unpredictable. It was a long time ago, though, and Hen now recognized that her desires from back then had been partly influenced by the manic side of her disease. She'd had a romantic notion of one of those marriages you read about in biographies: messy, creative, romantic, and laced with infidelities. It wasn't what she wanted now, not by a long shot, but she recognized the appeal. As it was, her years with Lloyd had been comfortable and stable and maybe just a little bit dull.

She stood up, weak with hunger, and made her way to the kitchen, Vinegar scurrying along with her. She noticed the half a grapefruit she'd left on the counter. Using her hands, she devoured the segments of the fruit, then squeezed the remaining juice directly into her mouth. Then she grabbed the Cheerios that Lloyd had left on the kitchen table and ate handfuls directly from the box until she wasn't hungry anymore.

After eating, she took her sketchbook with her out to the front porch and sat on one of the padded deck chairs, curling her feet up under her. It was an insanely windy day—according to weather reports, it was the tail end of a tropical storm that had climbed the coast from Florida—but the wind was warm, filled with traces of mist. Hen sat for a long time, watching the trees across the street bend and shake, leaves departing their branches. She saw an image suddenly—a tree losing all its leaves at once, but they weren't leaves, they were small birds, flying off as one flock into the turbulent sky. Then she pictured a sky full of birds, so numerous that they blocked out everything, forming dark chattering clouds. She shuddered.

Eventually, she allowed herself to think of Lloyd again, trying to decide what she should do. She could confront him, of course, cause a scene. She could kick him out of the house or demand that he stop seeing Joanna. She could ask for a divorce. She wondered what her younger self would have done. She would have fought for him, probably, tried to win him back. Or else she would have gotten revenge, had her own affair, taken up with someone new. It would have been easier back then, when the world was full of all those grungy, love-hungry boys in their twenties. But whom could she have an affair with now? Matthew, of course, the murderer next door. Hen laughed out loud, then quickly scanned the street to make sure no one had heard her. She checked her watch—it was a little after three o'clock, and she did wonder if Matthew was coming home soon.

She realized that that was part of the reason she was out on the porch, watching cars go by and leaves fall. And it wasn't an affair she wanted—again, the thought almost made her laugh out loud—it was that she wanted to talk with him some more, find out how exactly he'd known about Lloyd.

The gusting winds began to produce rain, sporadic bursts that pattered in the leaves. She began to sketch a tree, a flock of birds lifting off from its branches, but every time a car drove by she looked up.

At four o'clock Matthew pulled his Fiat into the driveway. Hen watched him, wondering if he'd seen her on the porch when he drove by. He got out of the car, reached back in to get his briefcase, then turned and looked toward Hen. Through the porch's screen and the now steady rain, she couldn't make out his face, but she waved toward him, and he waved back. He went into his house, and Hen wondered if she should go over and talk with him, but then he was coming back outside, wearing a crewneck sweater instead of a tweed blazer. He walked the short distance to the steps that led to Hen's porch, then stopped.

"Can I come up?" he asked, and Hen thought of vampires, how they needed to be invited in.

He sat across from her, on the old wooden rocker that had come with the house. He looked different today, paler, almost frightened. Maybe it was his hair, damp and pushed off his face, revealing a sharp widow's peak. Hen thought of vampires again.

"Why did you say what you said about Lloyd?" she asked.

He looked confused for a moment, then said, "So he *is* cheating on you."

"No, I didn't say that. I'm just wondering why you think he is." Hen felt a sudden lurch in her stomach, that maybe she shouldn't have mentioned Lloyd at all. Had she just confirmed to Matthew what he already thought?

"I didn't know. I guessed. He has that look."

"What look, exactly, is that?"

He pushed his lips together, thinking. "He looks like a man," he finally said, and smiled, almost sheepishly.

"I don't know what you mean by that," Hen said.

"It means that every woman he meets—every woman he sees, really—he instantly decides whether he'd have sex with her or not. He strips them naked in his mind. He wonders if they're thinking the same thing. I'll bet that the night after the dinner party your husband concocted an elaborate fantasy in his mind about my wife, wondering what would happen if I was out of town at the same time that you were out of town. Maybe they'd have dinner together, decide to have sex, promise to never tell another soul. He imagined every detail. Specific details. He pictured what my wife's breasts looked like, what her vagina—"

"Okay, I get the point."

"Well, that's what men do." He sounded a little defensive.

"That's what *you* do, you mean," Hen said.

Matthew rocked forward in his chair. "No, I don't, actually. I'm different."

"Then how do you know that men do it?"

"I just do. I had a very bad father. He was a . . . a sexual predator, and a sadist. And my brother, now, he's just like my father except for the fact that he doesn't have a wife. He doesn't have anyone to torture, but if he did, then . . ."

Hen placed her feet on the painted wood floor of the porch and leaned forward. "But still, that doesn't mean that every man—"

"That every man is the same? No, but it's a spectrum and every man is on it. Your husband is probably statistically average, not a bad man, but when he looks at a woman he just sees what he wants to do to her."

"So where are you on this spectrum?"

"I'm not on it."

"You don't objectify women? At all?"

"No."

"What did you think when you first looked at your wife, before you ever talked with her?"

"I thought she was beautiful, of course, but I didn't think about . . . other things, her body, the way most men would."

"And that's why you protect women, by killing all the bad men." Hen realized how sarcastic her words sounded, but didn't mind.

"Yes," he said. "If there's a man who has badly hurt a woman, and who will probably do it again, I don't mind killing him."

"You don't mind it?" Hen laughed.

"Right. It's not that I like it. Well, I do like it sometimes after I've done it. But the initial impulse . . . what allows me to kill someone in the first place . . . is that I don't mind it. It's a big difference."

"Lloyd's not a cheater," Hen said.

"Okay."

"I don't want you to hurt him. Ever. Okay?"

Matthew's face was serious. He said, "I'm going to stop, actually. That's what you want me to do, right? That's why you agreed to meet me yesterday. You think that if you can't convince the police to lock me up, then you can convince me to stop killing people."

"That was part of it," Hen said. "I also just wanted to hear what you had to say. It's a strange relationship, you being able to tell me what you want, and me unable to tell anyone."

"It is. It's very strange. It's liberating for me."

"How many men have you killed?" Hen asked.

Matthew slid back in his rocker and picked at the sleeve of his sweater. "I don't want to talk about that right now."

"Okay."

"I want to talk more about my brother."

"Okay."

"Have I mentioned him to you before?"

"Just now you did."

Matthew looked confused, like he'd already forgotten the words he'd just said.

"You said he's like your father."

"Richard is, not me," he said, and something about his phrasing made Hen feel suddenly nervous.

"In what way?" Hen asked.

"He's like my father, except that . . . as I said, he doesn't really spend a lot of time with people, besides me, so I never think of him as being dangerous."

"What does he do?"

"Richard? God, nothing. He says he's trying to write a book, but I'll believe it when I see it. Mira doesn't know, but I support him, financially. I've supported him for years. He's sick, just in his head, but now . . . I'm worried that he might be starting to act out, that he's getting braver—"

"You think he's hurt someone?"

"He might have," Matthew said, and Hen could tell he was holding back on her. "And I think he might hurt someone else. That's how it works with people like us. We're fine for a while, but then we get a taste of what it's like to take a life, and it's like a door opening, and you can never shut it again, not really. So at least I was able to control it by only killing men that deserved to die, but that's not how Richard's mind works. He's like my father. He wants to hurt innocent women."

"Maybe you should go to the police."

Matthew clenched his teeth. "I've thought about it, I really have, but you have to understand. He's still my brother. We survived our childhood together. I don't know if I can do it to him. I don't think he'd do well in prison."

It had stopped raining, but the clouds had gotten darker, and Hen didn't see the man walking down the street, then turning at their driveway, until he was coming up the steps toward the screen door. For one surreal second she thought it was Matthew's brother, but the door swung open and Lloyd stepped onto the porch, looking from Hen to Matthew on the rocking chair.

"Hello," he said.

"You're early," Hen said, before she could stop herself.

"You didn't get my text?"

"Oh, no. My phone's inside."

Matthew stood up, and Lloyd turned toward him. "Hi, Matthew," he said.

"Hi, Lloyd. I just dropped over a few minutes ago. Trying to clear the air, you know?"

Lloyd turned toward Hen and raised his eyebrows. "Okay?"

"I should go, though," Matthew said. "Nice talking with you, Hen. Nice seeing you, Lloyd."

He pushed his way through the screen door and walked rapidly to his own house.

Lloyd, still looking at Hen, said, "What the fuck was that about?"

"You're having an affair with Joanna Grimlund," Hen replied.

CHAPTER 30

Back in his office, his sweater damp and his heart still pumping from the sudden appearance of Hen's husband, Matthew looked again at the envelope his brother had left him. It was still there, as were the keys attached to the plastic *M*. He'd tried calling Michelle several times that day, her phone always going to voice mail. He'd tried calling his brother as well. No answer.

Matthew knew that all he needed to do was to drive to Country Squire Estates and try the key, see what had happened, if anything, in Michelle's apartment. If she was dead, then everything had changed, and his brother had finally done what he had been threatening to do for so long. But if he didn't go, if he didn't open up the door, Michelle might still be alive, driving to her parents' house, her phone going straight to voice mail because she wanted to pay attention to the road. That would be like Michelle, wouldn't it? Maybe if he went to her apartment he'd find nothing there, a clean apartment, Michelle long gone. It wouldn't be the first time that Richard had pretended he'd done something terrible only to reveal later that he'd been joking. Half joking, anyway, because it was always something that he *wanted* to do.

But what about the keys? Matthew thought. *Where'd he get them from?*

Mira called, and for the twenty minutes that they talked, Matthew felt okay, almost normal.

"I miss you," Matthew said toward the end of the call.

"Everything okay on that end?" Mira asked. "Anything more from the police?"

"Everything's fine. Is it okay if I just miss you?"

She laughed, and the sound of it made him feel even better. "I'll be back tomorrow night. Did you get the flight details I sent?"

"I think so," Matthew said.

"I'll see you then. And, Matthew . . ."

"Yeah."

"I love you so much. I want you to know that."

"I know," he said.

After the phone call Matthew went to the refrigerator. He wasn't hungry, but he thought he should eat something. The day had been awful. When he'd arrived at the teachers' lounge that morning all the talk had been about Michelle's sudden departure. Matthew got himself a coffee he didn't really need, while he listened to Sussex Hall's oldest teacher, Betty, half whisper, "She could have at least met with the sub and gone over her syllabus with her. It would have taken her all of half a day, at most."

"Her boyfriend was murdered and her father is dying," Matthew said from across the lounge. Betty and the three teachers she'd been gossiping with all turned and looked at him.

"I'm sorry," Matthew said. "I'm worried about her, is all."

"We're all worried about her," Betty quickly said. "But I'm also worried about her students' education."

Matthew moved through the rest of the day in an agitated haze. He taught his classes, occasionally forgetting the visit from his brother, but then he'd remember, suddenly see that key ring again in his mind, and his stomach would turn. When the day was finally over, Matthew got back into his car, tried calling Michelle—straight to voice mail ("Michelle here. You know what to do.")—then told himself that he should just drive directly over to her apartment complex, knock on her door. He could almost feel the relief that would come when she pulled the door open. He could hear her voice—"You came! I knew there was a reason I couldn't get my act together and leave here this morning"—and then he could hear his brother laughing at him later. "You didn't think I'd really do something like that, did you?" he'd say. "I bought that key ring at the drug store. Been waiting for months to use it on you." He replayed the scenario twice in his mind, then noticed one of his students, Billy Portis, watching him from across the parking lot. Matthew ignited the engine of his Fiat, wondering if he'd been moving his lips, talking to himself.

Instead of driving to Country Squire, he drove straight home, the wind driving the rain sideways, the inside of his car steaming up. He cracked a window, rain coming in and hitting his face, but the windshield began to clear a little. He parked, instinctively looking toward his neighbors' house as he got out of the car, and spotted Hen on her porch. She waved at him, and a feeling of relief spread through his body. He'd go talk with Hen, and he could make a decision about Michelle later.

Now, Matthew pulled a ginger ale from the refrigerator, plus two sticks of string cheese wrapped in plastic. He got some Triscuits from the cupboard and brought them with him to the living room couch, where he sat in the dark and ate his supper.

He couldn't quite believe that he'd told Hen about Richard, but it had felt good to do it. And it wasn't just that it was liberating for him. If Richard had actually done something to Michelle, then what else was he capable of? He'd mentioned Hen earlier, said how he'd seen her sitting on the porch one night, said he could see right up her skirt. What else had he said? Something about Hen being "up for it." At the time Matthew had barely paid attention. It was his brother speaking, his loser brother who was all words and no action. But what if that had finally changed? The thought made Matthew's stomach hurt worse than it had all day. He made the decision that he needed to go to Michelle's apartment; he needed to find out one way or another the truth of what had happened.

He checked the time. It was too early to go over to the apartment complex now. Too many people coming and going. He decided to go over at eleven at night, hoping that it would be late enough that no one would see him, but not so late that it would look suspicious if someone did. He went into his office, turned on the small Tiffany lamp by the sofa, and looked at some of the titles on his bookshelf, hoping to find something he could read to kill the next few hours. He touched the spines of his collection of Salinger paperbacks. *The Catcher in the Rye* was the book that saved him as a thirteen-year-old, the book that finally made him feel okay about the rage he felt toward his parents and toward the world in general. But the book he pulled out now was *Franny and Zooey,* equally important to him, the book that first made him feel protective toward a girl. When he'd read it, also at the age of thirteen, he'd imagined that he'd fallen in love with the troubled Franny of the first part of the book. He had, in a way. She was his first love, a girl who understood that the world we live in is all bullshit. Opening the frail, musty paperback now and reading the first line—"Though brilliantly sunny, Saturday morning was overcoat weather again, not just topcoat weather"—Matthew could feel the tension in his body begin to dissipate. He read the entire book, two long stories, really, then rose from the sofa, returned the book to its place on the shelf, and did some jumping jacks. Reading the book had worked, allowing him to enter a fictional realm for a time, something that had always been easy for him. It was what saved him, he sometimes thought; it was what got him through a childhood in which he'd been trapped in hell, and it was what his office represented now, with its books and talismans. It was a separate world.

It wasn't quite eleven at night, but Matthew knew it was time to drive to Michelle's apartment to discover the truth. He changed out of his chinos and sweater into his oldest pair of jeans and a sweatshirt that he only ever wore to do work around the house. He found one of Mira's fleece ski caps, pulled it on over his hair. If he did get spotted at the apartment, at least he wouldn't look too much like himself.

He drove to Country Squire, parking again in one of the visitor spots. Michelle drove a gray Honda Civic, and Matthew almost went to look for her car first, but decided against it. Whether her car was here wouldn't make any difference—he'd still need to see what was in the apartment. The rain had stopped, but the parking lot glistened. The sky was dark purple and starless. The complex comprised two separate L-shaped buildings around a large rectangular pool; it was quiet, most of the windows dark. Any light that leaked from the inside world to the outside world came through curtains or blinds, and most of the light was flickering and erratic, the light from televisions. Walking between the buildings with their cheap stucco siding, Matthew felt drawn to the entrance farther from him, a glass door illuminated by a dim light, a single moth battering dumbly against its side. A console by the side of the door had buzzers for apartment numbers 33 through 64. Matthew pulled the set of two keys from his jeans pocket. Neither had a number on it, but Michelle had told him on the phone to visit her in 41. He nearly pressed the buzzer now, but something stopped him. He needed to know if the keys that Richard had left for him were the keys to this complex. If they were he would have to prepare himself for the worst possible outcome.

The first key he tried on the outside door slid easily into the lock but didn't turn. Matthew felt a small burst of relief. But the second key, sliding in just as easily, turned and the bolt clicked open. Matthew pushed the door inward and stepped into the carpeted interior, the feeling of dread now at a fever pitch. He stood for a moment listening to the building's silence, his eyes adjusting to the harsh fluorescent glare of the overhead lighting, then he took two steps forward and turned left down a long hallway, the walls newly painted in an inoffensive beige, the carpeting showing dirt even through its elaborate red-and-gold pattern. The numbers started at 33, and about three-quarters of the way down the hallway Matthew came to 41. He pressed his ear against the wooden door but could hear nothing. He almost knocked but used the key instead, knowing somehow that if Michelle was still in the apartment she'd be dead. His only hope now was that she wasn't there, that she'd left with all her things, that she was safe at her parents' home, and Richard was not a murderer.

He swung the door inward. The apartment was dark but the window blinds were up, and Matthew could see a furnished living room area. A ceiling fan slowly spun, making a barely discernible clicking sound on each rotation. He quietly shut the door behind him and stood for a moment, breathing through his nostrils. There was a smell in the apartment, sweet and coppery, and Matthew almost decided to turn around right there. The smell was enough to tell him the worst had happened, but he told himself he had to see. He had to witness what his brother had done. He stepped quickly across the uncarpeted living room floor, noting the stack of boxes in the kitchen alcove. The bedroom door was cracked open, and Matthew pushed it inward with the toe of his shoe. The smell was more intense, and for a brief moment, before his eyes fully adjusted, he thought he was looking at a tapestry pinned up on the wall above the queen-sized bed. But it wasn't a tapestry; it was a high arc of blood, two arcs, dark and dripping.

Michelle was on the bed, lying in a puddle of even more blood, black and shiny in the light from outside.

CHAPTER 31

Hen lay in bed and watched the dawn fill the bedroom with light. Lloyd was downstairs on the couch. It was where she'd prefer to be, really, if she had a choice, but after he'd admitted to the one-year affair with Joanna, it didn't seem right to let him sleep in their shared bed while she took the couch.

It had been a long and draining night. As soon as she'd accused him of having an affair, his face had crumpled, and he'd begun to cry. Well, *cry* was not the best verb for what he had done. He'd doubled over and begun to sob, producing long rasping gasps of breath that only served to annoy Hen, who had to wait about ten minutes before they could start to talk. She told him she wanted the entire truth, and he nodded repeatedly, his face streaked with tears and snot. They sat in the living room, and Lloyd began by saying, "It's over, by the way. That's where I was last weekend when I said I was at Rob's party. I was with her in Northampton, and we both agreed . . . we both knew it was a huge mistake. She feels bad, too, terrible, but I promise you that it's finished."

"I'm not interested in how it finished, Lloyd, I'm wondering why it started."

So he told her the story, how it had begun a year earlier when Joanna had showed up at Rob's bonfire party and Lloyd was there by himself. They had hooked up that night ("it was just a stupid, drunken kiss"), but afterward they had begun to email back and forth, then talk on the phone, and things led to things. Lloyd said repeatedly that it was much more of an emotional affair than a physical one, that they had just found it easy to talk with each other.

"You talked about me, about us?" Hen asked.

"We did, yes."

"What did you talk about? Remember that you're telling me everything."

"I guess I talked about how our relationship has changed, how everything about us now is how we deal with things. So first it was your illness and taking care of that, and it made me feel like I was just a caretaker and nothing more, and then we bought this house together and everything was about mortgages and moving costs and decorating—"

"It's called real life," Hen said.

"I know. I'm not saying I'm in the right. I'm just saying how I felt. I know it's not fair. I know I'm the bad guy here."

"Okay," Hen said. "Continue."

Lloyd kept talking, and Hen was surprised to find herself almost bored listening to him. She could have told the story herself. It was just a midlife crisis, Lloyd wearied by the minutiae of his life—its health crises and financial decisions, and a job that was less creative than he thought it would be—and suddenly there was a new woman to talk with and sneak away to, and it kept things interesting for a while. And Hen even believed him when he said that it was really over, because it became clear that what happened between him and Joanna was no great love; it was just two semi-lonely people hooking up as though they were still in their twenties. Had she been hoping for more? Had some small part of her been hoping to hear that Lloyd was madly in love and wanted to leave, and that Hen would have to fight, *or not,* for her marriage? Maybe it was just that Lloyd's sordid little affair paled in comparison to what she'd learned in the last few days about her neighbor and the secrets that he kept.

"I'm tired, Lloyd," she said, interrupting another crying jag. "I'm going upstairs to sleep. We can talk about this more in the morning."

Before she left the living room, Lloyd said, "What were you talking about with Matthew Dolamore?"

"He kills people," she said.

"What?"

"That's not news. I've already told you that, but now he's told me about it as well."

"What? Are you going to go to the police again?"

"I can't, can I? He'd deny it, and they'd believe him. I have no proof, and the police know all about what happened in college. They'd never believe me."

"Is he dangerous?"

"To me? No, I don't think he is. I'd worry more about you. He knew you were a cheater, by the way."

"What the fuck are you talking about?"

"He told me he could tell as soon as he saw you. He could tell by the way you looked at his wife."

"Jesus Christ. You're not going to talk to him again, are you?"

"I don't know. Probably. He wants to stop what he's

doing and maybe I can help him do that. It's the only thing I can do."

"I think you should go to the police and tell them everything, even if they don't believe you. Put it on record."

"So you believe me now?"

"Yes! I mean, I believe that you've been talking with this creep, and he's been telling you that he kills people, and that you believe him."

"So now it's him you don't believe?" Hen was standing at the foot of the stairs, one hand on the bannister.

"I don't know what to believe." Lloyd took a deep breath, his mouth open. Hen noticed how dry his lips were, almost white at the edges.

"We'll talk more tomorrow, okay?"

Hen slept a small amount just after dawn. The light in the room gave the undersides of her lids a reddish tint, and she pretended she was lying at the edge of the lake in the Adirondacks where her parents owned a bare-bones cottage. It was one of her happy places, surrounded by pines, the cool lake water still on her skin, the distant sound of a motorboat. Then she was awake, and the motorboat was actually a lawn mower somewhere on Sycamore Street. She sat up in bed, realized she'd forgotten to take her meds the night before, so doubled up on them now, then went and took a shower. Afterward, she dressed, but couldn't bring herself to go downstairs and resume the conversation with Lloyd. It was exhausting and sad, and she was surprised to find that a part of herself didn't really care all that much. The shock of his infidelity had already worn off, and she was somehow numb to it. What she really wanted to do was to go downstairs, tell Lloyd that he should just go to work, and they could talk some more later. She wanted to be alone and maybe go to her studio, and she wanted to continue her conversation with Matthew, find out more about his brother and what was going on there.

She lay back on the bed and listened to the house. She wondered if Lloyd was up yet, but couldn't hear anything. Finally, she braced herself and went downstairs, expecting to see Lloyd still on the couch, probably still crying. *Why did he get to cry so much?* She was the one who got cheated on.

When she got to the first floor, the couch was empty, the single blanket lying on the floor.

"Lloyd," she said aloud, and as soon as she said it, she realized he wasn't in the house. She walked to the window that faced the driveway. The Golf was gone. There was no note in the kitchen, the place where he'd most likely leave one. Had he just gone to work, taking the car instead of the train? No, that made no sense. And if he had he would have let her know. He wouldn't have left while she was still asleep upstairs. She pulled her phone out. No text messages, and no voice mail. She dialed his number, and as she started to listen to it ring, a familiar noise came from the living room, the opening notes of "Coronado," the Deerhunter song Lloyd used as his ringtone.

She hit End on her phone and went and found Lloyd's cell, underneath the blanket by the couch. And then she began to really worry. Had he gone to the police to tell them about Matthew? Or maybe he'd gone directly to Matthew himself. But that didn't make sense, because why would he take the car to do that? *He's gone to pick up breakfast,* Hen told herself. *He's driven to that amazing bakery in Dartford Center to get those apricot scones that I like and two large coffees, and he just forgot to bring his phone with him.* She told herself this, but didn't quite believe it. It was something else, something bad.

She went to the living room window and looked across to Matthew's house. His car was gone as well, which made sense, since he'd be at school by now. There was nothing to see, but she stayed there anyway, looking out at her neighborhood, not knowing what to do next.

RICHARD

I didn't know that blood could jump like that, almost like it wants to leave the human body, get as far away as possible. I'd read about it, of course, in books, and I'd seen it in movies, the way arterial blood will spray. But to see it in reality, to see the life of it, that was something . . . something I can't even express in words.

DAD LOVED BLOOD, TOO. I know that not just because he showed me that bra once when he returned from his business trip—the bra with the bloodstain on it, the bra I still have, hidden away with Dad's things. No, I know it because after he broke Mom's nose at the dinner table, and she just sat there, immobile, and let the blood run out of her face and spill out over everything—the broken plate, the porcelain tabletop, the dinner napkins, the linoleum floor—I caught Dad pulling one of the napkins from the laundry basket. It was brown and stiff from all the blood, and when he saw me looking at him, he winked and said, "Another souvenir."

I wonder if Dad ever saw what blood can really do when you unleash it. I wonder that a lot, and for a time I sought out unsolved murders, looking at the places where he used to go most frequently on his business trips. I always found *something*—every town in America has murdered girls in it, their murderers unknown—but I could never know for sure that it was my father who had done it.

It's possible that I now know what he never did, that blood has a life all its own.

MATTHEW NOW KNOWS ABOUT what I did to his girlfriend Michelle. He knew it the moment I left him the keys, of course, but he had to go and see it for himself. I watched him from a distance, wondering what he'd do about it once he found out for sure. Would he go straight to the police and turn me in? So far he hasn't. At least not that I know of. I just don't think he will. Mom never went to the police, and Matthew is the one in the family who's most like Mom.

No, Matthew is much more likely to try to deal with me himself. Keep it in the family, he'd say. He killed Dad, after all, even though he swears to me that he didn't. But we both know that it was him. Matthew got bigger than Dad by his junior year of high school. He "sprouted," to use the word Mom liked to use. Dad must have noticed, because he got a little more careful around the house, a little more restrained when it came to the games he played on Mom. And Mom, never one to waste an opening, took advantage. I remember how she used to drop other men's names into conversations. "Oh, Porter," she'd say. "Ran into Dick Humphries this morning. He told me to tell you he hopes you're feeling better soon." This was when Dad had the bad back. It made him meaner, but there was less he could do about it. The last time he threatened Mom, grabbing her by the throat while she was doing dishes, Matthew shoved him so hard he went down on the kitchen floor and just stayed there for an hour, his back seizing up. Mom asked him if he wanted his dinner down on the floor.

The reason I know that Matthew was the one who shoved Dad down the cellar stairs was that Dad *never* went down there, at least not that I know of. Our cellar was just half the size of the first floor, a glorified fruit cellar, really, nothing down there but some moldy boxes containing the few keepsakes that Mom had taken from her parents' house after they'd both finally died. There was one of those giant freezers down there, where Mom used to keep frozen meat and Swanson dinners, but it had stopped working one summer, and after Mom threw out all the spoiled meat, she'd never gotten it fixed or bought a new one. No one in the family went down to the cellar, so it made no sense when Dad was found at the bottom of the steps, dead from a head wound. It happened when both Matthew and I were at school, and Dad was home with the bad back. I know how easy it would have been for Matthew to sneak away from the school, cut through the woods to our house. Matthew was strong enough then, and Dad was weak enough, that Matthew could have carried him to the cellar stairs and thrown him down himself.

I was the one who found him, of course. My father, reduced to a rag doll with a head that turned the wrong way. There was no blood anywhere. All the death that happened to my father happened inside of his skin.

MICHELLE THOUGHT I WAS Matthew, of course, just like Sally Respel had. By the time she realized I wasn't, it was too late. I was in her home, the door shut behind me. In the light of her sad apartment she could see my face.

I DREAM AGAIN ABOUT the dark house with its many rooms. I have the dream so often now that I know I'm dreaming when I have it. And I know that the person I'm looking for can't be found. There are too many hallways and too many rooms, too many places for him to hide.

But I don't really have a choice but to keep looking. The ceilings are low in this large house, and I've never given it too much thought, but there are no windows, just dark rooms that lead to other rooms. I tell myself to stop opening the doors, but I can't stop even when I find terrible things in them: a rabbit split down the middle, but still alive; a Thanksgiving turkey, its cavity filled with spiders; our mother giving birth on the kitchen floor, but all that's coming out is a river of blood.

Despite all this, I keep opening doors, keep hoping.

I'M IN HIDING NOW, even though it's only Matthew who's trying to find me. That will all change soon. The body will begin to smell and the neighbors will notice. Or someone will miss her and go check, and then I'll be in hiding from the police as well. It's only a matter of time.

Matthew calls me and calls me, even though he knows I'm not going to pick up.

I followed him back to his house after he went to Country Squire. I watched him get out of his car, and I saw the way he looked toward his neighbors' house with something like longing. *What has he told the neighbor?*

I peered through their window, and all I saw was some guy tossing and turning on the living room couch. I could feel the woman, though, Henrietta, in the house. She's cast some sort of spell over my brother. I know this much. I get it. I finally saw her up close during Open Studios at Black Brick. Matthew didn't know I was there, but I was. She wore tight black pants that showed her ankles and a large oxford shirt, the sleeves rolled up, and I bet she told herself that she looked like an artist, that all the men wandering into her studio weren't imagining what was under that oversized shirt and under those pants, that they were interested in her children's drawings. She crouched by one of her presses, pulling out a large sheet of paper, and I saw the skin above her pants, skin that looked as though it had never seen the sun, and her delicate rib cage.

I imagine all the blood that that skin, thin as tissue paper, must hold. I imagine she's warm.

IF I REALLY WANTED to get Matthew's attention, then I think I killed the wrong woman.

PART 3

BROTHERS

CHAPTER 32

Instead of panicking, Matthew remained calm. He left Michelle's apartment the way it was, but not before he called Michelle's number one more time and listened as her phone rang from her kitchen counter, where it was plugged into a charger.

He unplugged it and slid it into his pocket, then slowly backed out of the apartment, making sure to wipe anything he might have touched with the sleeve of his sweatshirt. When he got to the hallway, he locked the door, then moved as fast as he possibly could out to the apartment courtyard and his car. He drove away, finding himself on a back road surrounded by woodlands on either side, his headlights providing a tunnel of light against the black. He came to an intersection, and a sign pointed him toward Dartford. He knew where he was now, passing an ice-cream stand that was only open during the summer months, a place he'd been with Mira on several occasions. He pulled into its empty parking lot, dousing the lights, and walked steadily toward the back of the single-story ice-cream stand. There was a small dumpster and two or three picnic tables. Where the gravel ended, a weedy field began, bordered on one side by a stone wall and on the other by a line of trees, dark against the purple sky. Matthew walked a hundred yards out into the field until he got to a section that was particularly rocky. He crushed Michelle's phone between two flat rocks he found, shattering it so that he had to search through the weedy grass for fragments, then buried the busted phone and the keys underneath a larger rock he'd pried from the earth. The moon had crept out from behind clouds, and in its silvery light he could see earthworms moving in the damp black soil under the rock. He carefully put it back, then walked another hundred yards toward the line of trees. Just beyond the trees was a wire fence that marked the edge of a cow pasture. Matthew leaned over the fence and was violently ill. When he was done, he saw that one of the cows clustered together had turned her head to look toward him. Then the moon went back behind a cloud.

He drove home, trying not to think too hard about what he was going to do, trying to keep the panic from rising.

He doused the lights of the Fiat just as he pulled into his driveway, aware that it was very late and not wanting to be spotted by neighbors. He looked toward Hen's house, noticed that the living room lights were still on, wondered briefly what had happened after the husband came home and found the two of them talking on the porch. Her husband had looked concerned, of course, his dull eyes taking in everything slowly, passing from Matthew to Hen and back to Matthew, not quite knowing what to think or to say. Was he smart enough to see the intimacy between them? Did he think they were having an affair?

Back inside his dark house, Matthew paced, briefly allowing himself a fantasy of killing Lloyd. They were in a spotless white room—maybe it was an upscale hotel room in Boston—and Lloyd was wrapped in duct tape so tightly that the only part of his body he could move was his eyes. Matthew lifted him and put him in a deep bathtub, turned on the water, and watched Lloyd drown, watched all the swagger and lustfulness and arrogance disappear from those eyes as he began to realize exactly what was happening. The fantasy was only a little bit distracting, because Matthew knew that in all likelihood he'd never be able to enact it. Those days were long gone, thanks to Richard. Matthew did jumping jacks, then climbed the stairs to the second floor.

If I act like nothing happened—if I brush my teeth and wash my face and tuck myself into bed—then maybe nothing did happen.

It didn't work. Matthew lay in bed and thought about what was coming next. The police would discover Michelle's body, and because of her relationship with Scott Doyle, they'd instantly think the two murders were connected. It's possible they wouldn't, the murders being so different—but, no, that was just wishful thinking. They would. They'd link Scott's and Michelle's deaths together, and once they did that, then they'd remember that one of the first suspects brought in after Scott Doyle's murder had been Matthew Dolamore, who worked with Michelle Brine. Not just in the same school, but in the same department. Matthew could hear Dylan Hembree's voice: "Oh, they were always talking. Some people thought there might be something going on there. Plus, I remember a weird conversation when Matthew invited her to go to a bar with him, maybe it was even some night Scott was playing in the C-Beams." Of course the police would come back to him, and he wouldn't have an alibi this time. Not for Michelle's murder, anyway. And then the police would talk with Hen again, and maybe this time they'd believe her. She'd even tell them that he mentioned Michelle to her. And the closer they got to him, the closer they got to Richard.

Matthew could imagine one other scenario. What if he could convince the police that Henrietta Mazur killed Scott Doyle and Michelle Brine, that she did it to frame him for the murders, that it was all part of her weird obsessive fixation with seeing murderers everywhere, that she wanted to be right just one time. He thought it could work, but he'd never be able to do it, never be able to do that to her. She didn't deserve it. But what about Lloyd? What if he managed to get some evidence—a single hair, for example—and sneak back and leave it at the scene of the crime? It would be like killing two birds with one stone. Even if it turned out that Lloyd was never convicted, it would confuse the police, throw them off the track. The more he thought about it, the more it seemed like a good idea.

An hour before school began, Matthew got out of his bed. He hadn't slept at all, and all the muscles of his body ached. He worried for a moment that he was sick and touched his fingers to his forehead, but thought that he'd probably just been tensing his body so much that he'd exhausted it. In the shower, he slowly rotated his head as far back as it would go, his neck joint crackling and sending darts of satisfying pain down his back. He needed to sleep and let his body heal, but he also knew that he needed to go to work, that he couldn't do anything out of the ordinary now.

It was cold outside, the front lawn wet with dew. Half the sky was gray with clouds, and half was a milky blue.

He got into his car and turned on the engine, flipping through radio stations until he found a classical music station far to the left of the dial. He couldn't listen to normal human voices this morning talking about the weather or politics or postseason baseball. The windshield was fogged on the outside, and he flicked his wipers on, then rolled down his passenger-side window. He allowed himself one quick glance toward the neighbors' house and saw a figure in the window move away just as he was turning his head. *That's Lloyd,* he told himself. *Hen told him everything, about our meetings and what I said, and now he really does believe her, and he's keeping an eye on me. That's okay. If he comes after me he won't know what hit him.*

Matthew drove slowly out of the driveway, turned left on Sycamore Street. There were two ways he drove to Sussex Hall. The fastest was along Route 2, but he often took back roads, picking up Littleton Road in Dartford Center. Today he headed to Route 2, moving slowly, keeping his eyes on his rearview mirror. It was when he was halfway to school, having just gone through the Concord rotary, that he spotted the light gray Golf about three cars behind him. It didn't necessarily belong to Lloyd—this part of the world was full of Volkswagens—but Matthew knew that it did. He turned off on the exit that would take him to school. The Golf did as well. He wondered what Lloyd was planning on doing. Was he just following him to see where he went? No, Matthew decided, Lloyd was going to confront him in the school parking lot. He could picture it already, Lloyd sputtering out, "Stay away from my wife or I'll fucking kill you," or something like that, while other teachers and students gawked. So instead of driving through the main entrance like he normally did, Matthew went through the second entrance, the driveway that looped around toward the back of the school. He was hoping the back lot would be empty and it almost was, just a few cars parked there, probably belonging to the custodial staff. Matthew pulled up next to the loading dock, waited thirty seconds, then watched as Lloyd's Golf rounded the corner tentatively, pulling in two spaces away.

Matthew got out of his car, leaving his briefcase behind, and walked toward the Golf as Lloyd got out, underdressed in just a pair of jeans and a ratty T-shirt.

"Hi, Lloyd," Matthew said, trying not to smile nervously.

Lloyd looked suddenly surprised, as though he wasn't adequately prepared for what he wanted to say. He shut the car door behind him and said, "Stay away from my wife."

Matthew couldn't stop himself from smiling, the words exactly what he had expected.

"What the fuck you smiling about?" Lloyd said. His face was flushed.

"I'm smiling because you have no idea what you're talking about."

"I know everything. I know what you've told my wife, and she's going to tell the police everything. You're fucked. I'm just here now to tell you to stay away from Hen, or you're in even bigger trouble than you already are."

Matthew felt a familiar sense of calm and elation come over him. He walked steadily toward Lloyd with purpose, watching Lloyd's eyes shift back and forth, panicking, trying to decide what to do. When he was a step away Lloyd swung at him, a slow haymaker, hitting him inexpertly on the upper third of his left ear. Matthew grabbed Lloyd by his T-shirt—for some band called Scruffy the Cat—then put his right foot behind Lloyd's legs and pushed him backward, holding on to the T-shirt so that he wouldn't go down too hard on the pavement. Once he was on the ground, Matthew kneeled on his chest, pushing Lloyd's right arm down and using his other hand to press against the side of Lloyd's face. This left Lloyd's left arm free, and he grabbed hold of Matthew's neck, scratching at the skin just beneath his hair. It didn't hurt that much, and Matthew thought that Lloyd had probably clipped his nails recently and how that was a good thing. He leaned harder on Lloyd's chest, being careful to not break anything, until Lloyd passed out from lack of air.

Matthew stood, breathing heavily, pressing his hand against his neck where Lloyd had scratched him. It felt like a minor scratch, slightly sticky where the skin might have broken, but it wasn't too bad. He took two big gulps of air, then bent and pulled a hair from Lloyd's head. Lloyd's eyelids fluttered, and he began to cough. All Matthew would have to do was lean again on his chest, stay there this time, until Lloyd passed from this world to the next. It would be so simple and so satisfying. But instead, Matthew pocketed the hair, got back into his Fiat, and drove it around to the front of the school, parking in his usual spot. It was twenty minutes until his first class began.

CHAPTER 33

Hen had nearly called 911 about five times in the hour since she'd discovered Lloyd was missing, but each time she stopped herself, imagining the conversation.

Ma'am, how long has he been missing?

Just a few hours.

Is there any reason you can think of that he might have left? Had you two had a fight?

Yes. I found out he's been having an affair for the past year.

Don't you think, ma'am, that that might have some-thing to do with the fact that he's missing?

Well, let me tell you about the serial killer who lives next door . . .

Instead, she forced herself to make coffee and to eat a piece of toast, then went to the porch with her mug and her phone, telling herself she'd wait. He'd show up soon, even though part of her believed something really terrible had happened.

She was on the cusp of calling 911 again when she decided to call Detective Martinez in Cambridge instead. She'd mentioned his name to the local detectives investigating Scott Doyle's death and figured that maybe he'd been updated. If he hadn't, then she could tell him what was going on. His phone rang about six times, and just as Hen had decided he wasn't going to pick up, there was a click and then his voice saying, "Hi, Hen," almost as though they were old friends.

"Oh, hi, Detective," Hen said. "Do you have a moment to talk?"

"I do. What's up?"

"Did you hear about Scott Doyle, the man who got killed at the Rusty Scupper in New Essex?"

"Yeah, I definitely did. Couple of detectives each called me about it from there. Said you were an eyewitness and that you'd mentioned my name."

"I saw the whole thing."

"Yeah, I heard."

"It was Matthew Dolamore. I saw him as clearly as I've seen anyone, but that's not exactly why I'm calling you."

"Okay," the detective said.

"Did you hear the rest? How I have a previous arrest for stalking a fellow student in college and claiming she'd attempted murder?"

"I did hear about that."

"And that Matthew Dolamore and his wife now have a protective order out against me?"

"I'd heard they were going to apply for one."

"Well, it got approved. Not that it's stopped Matthew from coming to me. We've been talking, the two of us. And he's told me everything. He told me how he killed Dustin Miller, and he told me how he killed Scott Doyle. He's telling me because he thinks it's safe, he thinks no one will believe me."

"When did he tell you all this?"

Hen told him about their three meetings and every-thing that Matthew said, including the strange way in which he'd mentioned his brother the night before. She knew, as she was saying it, how crazy she must sound, but she kept going, telling it exactly as it had happened.

"I don't suppose you taped any of these conversations?" the detective asked.

"He patted me down the first time we met. He'd thought of that as well. No, I didn't. Look, thing is, what I'm worried about now is that my husband's missing."

"Your husband's missing?"

"Since this morning. I told him everything I just told you last night, and I got up this morning and he's gone, and the car's gone, and his cell phone is here. I'm worried he went after Matthew himself. I'm kind of freaking out, if you want to know the truth."

"Okay, Hen, calm down. When was the last time you saw him?"

"He was here last night. When I woke up he was gone." Hen decided that it wasn't the best time to talk about Lloyd's infidelity. "I was going to call 911, but I know that he's not officially missing at this point."

"No, it's good that you called me first, Hen."

She didn't like the way he kept using her name; it reminded her of times she'd been hospitalized, times when a counselor or a therapist was trying to make a connection with her. It made her feel like he was coddling her the way he'd coddle an insane person.

"You don't believe me, do you?" she said.

"I don't know what to believe," he said after a pause. "That's the best I can do for you. But it doesn't look good for you, I have to say. From what I heard, he has a pretty solid alibi for the night of Scott Doyle's death."

"From his wife."

"Yes, from his wife."

"She must be lying for him. She's his wife—doesn't that make you doubt her alibi? Just a little bit?"

"She could be lying, yes. But so could you, and that's the problem. You have a history of lying in a similar situation."

Hen, realizing that this call was futile, almost hung up. But she took a deep breath and said, "Okay. We don't need to have this argument. I know how it looks, and I know how I look. But for the record, I just want to tell you that Matthew Dolamore has killed several people, including Dustin Miller and Scott Doyle. I know this for a fact. I know that my testimony will never matter, but there has to be other evidence. There has to be."

"Okay, we'll—"

"And one more thing. Check out his brother. He said his name was Richard. Matthew claims that they both got messed up by their parents, but that Richard kills women, not men."

"He told you that his brother has killed people?"

"No, actually, he didn't say that. He seems to think his brother is like him, and if he started to kill people, he would kill women, not men. That's what he told me. He seemed worried, like maybe his brother had actually done something already."

"I'll look into it, Hen, okay?"

"You'll call me if anything changes, or if you find out anything?"

"Of course. And you can call me again if you think of anything else, and let me know if your husband doesn't show up."

As he was saying the words, Hen watched as a gray

Golf came down the street, slowly pulling into their driveway.

Deciding not to mention this to the detective, she said, quickly, "Thanks for listening to me, Iggy," using the name he'd asked her to call him, even though it sounded strange in her own mouth. She hung up.

As Lloyd got out of the car, Hen went and stood at the edge of the porch, watching him through the screen. All the worry she'd had about his safety had suddenly dissipated, and now she was just angry again. Angry at his affair. Angry that he'd made her worry about him this morning.

"What the fuck?" she said, as he took the stairs up toward the porch.

"Sorry, I . . . I, uh, left suddenly."

"You didn't take your phone. I was freaking out." Lloyd had come through the door now, and Hen saw how pale he was, how scared his eyes looked. "What happened? You okay?"

"I followed him. I followed Matthew to his school, just because I wanted to talk with him . . . Can we go inside? I'm so cold."

Once inside, she saw the way he was holding his right hand, trying to flex it, and she asked, "Did you two fight?"

Lloyd told her the story, how he had followed Matthew to Sussex Hall, and how Matthew had incapacitated him.

"Where? In the parking lot?"

"It was at the back of the main building. He drove there and parked, I think, because he knew I was following him."

"You hit him first?"

"I did, although I think I hurt myself more than I hurt him. He was so calm. He just pushed me to the ground and kind of sat on me, and I . . . I thought I was going to die. Everything went black, and I thought he was killing me, and all I could think about . . . all I could think about was you."

He was crying again, and Hen, despite not really wanting to do it, put her hand on his back and told him that it sounded scary. "Do you want to try and talk to the local police?"

"No. I don't. It wouldn't do any good. I was the one who followed him, and I was the one who hit him first. All he'd say was that he was defending himself. No, I've been thinking about it. I think we should just leave here. I'll call my office and tell them I've had an emergency and need to take some time off. We could get in the car and drive somewhere. What about up to Maine? We could go back to that place in Bar Harbor and spend a week. Work on our marriage. What?"

Hen was shaking her head. "I don't know, Lloyd. We'd still have to come back here. Besides, I don't know yet if I *want* to work on our marriage."

"Then we'll get separate rooms and at least we won't be here. I know I sound like a coward, but I don't care. I now believe he's dangerous—"

"Right, you now believe he's dangerous because you experienced it yourself. You didn't believe it when I told you I *literally* witnessed him killing someone. You weren't suggesting a vacation then."

"I'm not suggesting a vacation, Hen. I'm suggesting that you and I go away to protect ourselves. And while we're away we can figure out what's going on between us."

Hen noticed Vinegar on the couch, licking a paw and cleaning an ear while they argued. He saw her looking at him and stopped what he was doing, stared back at her, then yawned.

"I have work," Hen said. "I have deadlines still for this book, and I need to get to my studio."

"Fuck that," Lloyd said.

"You can go if you like. In fact, I think you should. It would make the most sense. Besides, it would be good for us to spend some time apart."

"I'm not—"

"Lloyd, I don't know if I even want you here. At all."

"You can't make me leave, not with him living next door. I'll move into the guest room if you want. I don't need to talk with you. I get it that you're pissed at me. I'm pissed at me. But I'm not leaving, not till he's behind bars."

"Who knows if that will ever happen?" Hen said. "I'm not a reliable witness. Neither are you. He has an alibi. He's our neighbor, for better or for worse, right now."

"Then we'll move," Lloyd said.

Hen was suddenly exhausted. Just the thought of it—the thought of trying to save this marriage, the thought of trusting Lloyd again, the thought of looking for a new place to live, a new studio—it all exhausted her beyond comprehension. "What do you think, Vinegar?" she said to the cat. "Want to move?"

He started cleaning his other ear, flattening it back against his skull with his paw.

"I'm not talking about moving right now, but eventually, if he's never arrested. But I still think we need to leave and go on a trip. Right now. It's too dangerous. You're coming with me, Hen. I don't care if you don't want to do it yourself. You need to do it as a favor for me."

"As a favor for you?" Hen said, laughing. "Okay, this conversation is officially ended. I need to go to the studio and get work done. You can stay here, or you can go to work, or you can drive up and watch the leaves change in Maine. I don't care either way."

"If you're going to the studio, then I'm going with you."

"That's not going to happen, Lloyd. Sorry, it's not. You're going to be in a lot more danger staying here than I'm going to be in at my studio."

Lloyd lowered his brow. "What do you mean by that?"

"I just don't think he's going to hurt me. We've gotten to know each other. Trust me on this."

"I actually do think you're losing your mind, Hen. I think there's something seriously wrong with you. Are you taking your meds?"

"Fuck you, Lloyd. Why don't you go to Joanna's house and stay there. Call her up and have her come get you. I'm going to the studio because I have work to do."

She walked into the kitchen and grabbed the car keys off the wall. Then she stood for a moment, thinking about what Lloyd had just said about her losing her mind. So many of the large emotional moments of her life related to her mental health, but this wasn't one of them. Even though some of the symptoms were the same—racing thoughts, paranoia, a sense of dread— she knew what she knew. *This is real,* she wanted to tell Lloyd. *I know exactly who Matthew is, and my condition has nothing to do with it.*

She went back out to the living room, wondering if Lloyd would try to physically stop her, but all he said as she passed by him was "I'll be here when you get home."

As Hen went out the door, she said, "I really hope you're not."

CHAPTER 34

With Lloyd's strand of hair still in his chino pocket, Matthew drove toward Country Squire Estates. It had been a long, miserable day of teaching, but he had gotten through it. One thing about spending your day with teenagers was that they were so consumed by their own internal dramas that they were oblivious to the fact that the adults had problems of their own. There were exceptions, of course. Katrina Benedict, motherly before her time, told him that he looked tired. "There's something going around, Mr. Dolamore. Are you achy?" And Jason Khoury was the only one who noticed the red welts toward the back of Matthew's neck, just under the hairline. He asked Matthew if he was okay.

"I woke up with it," Matthew said. "Probably had a nightmare and scratched myself."

It wasn't rush hour yet, but the traffic was heavy along Route 2A. He'd already swung by Gifford's Farm, the closed ice-cream stand where he'd buried Michelle's keys and phone. He knew how reckless it was to visit there in daylight, let alone go back to Michelle's apartment complex, but he was determined to leave evidence that implicated Lloyd Harding, even if it didn't stick.

He'd pulled his car in behind the shuttered ice-cream place, relieved that there was no one else there, and after twenty minutes, he found the spot where he had buried Michelle's keys and phone. It took him so long to find them he began to worry that maybe he'd imagined the whole thing, that he truly was losing his mind, but then he found the slightly loose rock and unearthed the keys. Holding them, his stomach twisted, and for a moment he thought he was going to be sick again. But the feeling passed and he got back into the car, the palms of his hands sweating and his mouth drying up.

Country Squire Estates was set about a hundred yards from the road, behind a line of pine trees. Matthew had already exited off Route 2A and was about to turn into the parking lot when he saw the two police cruisers parked close to the entrance to Michelle's building. Even from a distance he could see a line of yellow police tape between the cars and the building. A uniformed officer stood by one of the cruisers, talking on his radio, and a small group of residents had gathered nearby, all talking. Matthew pulled into the lot of the Whole Foods market that was adjacent to the apartment complex, finding a spot and parking the car. He needed a moment to just think. He was too late, obviously, and wouldn't be able to plant the hair. Part of him was relieved, mostly because it meant he didn't have to enter that chamber of horrors again, didn't have to smell all that spilled blood, but also because soon, one way or another, it would all be over. The important thing now was to get to Richard. He didn't know what he was going to do when that happened, but he knew he had to see him before talking with the police. He needed to make some decisions.

After parking in his driveway, he instinctively checked to see if Henrietta and Lloyd's car was parked in theirs. It wasn't, which only told him that one of them was away. Entering his house, he was amazed that it looked the same as it had when he left earlier that morning. He half expected to find a squadron of police officers brandishing search warrants. It was only a matter of time. He didn't think that Lloyd was going to report him for that morning's altercation, but he did realize that the death of Michelle was going to put the spotlight on him again.

His phone rang—a 617 number he didn't recognize—and he chose not to answer it, knowing that it would only be bad news.

He tried to reach his brother again, then checked the voice mail on his phone. It was from Iggy Martinez, the Cambridge police detective who'd come out to question him about Dustin Miller. "I was wondering if you could give me a call as soon as you possibly can," he said casually. "It's not a biggie, but I have a follow-up question for you. Okay, thanks."

Matthew went into the kitchen and poured himself a large glass of ginger ale over ice, then brought it into his office, found the bottle that he kept there for when Richard was visiting, and added just a little bit of whiskey to his drink, enough to maybe take some of his nerves away. He called the detective back.

"Thanks for getting back to me," the detective said, then cleared his throat.

"No problem. What's up?"

"I have a follow-up question for you from the conversation we had earlier. I'm not even sure it's relevant, but his name came up so I thought I'd ask you about it."

"Okay," Matthew said, not knowing what to expect.

"You have a brother named Richard Dolamore, don't you?" the detective asked.

Matthew's scalp turned cold, but he stayed calm and said, "Yes."

"What can you tell me about him?"

"I'm confused. Do you think Richard had something to do with what happened to Dustin Miller?"

"I don't. Not really. This is what we do with cold cases. We follow up every little detail, no matter how insignificant, and then we can eliminate all the possibilities. Eliminate enough possibilities and maybe what's left will tell you something." Matthew heard the distant bleep of a horn through his cell phone and thought that the detective was probably driving.

"No, I understand."

"Where does your brother live?"

"He lives in my parents' house, last I checked. They left it for him."

"And where's that?"

"Right here in Dartford, actually."

"Oh? So you see him quite a bit, then."

"Honestly, I don't. My brother keeps to himself. He's kind of a misfit. I see him, but it's pretty rare."

"Okay. Got it. I won't bother you anymore, except can I have his address? You said it was your parents' house."

"Sure. It's 227 Blackberry Lane. On the other side of Dartford from where I am."

"And what about a phone number? Do you have that for your brother?"

Deciding that any delay would be beneficial for Richard, Matthew said, "I don't. Sorry. For all I know he doesn't have one. The only way we keep in touch is if he drops by here or I drop by there."

"Thank you, Matthew. You've been very helpful. By the way, I did hear you had a little bit of trouble with your neighbor."

"Oh, that. I'm hoping I nipped it in the bud."

"So she's been leaving you alone, then?"

"Yeah, it's been fine." Matthew wanted to ask the detective how he even knew about the protective order, but he stopped himself. Of course, he knew. The police were putting it all together. "Look," he quickly said. "I actually have to—"

"Yeah, you go. Sorry about that, and thanks again for the information."

Matthew stared at the phone in his hand after the call had ended. He'd been pacing throughout the call and now was standing in the kitchen. Something smelled bad and he looked in the sink, where a cellophane-wrapped steak was floating in a bowl of pinkish water. He remembered taking the steak out of the freezer the night before for dinner and then forgetting all about it. He picked it up by one of its edges and dropped it into the trash. Back in his office, he stared at the one picture he kept of him and his brother, a faded print from when Richard was a baby. Their mother had insisted on the photograph: Matthew dressed in Sunday school clothes (chinos and a button-down shirt), holding Richard, bundled in a blanket, on his lap. Matthew was looking directly at his new baby brother, and he imagined that they were making eye contact, even though he knew that newborn babies had terrible eyesight. Still, it was a good picture, one of the few good pictures from their childhood. Looking at the picture now, Matthew wished he would hear from Richard. He needed to warn him that the police were coming. He needed to give him a chance to flee. Matthew kept calling.

"Yo, bro," Richard said.

"Jesus, finally."

"I've been busy. Also, I know exactly what you're going to say to me."

"I'm not sure you do, Richard. They're coming for you. The police are coming. I just talked with one of them."

"If they're coming for me, then they're coming for you, too. You know that."

"Yes, I do. That's why we need to get our stories straight; that's why I need to talk with you. I'm not calling because of what you've done. I just need to know. Did anyone see you there? How careful were you?"

"See me where? What are you talking about?"

"We don't have time for this, Richard."

"Maybe we should meet and talk about this face-to-face. I'd feel more comfortable."

"We don't have time for that. Are they going to find evidence at Michelle's apartment? They're there now, you know, picking through every fiber, looking at every blood spatter."

Richard was quiet for a moment, finally saying, "You were there, too."

"How do you know that?"

"I watched you. How did it make you feel to see all that blood?"

"You know how it made me feel. It was sickening. What *you* did was sickening. She didn't deserve to die, and you know that."

"I couldn't let you have all the fun, you know. It isn't

fair. And besides, just because you've killed a bunch of sleazy guys doesn't give you the moral high ground. You're like Mom that way. She thought her shit didn't stink because her husband was worse than she was, but that's not how it works, you know. Not in the real world. In the real world, you're as sick and perverted as I am."

"You're right, Richard. I agree with everything you're saying, now answer the question. What are they going to find in the apartment?"

Richard sighed. "We share the same DNA, you know. If I need to make a run for it, so do you."

"I think that's what you should do. I think you should run away. And do it soon, okay? I'm not going to help you if they come for you. I can't. You'll be on your own."

"Thank you, my brother. I expected nothing more."

"You killed Michelle!" Matthew screamed the words in a strange keening voice he didn't even recognize as belonging to himself. "You killed Michelle," he said again quietly. Then he waited for Richard's response, but none came. "Richard?" he said. "You there, Richard?"

But Richard was gone, and Matthew had the feeling—the terrible, reassuring feeling—that maybe his brother would do what he'd been threatening to do for years: to leave Dartford for good, to leave the past behind.

Matthew realized that he was in the living room, standing in front of the window that looked toward his neighbors' house, still no car in the driveway. It occurred to him that he could actually drive over to Blackberry Lane, to the house he'd grown up in, to the house where Richard still lived, but he couldn't bring himself to do it. He hadn't been there for years, and the last time he'd been there he'd been shocked to see how much rot had settled into the house. Richard lived there, but he did nothing to maintain it. He hadn't cleaned it or changed any of the furnishings for years. All the furniture, the shelves, the windowsills, were covered with a black film of accumulated dust. The upstairs rooms, including Matthew's old bedroom, still with its single bed and its strange beige wallpaper with patterns of ferns, were infested with animal droppings, the walls dotted with black mold. No, he didn't think he could bring himself to go back there. He'd done all he could, having warned Richard. Now he needed to protect himself. He needed—

He heard a click from upstairs. It was faint, but he heard it clearly, and it wasn't one of the sounds the house occasionally made, the gas heat turning on, the ice-maker in the refrigerator, the walls settling on the foundation. No, it sounded like a door shutting. He walked slowly and quietly to the base of the stairs. From there he could see up into the second-floor landing, see that two of the doors, the ones to Mira's and his bedroom and the one to the upstairs bathroom, were both wide open. He began to quietly climb the stairs, then realized how that sounded and sped up, trying to walk casually, a man just heading up the stairs of his own house. At the top of the stairs, he turned left and walked into the master bedroom, his eyes quickly going to the closet door, that door open as well, although it was tight against the doorjamb. Could the click he heard have been a door opening up? It was possible, he told himself, and walked, casually again, toward the closet, swinging the door open wide and stepping inside, between Mira's clothes on the right and his on the left. There was no one in there. He reached a hand up to the shelf above his hanging clothes, pushed aside a shoebox, and his fingers found the billy club made from hickory, one of the few items he'd brought with him from his parents' and the only weapon he kept in the house.

With the billy club in his hand, he walked steadily from the bedroom closet back out to the landing. The other two doors on the floor—the one to the guest room and the one to Mira's sewing room—were both open as well, but each had closets. He went into the guest room first. The closet door was closed. He walked to it, put his hand around the doorknob, and twisted, pulling the door open and taking a step backward, expecting . . . what, exactly? Hen looking for the fencing trophy? Lloyd waiting for him, eager to continue their fight from this morning? The closet was empty, and for the first time since he'd heard the click, he considered that it might have been nothing, maybe a branch striking one of the upstairs windows, or maybe just one of those phantom sounds that all houses make.

Matthew left the guest room and walked to the room at the front of the house, a small room with a sloped ceiling that once upon a time was going to be a nursery. It was now Mira's sewing room, the walls painted a cheerful yellow, made more cheerful by the late-afternoon sun streaming in through the room's single window. There was a closet in this room as well, a half-closet really, more of a crawl space. The door was shut, and Matthew stood for a moment, eyeing it. If there really was someone hiding up here, then this was where they were.

He put his hand on the doorknob just as the door flung open and a man bolted out, his head going directly into Matthew's solar plexus, knocking him backward, both men sliding along the floor.

With the billy club that he still held, Matthew took a swing at the intruder, catching him in the shoulder. The man roared, more from fear than pain, probably, and raised his head. It was Lloyd, his teeth gritted, his eyes wide. He pushed himself up off the floor with his arms so that he was on all fours like a dog. Matthew, sitting up now, swung the club again, catching Lloyd on the bridge of his nose. There was a splintery crack. Lloyd's roar turned into a howl, and blood spilled from his broken nose onto the hardwood floor.

Matthew, still sitting, scuttled backward, kicking out with his legs. Lloyd shook his head rapidly and blood sprayed from side to side, then he crouched, wiping at his face, smearing the blood. Both men stood, Matthew still holding the billy club, Lloyd clenching his fists, swaying slightly.

"I heard you," Lloyd said.

Matthew took a step toward him. "You're trespassing," he said.

"I heard everything, you freak," Lloyd said, as Matthew swung the billy club.

CHAPTER 35

Just being in the studio, with its low lights and clanking pipes, surrounded by everything she needed in order to create art, Hen was finally able to slow down her thoughts, to begin to rationally think about the events that had happened to her in the past few weeks.

She made herself chamomile tea, put on Iron and Wine on the CD player, and set about cleaning up and organizing her space, a ritual she often did before settling down to more serious work. As she became calmer, she internally listed out her current problems in order of importance, something she'd taught herself to do years earlier when small problems would sometimes make her feel as though her life was unlivable. The idea was then to focus on one problem at a time. The other purpose of the exercise, of course, was to show yourself that your problems—no matter how crippling—were often not so bad when you listed them out. But that was *clearly* not her current situation. Her number one problem right now wasn't even the cheating husband and whether her marriage could be saved; it was the psychotic murderer who lived next door. After those two issues, nothing else seemed to matter much. Still, she forced herself to list her additional problems. She needed to visit her parents more, especially now that they were getting older. Also, she was a little past her deadline for the next two illustrations for the *Lore Warriors* book, although she hadn't heard anything threatening yet from her agent so she wasn't too worried. Besides, it was only work. It could wait for a little while.

That left her two main problems, and they were big ones: what to do about Lloyd and what to do about Matthew. It made sense, what Lloyd had said, that they should go away. It would get the two of them out of harm's way for a little while and allow them to work on their marriage. The problem was that she didn't *want* to work on the marriage. Ever since she'd discovered what he'd done, a part of her knew, down deep, that they were over. She wasn't an overly jealous woman—she was pretty sure she could have forgiven a one-night fling—but there was something about the year of sneaking around behind her back, about the constant lies. And there was also something else: she felt wronged, definitely, and pissed off, but she didn't feel overly hurt. Her heart wasn't breaking. She loved Lloyd—she'd always love Lloyd—but she could imagine her life without him. And wasn't that an indication . . . that maybe it wasn't a marriage worth saving?

If it wasn't for the situation with Matthew next door—the potentially dangerous situation—then she'd tell Lloyd to go live somewhere else for a while, that they needed a break so she could figure things out. Maybe she should just make him do it anyway. He was the guilty party, after all, and she should be able to make him leave. Where would he go? she wondered. He'd probably wind up moving into Joanna Grimlund's place in—where was it?—Northampton. She tried to think about how that made her feel, and she wasn't sure. She just didn't care very much, although she did wonder if it really was over between Lloyd and Joanna, the way he'd claimed. She also wondered what their affair had been like. Was it intense, the two of them talking about their future lives together? Or was it one of those relationships that always felt stamped with an expiration date from the moment it started? What did Joanna think about what had happened?

Maybe I'll call her, Hen thought, and as soon as she had the thought she decided to actually do it. She wanted to hear Joanna's voice. She wanted to hear what she had to say for herself. Joanna had always been someone whom Hen had liked. As partners of two best friends, they'd been forced into a lot of time spent together, but happily, not reluctantly. Joanna had an irreverent and dirty sense of humor. While Rob and Lloyd got drunk and high and reminisced about shit they'd gotten up to in college, Joanna and Hen would drink wine and have intense conversations. Hen had told her almost everything about her psychotic episode in college, and Joanna told her about her alcoholic father who was now in prison for securities fraud. When Rob and Joanna split up, Hen had thought about getting in touch with Joanna directly, maybe even meeting up, but she'd never done it. Lloyd, clearly, had had the same thought.

Hen didn't have Joanna's cell phone number, of course, and she almost considered calling Lloyd and demanding he give it to her, but even if he did give her the number he'd probably manage to call Joanna up first, or at least text her, and warn her about the impending phone call. Hen wanted the element of surprise.

She called Rob, who picked up almost instantly.

"You couldn't open them?" he said into the phone.

"What?" she said, figuring he thought she was someone else.

"The pictures I sent you. I realized after I sent them that maybe I should have reformatted them."

"Oh, the *bonfire* pictures," Hen said. "I haven't even gotten them yet, but I'm calling for another reason."

"You haven't gotten them yet? I sent them right after we talked."

"Maybe it went to spam, Rob. Listen, I'm calling because I need Joanna's phone number, and I thought you'd probably have it."

"Sure," he said. "It's her phone number from a year ago, but I doubt it's changed. What do you need it for?"

"I just need to talk with her. It's important." Hen hoped that the truth, however vague, would be enough.

"Let me get it for you," Rob said, his voice already faint, Hen realizing that he was probably scrolling through his phone right now. "Okay, ready?"

He read her the number while she wrote it down in her sketchbook with a pencil.

"Thanks, Rob, you're awesome," Hen said.

"Not a problem, but I'm confused. Why do you want to talk with her?"

"She's been having an affair with Lloyd for a year and I wanted to hear her side of the story."

Rob laughed, more of a snorting sound, then said, "Really?"

"Really."

"Oh, shit."

"Thanks for the number."

Hen didn't think that Rob would call up Joanna to warn her, but just in case, she instantly dialed the number she'd written down in her sketchbook. After two rings, Joanna's voice, deeper than she remembered, said a tentative "Hello?"

"Joanna, it's Hen Mazur . . . Lloyd's wife."

There was about a two-second pause, long enough for Hen to think that Joanna had quietly ended the call, but then came Joanna's voice, saying, "Hi, Hen."

"Joanna, I don't know if Lloyd's talked to you, but I'm guessing he has. I know everything. He told me everything." Even as she said the words, she knew they were untrue. No one knows everything.

"Hen, I just want to say that I am so, so sorry. I don't expect you to ever forgive me. I don't deserve it, I know, but please understand—"

"Joanna, it's okay. I'm not calling to yell at you. I'm just calling . . . I don't know why I'm calling. I guess I want to hear your side of the story and not just Lloyd's."

"Okay," Joanna said, and took a long, audible breath. "When did . . . What did Lloyd tell you?"

"You haven't talked with him yet?"

"Um . . . briefly. He'd told me that for a while he'd been planning on finally letting you know about . . . what had happened."

"He didn't let me know, actually. I figured it out, and then he confessed to it."

"Oh."

Hen could tell Joanna hadn't been told about these recent developments and that she was trying to catch up, trying to figure out what she should and should not say.

"He hasn't talked with you, has he?" Hen asked.

"I think I should go."

"Joanna, he told me you two were over, that you broke up over the last weekend you were together."

"He told you that?"

"Yes."

Hen heard what sounded like an exasperated sigh. "Can I ask you something, Hen?"

"Okay."

"Have the two of you been talking about getting a divorce?"

"What do you mean? Like recently, now that I know about you and Lloyd?"

"No, I mean before. Like for the past six months."

"We just bought a fucking house together. No, we haven't been talking about divorce. Is that what he's been telling you?"

"Maybe he's implied—"

"Implied that we were going to get divorced?"

"Is that not happening?" Joanna actually laughed. "He told me you were both unhappy, that things weren't going well, that you bought the house to try and save the marriage."

"None of that is remotely true. I mean, maybe it was true in his own mind, but we never had a conversation about any of that. He's never told me he's unhappy. It was a total shock for me that he was having an affair."

Silence again. Then Joanna said, "I'm sorry. I never would have—"

"You can stop saying you're sorry. Did you think . . . Are you planning on being with Lloyd?"

"I hadn't planned anything, exactly, but I did think that you and him were breaking up. And I did think that it might work out between us. Jesus, have I been a total idiot?"

"Well, if you've been an idiot, then so have I."

"It's still my fault. I was the one—"

"Let's just say it's all Lloyd's fault and leave it at that, okay? I'm kicking him out of my house, by the way. I just decided. Just wanted to give you a heads-up that he might be looking for a place to stay."

"He's not staying here."

"I don't really care where he stays, Joanna, so you don't have to say that for my sake."

"Okay," she said.

There was another pause, and Hen realized that there was nothing left to say. She said, "I've got to go now. Thanks for talking with me."

"Stop being nice. I think I'd feel better if you yelled at me or something."

"Well, thanks for talking with me, and fuck you for everything else."

"Thanks, that's better. Sorry again."

Hen hung up, put her phone down on the arm of the ragged upholstered chair she was sitting on, and felt a surge of energy, half anger and half . . . something else—maybe excitement, although that wasn't the exact word. It was more like anticipation. Everything was changing so rapidly. Lloyd was not who she thought he was. Not even close. The cheating was one thing—people were flawed and made mistakes—but the outright deceit, not just toward her but also toward Joanna, who suddenly seemed more like a fellow victim instead of the enemy, was something else altogether. She stood up, shook her hands out, and wondered what to do next. Her body was buzzing, like there were tiny wires sparking just under the surface of her skin. In a way, it reminded her of times when she was manic, but that wasn't the case now. Any mania she was experiencing was strictly related to what was going on in her life.

She decided that what she really wanted to do was to just go home and send Lloyd packing, but she knew he was going to resist, claiming she was in danger. Maybe *she* should go somewhere else—a nearby hotel or maybe a friend's house (Darlene, their old neighbor in Cambridge, would definitely welcome her)—and not tell Lloyd where she was going to be. She was excited by the thought, decided that she should do it, then realized that she would need to go home and pack first. She had to pack clothes, but more important, she needed her meds. The problem with going home, of course, was having to deal with Lloyd. She decided to call him first, tell him she was coming home to get some things but didn't want to have a conversation. His phone went to voice mail; she didn't leave a message. They had a landline in the house—it was part of the bundle that got them cable and Wi-Fi—and she tried that number, just on the off chance that Lloyd wasn't near his cell phone. But there was no answer on the landline, either.

Maybe he's gone for a walk, she thought, and wondered if she had time to drive home, get her things, and leave before he came back. While she was thinking this, the lights in her studio suddenly went out, and the room was plunged in darkness.

"Hey," she said aloud.

A hollow, distant "Sorry" came back, and the lights turned back on. Yuma something or other, who was a watercolor painter on the other side of the basement level, came and popped her head into Hen's studio.

"Sorry 'bout that," she said. "You didn't hear me call out? I thought I was the only one down here."

"No, sorry, I didn't hear you. No big deal. Am I the last one here?"

"As soon as I leave, you will be."

Hen almost asked Yuma to wait up, that she was leaving, too, but instead said, "I'll make sure to turn the lights out when I leave."

She listened to Yuma's footsteps as she made her way down the hall. The CD in her player was changing over and a Morphine album began to play. She looked at the copper plate that she'd begun to prepare earlier, briefly considered trying to do just a little bit of work, but knew she should go home and pack. It was going to be another scene with Lloyd, but the quicker it began, the quicker it would end. She could come back tomorrow and get work done.

Hen grabbed her jean jacket from the back of the chair, put her sketchbook in her bag, and was about to turn out the lights in her studio when she heard footsteps coming back down the hall. Was Yuma back? No, the footsteps were louder and heavier. She kept her hand on the switch, listening to where they were going. She almost shouted out "hello," but something stopped her. The footsteps were coming toward her studio.

CHAPTER 36

At Logan Airport, Mira stepped out through the automatic doors into the cool air and turned left toward the line for taxis. She wondered briefly how much it was going to cost to take a cab all the way to West Dartford, then pushed the thought away. That was the least of her worries. When everything turned out to be fine, she and Matthew could laugh at the credit card bill, laugh at how Mira panicked during her trip to Wichita and returned early.

That will most likely never happen and you know it. Where there's smoke, there's fire.

Mira had woken early that morning in the hotel room. She'd left the curtains open and was greeted by the enormous Midwest sky, its clouds edged in pink. She'd had terrible dreams, the most vivid being one in which her house had burned down. In the dream Matthew and she had toured the remains. Everything was gone except for charred bodies, hidden everywhere in the smoldering house. Most were men—Jay Saravan, a frequent visitor in Mira's dreams, was there, of course—but some were children, small blackened bodies that Mira knew were her own, the babies Matthew and she had never been able to have.

Lying in bed, staring at the window, a phrase kept going through Mira's mind: *Where there's smoke, there's fire.* She knew what she was telling herself: it was all true; her husband killed people. There was just too much smoke. Even last night, when they'd had such a seemingly normal conversation on the phone, he'd come out and said that he missed her. It wasn't the words so much, but the way in which he had said them, his voice childish and sad. Something inside of him was unraveling. She knew it. It was no longer doubt she felt but dread.

She'd packed, checked out early, texted Linda at the local office that she thought she had food poisoning and could someone man the booth for her that day, then taxied to the airport to catch the next flight to Boston. The best one she could find didn't get her in until midafternoon—she had to connect in Charlotte—but there was one seat left and she took it.

In the cab on her way to her house she fought the urge to call Matthew and tell him she was on her way home. The whole point of returning early was to catch him off guard and to confront him. To tell him she was beginning to have doubts and give him a chance to confess. Or give him a chance to convince her that she—like their neighbor—had become unreasonably paranoid. Convince her that there was no fire.

The cab got caught up in stalled traffic right before the Concord rotary, and the driver, a jowly, red-faced man, muttered under his breath about the traffic as though he were the one who needed to get home.

Mira cracked the window in the back, not because it was too warm but because the air in the cab felt thin, as though she wasn't getting enough oxygen. The cab jerked its way through the rotary, the driver still grumbling, and then they were on the relatively empty road toward West Dartford. She checked her watch; on any normal day Matthew would be home from school by now. What would he be doing? If she were there he'd be working on that day's crossword on his iPad while she started dinner, or else he'd be in his office grading papers.

The cab pulled onto Sycamore, the low sun casting long shadows across the street. She directed the driver to her house, noticing right away that Matthew's car wasn't in the driveway. She felt a combination of increased fear but also relief. After putting the giant fare on her credit card, she rolled her luggage to the front door, trying to remember where she'd put the house key. She didn't need it, though; the front door swung open, and she stepped across the threshold, calling out Matthew's name even though his car was gone. He didn't answer back.

The door being unlocked, along with the slightly offputting smell in the house, raised Mira's already elevated heartbeat. She shut the door behind her, shouted out another "Hello?," then walked through the living room toward the kitchen, where the bad smell seemed to be coming from. The kitchen looked relatively normal except for a line of empty ginger ale cans across the granite countertop, as though those were the only sustenance that Matthew allowed himself when she was gone. She looked into the stainless steel sink. It was dry and empty, so she pulled open the cabinet that held the garbage can and was immediately hit with the strong smell of rotten food. On the top of the garbage was a rib eye steak still wrapped in its container, beaded with drops of reddish water. Had Matthew taken it out of the freezer, forgotten to eat it, then thrown it away? If so, it was so unlike him. He was a man who hated wasting food.

Next, she went to Matthew's office, almost considered knocking, but turned the doorknob and swiftly entered. She flicked the switch on the wall, turning the ceiling light on. At first the room looked normal, but as she looked around she realized that all of Matthew's little knickknacks had been moved. Where the vintage typewriter had been, on the side table, there was now his art deco greyhound sculpture. The typewriter had been moved to the desk. It wasn't unusual for Matthew to move things around in his office, but she knew that he tended to do it when he was anxious about something. And then Mira looked at the corduroy sofa, noticing first that the red velvet pillow was indented as though someone had been sleeping on it and that there was a wool blanket bunched up on the floor. She hadn't thought about Richard for years, but Mira thought about him now, wondered if he'd been the one who'd spent the night on the couch. She left the office and climbed the stairs to the second floor, wanting to check their bedroom to see if their bed had been slept in. It looked like it had even though it had been made, and the tight corners and the lined-up pillows told Mira that it was Matthew who'd made it.

Tired suddenly, she sat on the edge of the bed and looked at her phone, reading through the string of concerned text messages from her colleagues asking about the food poisoning. Mira was never sick, never missed a day of work. Ignoring the texts, she went to her contacts list so she could call Matthew. She'd tell him she'd returned early and wanted to talk. With her thumb hovering over the Call button, she found herself reciting Ayat al-Kursi, the only Muslim prayer she knew, taught to her by her grandmother who had come to live with them in California for the final years of her life. She hadn't thought of the words in years—she barely even knew what they meant anymore—but she spoke them now, the simple act of recitation causing her body to somewhat relax. Opening her eyes again, she noticed that the closet door was swung all the way open. It wasn't alarming that it was open, but it was unusual. Except for the morning when they were getting ready for work, the closet door was usually shut. She walked into it, running her hands along the hung clothes on either side. Everything seemed normal, but when she looked up at the shelving above Matthew's side, she noticed a shoe box hanging over the edge. He'd been up there, clearly looking for something. Mira, standing on her tiptoes, wasn't even able to touch the shelf, let alone anything on it. She immediately thought of the wooden chair in her craft room. She walked out of the bedroom to the landing and pushed through the door into the sloped-ceilinged room.

The chair was under the window, and Mira was halfway into the room before she noticed the body on the floor. She screamed out loud, more like a sharp bark of panic that she cut off instantly. It was definitely a body, lying diagonally, its feet just under her sewing table. There was no way to know who it was since the body had been entirely wrapped in duct tape, from the feet all the way to the head, so that it looked like a silver mummy.

Trembling, Mira took two quick steps to the body,

lowered herself onto a knee, and pressed the palm of her hand against the chest of the body. It was a man—she could tell that much by his size and the flatness of his chest—and there was no movement in his body and no heartbeat. Close up, she could see that blood had seeped out between the folds of duct tape around the head. *Call 911,* she told herself, thinking of her phone back on the bed. But she had to know who was under the tape. She had to know if it was Matthew.

Her fingers found the sticky edge of the end of a piece of duct tape plastered across the center of the dead man's face. And she began to pull the tape away.

CHAPTER 37

Richard Dolamore pulled into the liquor store parking lot. It was late afternoon, the air cold in his nostrils as he walked across the lot and through the automatic doors. He loved this liquor store, as big as a warehouse, full of suburban boomers filling carts with gallons of trendy gin and cases of wine with names like "Mommy's Best Friend." Before it became a liquor store it had been a movie theater, years ago, a cheap independently run place with one screen that had been converted to two by putting up a shabbily constructed wall. Richard had come here as a teenager, mostly alone, but sometimes with dates, and he remembered that during quiet moments of whatever movie you were watching, you could hear what was happening on the other screen.

But the theater had been gutted, and now it was filled with row after row of colorful bottles. Richard wandered up and down the aisles looking at all the labels, designed to sell you a little something more than the alcohol inside. Dad had been a liquor rep, selling mostly down-market brands—vodkas with names like Romanov, and whiskey called Old Scotsman or Gold Rush—at bulk discount to chain restaurants and hotel bars. These types of brands still existed, always on the bottom shelf. You could stand in an aisle at the liquor store and run your eyes from the top to the bottom shelf, and you'd see bottles trying to attract a whole spectrum of customers—from the asshole who bought barrel-aged rum for a hundred dollars a bottle to the alcoholic on disability whose rum came in a gallon bottle made from plastic.

"They're all the same," Porter Dolamore used to say to him. "People are fools. Put rotgut in a pretty bottle, and everyone thinks they're living like kings."

Richard went to the Scotch aisle. A woman about his age studied the bottles, looking like she was trying to read a menu in a language she didn't understand.

"That's a good one," Richard said, tilting his head toward the bottle of single malt she'd just picked up off the shelf.

"Oh, yeah?" she said. She wasn't pretty. Her nose was too big and her eyes were too close together, but it was clear that she worked out and took care of herself. She had long brown hair with blond highlights, and she wore a pumpkin-colored sweater with a plunging neckline. Richard let his eyes scan the exposed tops of her breasts, nicely tanned. *Dark brown nipples,* he thought.

"Super smooth," he said. "Like silk. Is it for you or for . . . ?"

She'd caught him looking down her sweater, and Richard thought she hadn't decided yet how she felt about it. But she bit her lower lip and said, "It's for a new friend in my life. He loves Scotch, and I don't know anything about it." Then she laughed, as though she'd said something funny.

"Does he like peaty Scotch?"

She grimaced, said, "I don't even know what that means."

Richard explained the difference between peated and unpeated Scotch, asked her if she could remember any particular brand he'd ordered at a restaurant. "Macallan, I think."

"Right, Macallan," Richard said, and grabbed a Scotch at random off the top shelf and handed it to her. "Get him this. He'll love it. Just like Macallan but a little bit better."

"You sure?" she said.

"Trust me," Richard said, then thought, *I could do this for a living. Easy peasy.* The bottle he'd handed to the woman came inside a very tasteful box, and he could tell that she was impressed.

"All right," she said. "Sold."

"And if it doesn't work out with your new friend, I'd be happy to take his place."

The woman frowned. "You're married," she said, looking down at his hand.

"I wear a ring," he said. "Doesn't mean I'm married."

"It usually does," she said, and headed toward the front of the store.

Richard whispered, "Cunt," and wondered if she heard him. He thought he saw a twitch in her upper back.

From the second shelf up from the bottom he grabbed a bottle of J&B for himself, then waited a couple of minutes to give the woman a chance to buy her overpriced swill and get away from the big bad wolf. When he got to the checkout himself, he almost told the teller—an old guy with a mustache stained yellow from cigarettes—that he should get a commission for talking the previous customer into a hundred-dollar bottle, but decided against it.

Back in his car, he stowed the Scotch in his glove compartment. It was nice just knowing it was there, even if he decided he didn't need it.

From the liquor store, he drove through Middleham back toward Dartford, taking Sudbury Road over to Blackberry Lane. He almost didn't turn down his own street for fear that the police were already there, but decided to take a chance. If there were any suspicious vehicles, he'd simply pull into another driveway, then turn around and leave. And if they weren't there yet, then he'd have a chance to do what he should have done a long time ago. He took the turn down Blackberry, all the properties except for one—a monstrous new pillared house—built in the decade after World War II, charmless boxes designed to contain an average American family. The lane dead-ended at a cul-de-sac that was ringed by four properties, including Richard's childhood home. It belonged to him now; well, technically it really belonged to Matthew, who paid the taxes on it. The house—half brick and half white siding—was set back behind a cluster of white pines. The front yard was covered with a layer of brown pine needles, and the driveway asphalt was cracked and choked with weeds. The house itself, at least from the outside, still looked decent, although the white vinyl siding had begun to turn a mossy green. A blank, dumb house, Richard thought, not for the first time. He swung the car around the circular dead end and parked it so that its nose was facing back toward Sudbury Road. Before getting out of his car, he took a little sip from his bottle of Scotch.

After entering through the front door, he called out,

"Hey, Mom. Hey, Dad. I'm home," like he always did. It cracked him up, although he always had a little bit of fear that one day his greeting would be returned. It never was, though, and this would be the last time he'd ever enter this house. He went up the stairs, the air changing as he got to the top. It was stagnant, smelling of mildew, but underneath that smell was the unmistakable tang of something dead, a sweet, cloying odor. Probably a dead squirrel in one of the walls, he told himself. He didn't want to stay upstairs too long—it disgusted him, and not just because of the rot—but he did want to get one of his dad's suitcases from his parents' old bedroom. He pushed the bedroom door open with his foot. It was dim inside the room, the curtains pulled, and as Richard entered, he heard something scurry along the floorboards. Ignoring it, he took out his phone and, using its flashlight, walked to the closet, the door already open. He spotted the large plaid suitcase tucked toward the back. He grasped its leather handle and pulled it out, glad to discover that it was empty. He put the suitcase on the bed, the air in the room now swirling with disturbed dust. It tasted almost bitter at the back of Richard's throat. There were two things in this room he wanted: his mother's framed picture of her own parents—a short, dour man in a felt hat with a feather in its brim and a woman in a house dress, a sad smile on her lips—and his father's old billfold. He knew right where it was, in the top drawer of the bureau. It contained a two-dollar bill, his father's driver's license, his AAA card, a few business cards, plus a folded-up clipping from a magazine of Bo Derek on the beach.

Richard took the wallet and the picture and put both of them inside of the suitcase, then zipped it back up and left the room after taking one final look around. It was, after all, the room where he'd found the body of his mother. He'd known she was dead as soon as he saw her outline under the chenille bedspread. She was curled into a tight ball, like an animal that knows it's dying and goes to ground. Still, he'd lifted the bedspread off her and taken a long look. Her yellowed nightgown was bunched up around her waist, and there was dried vomit around her head. In one hand was a vodka bottle—Smirnoff, if he remembered correctly—and there was an empty pill bottle on the bedside table. Her other hand was up against her face. When Richard had taken a closer look he realized that she'd been sucking her thumb when she died.

Back downstairs, he filled the suitcase with the few other things he wanted. It wasn't much, just framed photos mostly, a family Bible that had been passed down to his father, the set of Ginsu knives his mother had bought from the television, and the mason jar that was hidden under the loose floorboard in the pantry. Richard had found it there only a few years ago. There was about a thousand dollars in cash in the jar.

With the suitcase full, Richard went down into the basement, again using his cell phone flashlight, and got the two gallon cans of gasoline that had been down there for as long as he could remember. He used the first can on the curtains and along the runner carpet that went up the middle of the stairs to the second floor. It was empty much sooner than he expected, and he was more careful with the second can, splashing a little bit here and there around the first floor of the house, saving most of it for his father's recliner, first pushing it over toward the wall so that it touched the heavy velvet curtains that draped across the front windows. The fabric had split from the recliner's seat, revealing crumbling yellow Styrofoam, which he soaked with the remaining gasoline. The smell of the gas bit at his nostrils and his throat and made his eyes water.

He had a set of matches from the Owl's Head Tavern in his pocket and he lit one, dropped it onto the soaked cushion. It just sat there for a moment, the flame flickering weakly, then there was a loud *whump,* and the cushion was fully ablaze. He grabbed the suitcase and exited out the front door, walking at a normal pace back to his car, catching movement in one of the windows of the closest house, probably Mrs. MacDonald watching his every move. Maybe he'd be lucky and the fire would spread to her house as well.

He'd been driving for ten minutes when he realized how hard he was gripping the steering wheel. He told himself to relax. Things were in motion and he just needed to let them play out.

He cruised down Sycamore Street, curious to see if Henrietta Mazur's car was parked in front of her house. It wasn't, so he kept going, his window cracked, expecting to hear the distant sound of sirens, but maybe he was too far from the other side of Dartford. Maybe the house hadn't burned, the flames just sputtering out before they ever got going, but he didn't think that was the case. He did a loop that took him up near Scituate River and did hear the distant sound of some kind of siren. It could be anything, of course, but it could also be his childhood home burning to the ground. He rolled the window all the way down. There was smoke in the air, but it had the fruity, pleasant aroma of chimney smoke, a common smell on a brisk fall afternoon.

He drove a short distance to Black Brick Studios. He knew where Henrietta usually parked, near the entrance to the basement. He left his car a block away on a side street, then walked down the hill to the lot. The gray Golf was there, along with one other car, a light blue Prius. The back parking lot was bordered on one side by a high embankment and on the other by a sloping embankment that led down to the river. A huge willow tree, beginning to turn yellow, rustled in the cold breeze. Richard stood about halfway between the willow tree and the locked back door of the studios, trying to look casual. One of two things would most likely happen next. Either Henrietta would come out from those doors and he'd be waiting for her, or whoever owned the Prius would emerge and, if that was the case—he was hoping it would be—he'd make sure he was walking toward the door with purpose, and hopefully whoever it was would let him in.

He stood for about thirty minutes, the clouds building up in the sky, till he saw the doorknob of the metal door turn. He began to walk swiftly toward the door, his phone in his hand, and watched as a woman with short gray hair emerged.

"Oh, hey," Richard said, approaching. "Can you hold that?"

He saw the doubt in the woman's eyes, but she held the door because he'd asked her to do it. "Visiting Hen," he said, and held up his phone. "Does *your* phone work down there?"

"No, not really," the woman said.

Richard slid past her, saying thanks, and the door closed behind him. He stood for a moment in the dim hallway and breathed deeply through his nostrils; he could smell paint and turpentine and the lingering scent of patchouli from the woman who'd just let him in. He wondered how long she'd be haunted by what she had just done. Probably for the rest of her life, he thought.

He began to walk toward Henrietta's studio, not attempting to walk quietly. It didn't matter if she knew he was down here. They were alone, and there was nothing she could do about it. He turned a corner, saw the light coming from underneath the door of her studio, then heard her door open. She poked her pretty head out and saw him. He kept coming.

"Hi, Matthew," she said, a little bit of uncertainty in her voice.

"I'm not Matthew," Richard said.

CHAPTER 38

Hen almost ran, but something stopped her. *You run, you die,* a voice was telling her, so instead she stepped out into the hallway and faced the man who just told her he wasn't Matthew.

But it *was* Matthew, even though there was something different about him, in his eyes maybe, even in the way he was walking, the set of his head.

"Who are you?" she asked.

"I'm Richard," he said. "We haven't officially met yet."

"No, we haven't." Hen's entire body had turned icy cold, yet her brain was clicking along calmly, trying to assess the situation. "Where's Matthew?"

"Matthew? Who knows? Who cares?"

He was taking a step forward, his face completely illuminated by one of the hallway's hanging lamps. *Maybe Richard is his twin,* she thought, but then she saw the scar below his mouth, the one that made him look a little like Harrison Ford, and she realized that there was no brother named Richard. There was just Matthew, and he was far more insane than she had realized. Again, she thought of running, but she also realized almost for the first time how strong Matthew was, with his broad shoulders, his large hands. She could bolt toward the other side of the studio, toward the metal steps that led up to the first floor, but now Matthew was only about two feet away from her.

"I'd like to see your studio," he said. "See where you make all your dirty pictures."

He ran his fingers through his hair, and it stayed standing up, as though he hadn't washed it for a few days. He was now close enough that she could smell alcohol on his breath.

"I actually have to go," she said, wondering if maybe he'd let her just walk past him. Maybe if she did it quickly, nonchalantly, but as soon as she began his hand flashed forward and he grabbed her by the neck, pinching hard with his thumb and forefinger. She kicked out at him, hoping to hit him in the groin, but caught his shin instead. His face flinched, his lips parting but his teeth clenched, and, still gripping her neck, he pushed her into her studio, then shoved her hard so that she went flying backward, landing on her back and sliding a little along the concrete floor. A jolt of pain radiated up her spine.

Hen pushed herself back along the floor until she was leaning up against her chair. Matthew was looking around the studio, eyes flicking over everything.

"Go ahead and take a look around," Hen said.

"Don't you want to fuck me first?" Matthew said, a wide grin on his face, his eyes darting.

"We've only just met, Richard. Why did you think I'd fuck you?" Hen said, not really thinking about it. Matthew's eyes dropped down to her, and he looked amused and interested, and she realized she'd said the right thing. If she pretended he was Richard, if she engaged with him, maybe she'd stall him. And if she could stall him, maybe she could get away from him.

"Well, you want to fuck Matthew, don't you?" he said.

"Actually, I don't. Matthew and I don't have that kind of relationship, and besides, we're both married."

"You can sit in the chair, if you'd like. You look pretty pathetic there on the floor."

Hen slid up into the chair, settling onto its cushion. How many times had she sat in that chair, relaxed, thinking about art, drinking tea? And now she was sitting here and it could be the last thing she ever did.

"To Lloyd and Mira," Matthew said suddenly, and Hen was confused, until she realized he was responding to her saying that Matthew and she were both married.

"Right, to Lloyd and Mira."

Matthew held his hands out, palms up, and smirked at her. "I mean . . ." he said.

"What?"

"I'm not too impressed with Lloyd."

"But Richard's never met him," Hen said, and knew almost immediately this was the wrong thing to say. Matthew frowned, his eyes going from amusement to controlled rage with one flutter of his eyelids. *Don't question him,* she told herself. *Don't question his logic. Just go with it. Go with whatever he wants to talk about, and maybe if he wanders far enough away from me . . .*

"Matthew told me all about him. He still tells me things, you know, even though he doesn't quite trust me with the information."

"What did Matthew tell you about Lloyd?"

"Nothing you don't already know about at this point. He's been putting his pee-pee where he shouldn't. It's pretty easy these days, you know. Back in the day you had to go to a brothel to get some pussy. Now you can find it anywhere." Matthew was staring intently at her, maybe trying to see if she was shocked by what he said.

"Where do you go?"

"Where do I go for what?"

"Where do you go for pussy, Richard?" she asked, holding his eye contact. He flinched, just a little. "Do you go to brothels?"

"My dad went to brothels. He told me all about them. But it's like I told you, every girl walking down the street now is up for it."

He looks nervous, Hen thought, and tried to decide whether to push him down this conversational road. She could tell that it unnerved him when she challenged him, but she wasn't sure if it was good to unnerve him. She didn't want to go too far, but she did want to keep him talking about topics that interested him. What she really wanted to do—and she knew it would be dangerous—was to reach the real Matthew, get him to come out, and then she'd be safe, at least temporarily. Was he *pretending* to be Richard, his brother? Was it a true split personality? If she could get him to revert to Matthew, she thought she could talk her way out of whatever he had planned. If he stayed in his current personality, then she thought there was a chance she could run to the door, slam it shut, and lock Matthew inside. It was a peculiarity of all the studio doors on the basement level: the dead bolt lock needed a key on both sides of the door, and Hen's key—the only copy she had—was in her jacket pocket.

"How come you're so different from Matthew," Hen said. "I've gotten to know him pretty well, and I think he's a gentleman."

A huge smile crossed Matthew's face. She could see his gums. "He kills people, you know."

"I know he does. He told me. But he also told me that he would never hurt a woman, and that he would only hurt a man who would hurt a woman. That's why I said he's a gentleman."

"He was a mama's boy," Matthew said, and turned his eyes up to the ceiling of the studio, as though he were remembering.

Hen almost thought about bolting for the door, but he quickly turned his gaze back toward her. Was he carrying a weapon? she wondered. It didn't really matter if he was or wasn't. She remembered the strength of his hand around her neck, the way he could have crushed her throat with a simple squeeze.

"And you weren't?"

"Mom was a whore all over town. I even heard once that she was fucking the minister at the church, the same minister that married her and Dad."

"If that was true, then why was Matthew a mama's boy? He must have known all about that as well."

Matthew shook his head, glanced toward the larger of Hen's two printing presses, and took a step toward it, leaning against its metal edge. It gave Hen a slightly better chance of getting to the door if she decided to make a run for it. "He knew all about it, but he says that Dad made her that way. He says that Mom figured if she was going to be called a whore, and treated like a whore, then maybe she should act like one, too."

"Your dad used to call your mom a whore?"

"He knew what she was. He knew what all women are."

"Did your dad kill women?" Hen asked.

Matthew appeared to think for a while. "I don't think I want to talk about my dad anymore," he said.

"That's okay," Hen replied. "I'm curious, that's all."

"You just want to keep me talking until you can decide whether you can run faster than me."

Hen forced herself to smile. "A little bit," she said. "I mean, more than a little bit. I'm scared of you, Richard. I'm sure you realize that. But I'm also curious. You're so different from your brother, and I want to know why. You grew up in the same house with the same parents."

"We're not that different," he said. "Matthew pretends to be all noble and good, but down deep he knows he's just like his dad. He has bad thoughts, too, you know. He probably had bad thoughts about you."

"But he doesn't act on them."

Matthew blinked and pursed his lips. "No, he doesn't act on them with women. He doesn't do that. But he still kills people. He gets off on it, too. He'll tell you he doesn't. He'll tell you that he hates blood, and he really just wants certain people to go away, people like Dad, people who hurt other people, but it's not true. When he killed Dad he got a taste for it, and now he gets to keep doing it."

"And what about you? You don't act on it?"

"I didn't, no. I didn't for years and years and years. Matthew got to have all the fun, and all I got was an occasional fantasy. He wouldn't even let me know what I was missing, wouldn't tell me about it. Pretended he was perfect. But I knew his game. He made a mistake and told me about Michelle, his fellow teacher, and how he gave her advice, and she had this crush on him, and as soon as I found out that Michelle had some creepy boyfriend, I knew. I knew that he was gearing up again.

So after he killed Scott Doyle, I went and paid a visit to Michelle. I can't tell you . . . she was so happy to see me because she thought I was Matthew at first, same way you did. But she didn't like Richard. She didn't like me at all."

"Was that the first time you hurt a woman?" Hen asked.

"Pretty much." Matthew smiled at her, but Hen thought it was a fake smile, the rest of his face grim and uncertain.

"I don't think you liked it," Hen said, bracing herself. She now thought she could make it to the door if she needed to. She just wasn't sure she could swing it open and get through it before he got hold of her with his big hands.

"I didn't like it, I loved it."

"I don't believe you, Richard. I think a part of you is upset about what you did."

"Dad loved blood, too," Matthew said.

"But Matthew hates it," she said.

"Matthew hates blood because he saw Dad make Mom bleed and he never got it out of his mind. She just sat there with the blood coming out of her nose, and she didn't do anything to stop it. There was a napkin right on the table, and she never picked it up, just let it sit there. Can you imagine doing that in front of your own kid? Imagine letting him see that."

"But it was your dad who made her bleed, wasn't it?"

"She was asking for it."

"What about Michelle? Was she asking for it as well?"

Matthew ran his fingers through his hair. "She called up a married man and asked him over to her apartment all alone. She did it when she knew his wife was away. What kind of woman does that?"

"Maybe she just wanted someone to talk with."

"There's no such thing. She wanted Matthew all to herself so she could suck his cock."

"I don't believe you," Hen said. "I'm friends with Matthew and Matthew is friends with me, and it has nothing to do with sex."

"That's bullshit. He's had dirty thoughts about you, and I bet that you've had dirty thoughts about him."

"I haven't, Richard. I haven't had any. I'm not lying to you. I'm telling you the entire truth, I promise. And maybe it was the same way with Michelle, maybe she just wanted a friend."

Matthew shook his head.

"What did Matthew think?" Hen asked.

"About what?"

"What did Matthew think about Michelle? Did he think she deserved to die as well?" Hen pulled her legs a little farther in toward her so that the balls of her feet were pressed against the ground.

"He knew what she was."

"But I want to know what he *thought*. Can you tell me that, Richard? Can I talk to Matthew, just for a little bit?" She pressed her feet harder against the floor.

"No."

"Why not? I don't need to talk with him for long, but I want to talk with him. I have something to say to him."

"What do you have to say to him?" Matthew asked.

"The last time I talked with him, when we were on my front porch, he told me that he wanted to stop all the killing. He told me that he was done, and I want to know if he really meant it. I want to know if he was telling me the truth."

"He wasn't."

"But I want to hear it from him. I don't want to hear it from you."

"He's not here," Matthew said, and he pushed his chin down against his chest and swallowed heavily, as though he was trying to keep himself from being sick.

"I know that he's there, somewhere," Hen said. "If you let me talk with him, just for a minute, that's all I'm asking."

"I know what you're up to," Matthew said.

"What am I up to?"

"You think that if you talk with Matthew that you can talk your way out of here. You're probably thinking that he'll let you walk out that door, and then you'll go and tell the police everything."

Hen paused, trying to figure out the best thing to say. *Keep being honest,* she told herself. *It's working. Keep being honest.*

"I *am* going to tell them everything, you're right," she said. "And I *do* want to walk out of here. I don't want to die. Not yet. But I'm not going to hurt you or Matthew. I just think that down deep you both want to stop what you're doing, that you know it's wrong, and that you know that it's over."

"Matthew's a pussy. He probably *would* let you go."

"That makes him strong," Hen said. "You were strong, too. All those years you wanted to do bad things just like your dad, but you didn't do them."

"That's all changed. I've changed now."

"That doesn't mean you can't change back, you know. It's not too late."

"I'll go to prison."

"You'll go to prison, or you'll go to a hospital. Either way someone will help you."

"It's Matthew who needs help. Not me."

Hen, without thinking, yelled as loud as she could: "Let me talk to Matthew. Right the fuck now!"

Matthew blinked rapidly, pushed his chin down against his chest again. His eyes welled up with tears. "Hi, Hen," he said after a while, his voice quiet.

"Matthew?"

"Uh-huh."

"I just met your brother. He's different from you."

"It's not all his fault. It was our upbringing. He idolized our father, and I think it twisted him."

"Did you hear everything we talked about?" Hen asked.

"No," Matthew said. "Was he going to hurt you?"

"I think so, yes. He scared me."

"He scares me, too. He's gone now."

Hen relaxed a little, and as soon as she did, she could feel her body physically reacting to the fear, her breath shortening, her limbs flooding with a terrible heaviness. "Let's get out of here, then. We'll go to the police, if that's what you want." Her voice trembled now.

"What were you going to do?" Matthew asked. "To get away from Richard?"

"I was going to try and run through the door, bolt it behind me."

"Could you have locked him in?"

"Uh-huh. You need a key for both sides of the door."

"Lock me in," Matthew said.

"What?"

"I want you to lock me in here. I want to give my-self up."

"Are you sure?"

"Please, just do it. Before I change my mind."

Hen stood up from her chair, her legs trembling now as well. "Okay," she said.

"Don't leave me down here for a long time," he said. "You'll send someone soon for me, won't you?"

"Yes, right away."

Hen walked to the door, swung it open. She turned and Matthew was now sitting on the floor, holding on to one of the legs of the press.

"I'm sorry about Lloyd," he said. "He was in my house."

"What?"

"This afternoon, when I came home, he was hiding in my house, upstairs. I guess he was looking for something to incriminate me. Maybe he was looking for that fencing trophy."

"Is he dead, Matthew?"

He breathed in wetly through his nostrils. "I'm sorry, but he was in my house."

Hen stepped through the door and locked it behind her. She ran down the basement hallway toward the exit.

CHAPTER 39

Matthew spent most of the next forty-five minutes looking through Hen's prints. He felt bad, violating her space that way, but he really did love her art.

In one corner of the studio was an old metal file cabinet with three drawers. On top of the cabinet was a desk lamp with a long, bendable neck, and in each of the drawers was a hefty stack of prints done by Hen. He turned the lamp on and went through the prints one by one. They didn't seem to be organized in any specific way, although the prints in the bottom drawer seemed to be older. The images were more disturbing, clearly not intended for children's books, but they all had captions on them, some inexplicable, some funny. The print that Matthew looked at the longest was of a fox caught in one of those leg traps. The fox, grimacing in pain, wore a shabby suit, his tie askew. Around him, in a circle, stood more anthropomorphized foxes wearing a variety of clothes—dresses, suits, children's outfits, a butcher's smock. They were just observing, eyes wide and scared. The caption read: "The other foxes of the village watched, as it had been decreed."

Matthew touched each of the foxes on the print with

his index finger and said, "Fox face, fox face, fox face, fox face, fox face, fox face." Then he laughed. He wondered if these few minutes he was spending right now in Hen's studio, alone, were the last unobserved moments of his life. A feeling of sadness swept through him, now that it was all over. But there was also relief. He knew he would never stop thinking about what Richard had done to Michelle, what Richard had almost done to Hen. And when the police—with their pig faces, he thought, and almost laughed again—came and got him, he'd make sure that Richard came along as well. They were brothers, after all. They were in this thing together, just as they always had been.

CHAPTER 40

After Hen dialed 911 and gave them Matthew's address, saying she believed her husband was in the house and that he was injured, she got into her car, found the number for Detective Martinez.

"Where are you?" he said immediately after answering.

"I'm at my studio. Why? Where are you?"

"I'm on your street."

Hen started the car. "You need to go into Matthew Dolamore's house right now," Hen said. "Lloyd's in there, and I think he's hurt."

"The police are already there."

"What do you mean?"

"There's something happening at Matthew's house. I'm going to check it out now. I'll call you right away—"

"Don't hang up. Matthew Dolamore is in my studio."

"What?"

Hen put the phone on speaker and began to back the car out of Black Brick Studios' parking lot. "He came to see me at my studio. He wants to confess to everything, and I locked him in. He's there now." Hen made a sudden decision to not tell the detective about the split personality. Not right now, anyway. "He told me Lloyd was searching through his house, and they got into some kind of fight."

"Are you on your way?"

"I am."

"I'll be here," the detective said, and ended the call.

There were no stop signs or lights between Black Brick Studios and Sycamore Street, and Hen was pulling onto Sycamore only a minute or so after the detective had ended the call. When she saw the semicircle of police cars, plus the ambulance with its flashing lights, she knew that something bad had happened to Lloyd. She felt it in her stomach—a hollow ache.

She pulled the car into her driveway and sat for a moment; it couldn't have been more than five seconds, but it felt longer. Then she opened the door and got out, began to walk toward the cluster of officers, some in uniform, some not. She watched as Detective Martinez turned toward her, then disengaged himself from the group, meeting her halfway across the Dolamores' yard. A dog barked in the distance, the sound of it oddly sharp in Hen's ears. The day was bleached of color and clouds had filled the sky, but Hen found herself squinting as the detective approached.

"I'm sorry," he said.

"He's dead?"

"He is, Hen. I'm so sorry."

There was movement over his shoulder, and Hen watched as a female police officer led Mira Dolamore down her front steps. Mira looked dazed, her head swiveling to take in the scene around her, then settling on Hen. Their eyes met, and Mira seemed to open her mouth to say something—not that Hen could have heard her from that distance—but instead of speaking, Mira lowered her head.

Hen felt the detective's hands, one on each of her arms. She wondered why he was touching her, then realized that she'd been falling.

CHAPTER 41

After they let him out of the studio, Matthew was brought to an interview room at the Dartford police station, where he waived his rights to have an attorney present.

He told Detective Shaheen everything about the killing of Scott Doyle, making sure that she understood that Mira, his wife, had not been lying for him, that she truly had thought he'd been next to her in the hotel room all night. Speaking the words out loud, looking at the placid face of the female detective, and feeling the presence of all those other detectives and officers listening in, his words and gestures recorded, he felt a sense of relief wash over him. His muscles relaxed; his pulse slowed.

"So you did it for Michelle Brine?" the detective asked.

"Killed Scott Doyle?"

"Yes."

"Yes and no. I felt bad for Michelle because he was a shitty boyfriend, but it wasn't just for her. It was for all the other women that Scott Doyle was going to pollute in the course of his life. He was toxic."

"I get that," she said. Both her hands lay on the table that separated them, and Matthew watched her occasionally spin her wedding band with her thumb. He wondered if she'd recently lost weight and hadn't had the ring resized yet. "But, still," she continued. "I want to know more about your relationship with Michelle. You must have been close if she told you about her boyfriend."

"We weren't really close, I'd say. We were work friends. We worked with one another."

"I notice you are using the past tense."

"Right," Matthew said. "She's dead now, too."

"How do you know that, Matthew?"

"Because I saw her body. I went to her apartment and saw her body."

"When you killed her, you mean?" the detective said.

Matthew shook his head. "No," he said. "God, no. Of course I didn't kill her. I'd never hurt a woman. Never."

"Do you know who killed her?"

"It was my brother, Richard," Matthew said.

"Your brother killed Michelle Brine?"

"Yes."

"How do you know that?"

"He told me. After he killed Michelle he came to my house to visit and he left me the keys to her apartment. It was his way of letting me know what he had done. He was taunting me. That's how I got into her apartment. I needed to see for myself what he had done."

Matthew covered his mouth with his hand. He was thinking back to all the blood on the wall, all the blood on the bed, Michelle's skin gray in the dim light. She would have thought that Richard was him, that he'd come to support her, maybe even make love to her, and then . . .

"Are you okay, Matthew?"

"Sorry, yes. It's just upsetting to me. She didn't deserve it. She'd done nothing wrong."

"Why do you think your brother killed her, then, if she'd done nothing wrong?"

"He doesn't think that way. He doesn't think the way I think. He's like my father was. I think . . . I think that he always wanted to know what it felt like to kill a woman because down deep he hates all women. He'd never done it before because he didn't have the nerve. He'd thought about it . . . a lot. And then I should never have told him about Scott and Michelle, but he kind of figured out what I had done, and then I think that he knew . . . that he knew that Michelle . . . I think he knew that Michelle wanted me."

"That she *wanted* you?"

"The night that Richard went and killed Michelle, she'd invited me over. That's how he got into her apartment, you see. She thought he was me."

"Why did she invite you over?"

"I talked to her on the phone, and she told me that she was leaving Sussex Hall for a while to go back home and be with her family, that she couldn't handle being a teacher anymore. So she asked if I wanted to stop by and see her, just to say good-bye. She knew that Mira was out of town."

"Did you go?"

"I thought about it. I actually drove over to her place, but then I realized it wouldn't be appropriate. I'm married, and I think that Michelle thought there was more between us than there was. So, no, I didn't visit her."

"But Richard did?" The detective's hands were off the table now, out of sight. She was leaning in slightly.

"Yes, Richard did."

"Matthew, where is Richard right now?"

Matthew didn't speak right away. His body was tense

again, for the first time since he'd been brought into the interview room. He'd told himself that he was going to be entirely truthful, that it was time. No more lies, no more pretending. He wanted to tell the detective that he didn't know where Richard was, but that wasn't entirely true.

"He's sleeping," he finally said.

"Richard's sleeping?"

"Yes."

"Where is he sleeping, Matthew?"

Matthew could feel his face frowning. *Be truthful,* he told himself. "Um, I don't know how to answer that question exactly. He's asleep right now, and I can't tell you any more than that."

The door to the room opened, and in came the detective who'd come to Matthew's house and interviewed him about Dustin Miller. He bent down and said something into Detective Shaheen's ear that Matthew couldn't hear. When he stood up again, he looked at Matthew, his eyes intense, and Matthew remembered his name—it was Martinez, and he was a Cambridge police detective.

Detective Shaheen stood and said, "We'll be right back, okay, Matthew? Can we get you anything? Water? Coffee?"

"Water would be good."

They left, and Matthew was alone, even though he knew the camera in the corner of the square room was watching him. He knew what they were talking about. He knew they wanted to pin everything on him, and that included what had happened to Michelle. But that wasn't him—it was Richard—and they needed to understand that. His stomach started to hurt, and he knew that if he pressed against it he'd feel better, but they were watching and he didn't want them to see that.

Some time later Detective Shaheen and Detective Martinez reentered the room, the man carrying a bottle of water. He pushed it across the table to Matthew as they both took seats.

"Hi, again," the detective said. "You remember me?"

"Of course. Detective Martinez, right?" Matthew twisted the top off the water and took a long swig. It was lukewarm.

"Right. I've been told you waived your right to an attorney. Is that correct?"

"Yes. I don't need an attorney right now. I just want to tell the truth."

"I understand." Detective Martinez was tall and rangy, and he made the molded plastic chair he was sitting on look small. "We have a lot of things to get to, Matthew, but for right now, I was wondering if you could tell me about what happened between you and Lloyd Harding today."

"He broke into my house and attacked me. I was defending myself."

"Why did he break into your house, you think?"

"Hen must have told him everything. This all started when they came over to our house for dinner."

"What all started?"

Matthew took another long drink of his water. "Hen and Lloyd came to dinner. Just a neighborly thing. As you know, Hen spotted Dustin Miller's fencing trophy that I'd left out in my office, and it made her suspicious. That's why she called you. I should never have left that trophy out. It was arrogant of me, but I have to wonder if maybe, just a little bit, I wanted someone like Hen to come along and see it. That I wanted someone to know."

"Matthew, I don't want to interrupt, and I eventually

want to hear all about Dustin Miller, but right now I'd like to hear more about Lloyd."

"I didn't mean to kill him—not that I don't think he probably deserved it, in some way—but I didn't mean to do it. He attacked me, and I defended myself."

Matthew thought of the sound of the billy club as it hit the side of Lloyd's head, then the way he had dropped to the floor, his legs giving way as though their tendons had been sliced.

"Why was he in your house?" Detective Martinez asked.

"He was probably trying to win Hen back, trying to find something on me. I don't think he was planning on attacking me, because he was hiding. I found him because I heard him upstairs. He came out of one of the spare room closets and just attacked me. I hit him in the shoulder, and I thought that might be it, but he kept coming. So I hit him in the head."

"Why did you wrap him up the way you did with the duct tape?"

Matthew was quiet, looked at the ceiling.

"You with us, Matthew?"

"I am. There was a lot of blood coming from his head, where I hit him, so that's why I used the duct tape. At first it was just around his face, but then I figured why not cover his whole body? It looked better that way."

"And after you did this you went directly to Henrietta Mazur's art studio and threatened her?"

"That wasn't me. That was Richard."

"Richard's your brother?"

"Right."

"Do you want to know why I came out here to Dartford, Matthew, today? Hen called me, and one of the things she told me was that you'd mentioned a brother and that you were worried about him, and I think it kind of freaked her out. So I looked into it. There were police reports on both of your parents' deaths, and both of those reports only mentioned you, Matthew. Neither mentioned a brother. Neither mentioned any siblings. I called the detective who investigated your father's death—he's retired now—and he remembered the case, only because he said he suspected that you had something to do with it, even though he could never prove it. I asked him if you were the only child, and he said that you were, that there had been a brother called Richard, but that Richard had died in infancy. It was a crib death, he said, sudden infant death syndrome. Is that the same Richard that you're referring to, Matthew?"

"He didn't die," Matthew said, his chin closer to his chest.

"He didn't die when he was an infant?"

Matthew didn't immediately say anything.

Detective Shaheen said, "Tell Detective Martinez what you told me about Richard earlier, how he was responsible for Michelle Brine's death."

Matthew sighed. "Richard killed Michelle, and Richard went to Hen's studio because he wanted to kill her, too. That's all I can tell you about him. I wasn't there."

"I'm confused, Matthew," Detective Martinez said. "If Richard went to Hen's studio, then how was it that you ended up in there?"

"I don't remember how I got there because that was all Richard. Then he went to sleep. I haven't even talked to him. I don't want to talk with him, frankly. I'd be perfectly happy if I never talked with him again."

"Matthew, are you and Richard the same person?"

"No. I mean, we're brothers, so we both survived our parents, and that means we have something in common. We're survivors. But Richard takes after our dad. He thinks like our dad, and he thinks that Mom . . . that she had something to do with the way Dad acted. I don't think that myself. Not at all."

There was a quick knock on the door and it swung open. Both detectives turned their heads as an older man in a pin-striped suit entered, taking one step into the room but holding the door open behind him. "Maggie, Iggy, a moment?" he said.

They left the room, and Matthew was alone again. He had finished his water and was now squeezing the plastic bottle so that it made a crinkly sound. He was very tired all of a sudden, tired of talking and explaining. He knew that an endless stream of people was going to want to talk with him now. It was inevitable. So much was inevitable now. Police detectives and psychiatrists and lawyers. There would be no trial. He would make sure that there never was a trial. He'd confess to everything. He knew that confessing wouldn't keep the stories out of the papers, though. He was going to be all over the news. "Popular History Teacher at Private School Convicted of String of Murders." No, it would be worse than that. "Private School Teacher Hid His Insanity from the World." That was the part that bothered him, that no one would really understand that he had no control over what Richard did. They'd think he was pretending, or that he knew, or that he could have stopped him. He would never really be able to explain it to them.

Richard spoke to him, then, for the first time since he'd been in the studio: *I'll explain it to them. I'll give them what they want.*

Matthew said nothing back. He didn't want to get into a conversation with Richard, not right now.

Take a break, big bro. I can tell you're exhausted. It would be nice to catch a little nap, wouldn't it?

"I don't want to talk with you anymore," Matthew said, and when he realized he'd said it out loud he threw up all over the table.

MATTHEW WASN'T INTERVIEWED AGAIN that evening. He was officially charged by Detective Shaheen, told he could have a lawyer again; then he was allowed to clean up under supervision in the station bathroom. They took his clothes and gave him a green prison uniform that smelled of bleach, a pair of clean socks, and a used pair of sneakers without laces. In his holding cell in the basement level of the precinct, they brought him dinner—a microwaved hamburger with a side of mixed vegetables. He didn't feel hungry, but after he took one bite of the rubbery burger, he found himself devouring the rest, almost like a dog bolting down its food. Afterward he felt nauseated and decided to lie down on the thin cot. He kicked his sneakers off and fell asleep without having to tell himself any stories.

After breakfast the following morning, a uniformed officer told him he had a visitor. He recognized Mira's footsteps, the clack of her nice shoes, as she was brought down the short linoleum hallway. She turned and looked at him, her eyes puffy from crying, and the police officer took two steps backward but stayed in the hall.

"Oh, Bear," she said, stepping toward the bars.

And then he was Bear, and he was crying.

CHAPTER 42

After two weeks at her parents', and then three quick days back in Boston for Lloyd's memorial service, then another two weeks at her best friend Charlotte's house in Burlington, Vermont, Hen returned to West Dartford for the first time since Lloyd had been killed by Matthew Dolamore.

It was late November, the days now getting dark before five o'clock. All the bright colors of fall had coalesced into a hue that could only be described as rust. Dull, dead leaves were piled and strewn everywhere, and the few leaves that were still attached to trees had died as well, just waiting to be liberated by the next burst of cold wind. Hen pulled the Golf into her driveway at noon on a Thursday. The front yards of both her house and the Dolamores' were covered in a thick mat of orange-brown needles. There was a For Sale sign in front of the Dolamore house. She was surprised, not that Mira was selling the house, but that it was already on the market. Maybe she needed money fast.

Walking from the car to her front door, carrying a mewling Vinegar in his carrier, she could smell chimney smoke in the air. There was an uncarved pumpkin on her front step, rotten and collapsing. She didn't remember it being there—had Lloyd bought it?—but she didn't entirely trust all of her memories from that surreal period during which she'd gotten to know Matthew. She unlocked the door and pushed it open, the door jamming briefly on the pile of mail that had accumulated in the foyer. She put the carrier on the floor and unlatched the top. Vinegar sprung out and raced toward the cat door that led to the basement. The house was cold inside, and Hen went immediately to the thermostat, raising the temperature till she heard water starting to move through the pipes. Not knowing what else to do, she gathered up all the mail—mostly catalogs and credit card solicitations—and brought the pile into the kitchen. On the counter was a bowl of apples that had sat untouched for the last month. They were still bright red, and she plucked one from the bowl, its flesh fairly firm. *It's been no time at all,* she thought, and allowed herself to cry, briefly, before touring the rest of the house.

That night she crawled into the bed she'd shared with Lloyd and lay on her back. The full weight of his death, the enormity of his absence, pressed down on her. She didn't really know whether the marriage could have been saved had he lived, but that didn't seem to matter anymore. His affair seemed quaint now, unimportant. What was so painful was that she could never speak to him again, that they would never relive what they had gone through together. He was gone, and when she really comprehended that fact her whole body hurt. Yes, she was depressed—a feeling she easily recognized— but she also thought that the depression was mostly the result of grief and trauma, and that her brain was working okay. She'd need to find a therapist—she knew that—but she wasn't too worried that the recent events would trigger a depressive episode or a suicidal one. She felt sane.

She slept through the night, much deeper than she thought she would, and when light flooded in through the bedroom window, she pulled herself up out of a complicated dream that involved Matthew. She never dreamed these days about Lloyd, but she dreamed constantly of Matthew. In the dreams he was always coming to find her, and she was always asking him if they'd released him from the hospital. *No,* he'd say. *That's my brother in the hospital. You have us confused.*

Maybe because of the dream, or maybe because of waking up in her old house, Hen called Detective Martinez and asked him if there was anything new in the case.

"He's not going anywhere," he said. "He's going to be hospitalized for a very long time, and there's never going to be a trial. You won't have to testify."

"Is that a good thing?" she asked. "Maybe I want to testify."

"You really don't, Hen. Matthew Dolamore is where he should be right now."

"I know he is."

"Where are you calling from?" he asked.

"Home," Hen said. "I'm back in the house on Sycamore Street. Spent my first night here last night."

"How'd it go?"

"Not bad. Had a couple of nightmares, but I have those anywhere I sleep."

"So you're going to stay?"

"I am," Hen said. "I'm going back to the studio today to see how that feels, but, yes, I want to stay, Iggy."

"Good for you," he said.

Hen ate an apple for breakfast, then stepped onto the porch to see what the day felt like. It was in the mid-forties, the sky a patchwork of thin clouds. Back in the house, she pulled on a thick wool turtleneck, then her old jean jacket, the one with the frayed collar that she'd been wearing the last time she went to her studio. She was grabbing her sketchbook when Vinegar emerged from the basement. She scooped him up and held him for a moment. He meowed at her—his protest meow—and she replied that it was just the two of them now, but they were home.

It was a school day and Sycamore Street was quiet, most of the driveways empty of cars. Walking toward the studio, however, she felt eyes on her, neighbors peering through curtains, wondering if that really could be that poor woman whose husband had been killed by the now infamous psychopath. Whether she was being watched or not, she still felt the eyes on her. It was going to be the hardest part of coming back to this town, but it wouldn't last. Nothing lasted forever.

After buying coffee at the Starbucks two blocks past Black Brick, Hen doubled back and let herself into the basement level of the studios. The lights were on, which meant that someone else was down here, a comforting thought even though she didn't necessarily want any social interaction. When she got to the door of her studio, she tried it first but it was locked, and she used the key the police had returned to her and entered, turning on the lights. She quickly scanned the room for anything out of the ordinary, but it looked exactly the same as when she'd left it last. She went toward the chair she'd been sitting on when Matthew/Richard had her trapped, when she thought she was going to die in this room, and touched it, dropping her sketchbook onto its fraying seat. She had already decided that the first half of her day was going to be spent clearing out some of the junk from the studio. It would be symbolic, in a way, but she also wanted to do some physical work, to move a little bit, before settling back into artwork. She flicked through the pile of CDs by her player and finally decided to listen to *Exile in Guyville*. She set the volume low, then went to the back of the studio, where there was a stack of boxes that had been sitting there since she'd moved in to Black Brick over the summer. Some of the boxes went all the way back to college, and she'd been meaning to go through them, to throw away what she could, and to put what she wanted to save into one of the new Tupperware boxes she'd bought for her old artwork.

She pulled the top box off the stack and onto the floor, then sat down next to it and started to sort. Most of what was in the box were failed prints, either too dark or too light, or simply images that didn't work. She recognized the pieces as being from a few years ago, back when she lived in Cambridge. Some were worth keeping, but most she put into a pile that would go into the large recycling bin on the ground-level floor of the studio.

At the bottom of the box there was a sheet that had clearly been pulled from one of her sketchbooks. She turned it over and there was the sketch she'd made of Dustin Miller, a few months before he'd been killed by Matthew Dolamore. In the sketch he sat on the edge of his bed in his apartment, his chin raised, his eyes humorless and arrogant. She'd done it the only time she'd been to his apartment. It was during a week in which Lloyd had traveled down to Fort Myers with two high school friends to attend some Red Sox spring training games.

Two nights that week she'd walked to the Village Inn, sitting at one of the booths with her sketchbook, sipping at a bourbon sour, and drawing people at the bar.

Dustin had approached her during her first night there and asked to look at her drawings. He was younger than her, and so ridiculously handsome that she didn't particularly find him attractive. But she let him look at some of her sketches and buy her drinks. In retrospect, she was already manic at that point and immensely flattered that he had approached her. He radiated a kind of green aura of energy, and when he sat across from her at the booth she could feel that energy pricking at her skin.

"Can you do a drawing of me for me to keep?" he asked, on the second night they were hanging out.

"Sure," she said, and flipped to a blank page.

"No, not here. At my place."

"Why?" she asked, instead of simply laughing at him or telling him no.

"It'll be more special. For me. Come on. I want you to see where I live. I promise I won't be creepy."

"You're already being creepy," she said. But she went with him anyway, pulled by something she didn't totally understand. Maybe it was the thrill of embarking on something in which the outcome was not known. Maybe she was challenging the strength of her love for Lloyd. Or maybe it was something far less complicated.

He didn't live far from the Village Inn, and when they got to his second-floor apartment in a Victorian very close to Hen's own house, Dustin rushed in first, quickly tidying things, then getting them each a beer.

"Where do you want me?" he asked.

"Wherever," she said.

"What if I sit on the edge of my bed and you can

sit here," he said, leading her toward his bedroom, then clearing clothes off a T-back wooden chair. Hen sat down, sketched for about twenty minutes, then tore it out of her book and gave it to Dustin. She thought she'd caught him: his confident youth, the lines of his face, his posture, the intimacies of the setting.

"I love it," he said, then awkwardly lurched in toward her for a kiss. Hen laughed, but kissed him back, telling herself that she just wanted to see what it felt like, getting close to all that springlike green energy; to see what it felt like to be really wanted, really physically wanted, one more time. He scooped her up and rolled her expertly onto his platform bed, one of his large hands already sneaking underneath her top.

"Dustin," she said.

"Uh-huh."

"I'm married."

"You told me. I don't care. It's hot."

"Slow down a minute, okay?" Hen said. "I need to use your bathroom." She did need to go, but she also wanted a moment to think. Was she really about to make this colossal mistake? Did she even want to?

"Okay," he said, then added, when she got to the bedroom door, "Don't fucking change your mind."

She spun reflexively; his voice had changed so much with those last five words that for a moment she thought someone else had spoken from the room. But in the light from the single bedside lamp she saw that his face had changed as well, his eyes gone dead. And he had slid a hand down his own jeans and was touching himself.

"I'll be right back," Hen said, trying to keep her own voice normal, and went into the bathroom—she could still smell it, cologne and stale urine—and sat on the toilet. She managed to pee, telling herself to stop panicking and form a plan. She'd made a huge mistake; Dustin was not some dopey, horny guy. He was something else altogether. If she told him she wanted to leave, he would rape her. She was sure of it. She could go through with it, she thought. Just have sex with him and get out of here alive, but the thought made her nauseated. She still had her clothes on, so if she wanted to she could exit the bathroom and head straight toward the front door, get out of there before he could grab her. But her sketchbook was in the bedroom, and something about leaving that behind was unthinkable. It had her address in it, for one, but it was also filled with personal sketches, even a couple of Lloyd. She flushed the toilet, then looked in the medicine cabinet, hoping there was some kind of weapon she might be able to brandish, a straight razor or a can of shaving cream, but there was nothing that looked remotely effective.

There was a thumping on the door, Dustin's voice saying, "Hurry up. I gotta pee, too."

Hen thought, *Here's my chance.*

She came out of the bathroom. He was shirtless and he slid past her, leaving the door open. She heard a stream of piss hit the side of the toilet before splashing into the bowl. She moved as fast as she could into the bedroom, grabbing her sketchbook from the chair and the torn-out sketch that was now lying on the floor, then walked rapidly across the living room to the front door.

"Where you going?" he said, his voice threatening again, as she twisted the doorknob. For a moment she hesitated, almost told him she was leaving, out of some ridiculous fear of not being polite, but kept going instead.

She raced down the stairs, but he caught her at the bottom, his hand twisting the soft flesh of her upper arm.

"I'll scream," Hen said. "I'll fucking scream so loud."

Dustin's eyes flicked to the side door at the bottom of the landing, a door that most likely led to a first-floor apartment. Hen thought she could hear the sound of a television coming from within. "I'm serious," she said, and he let go of her arm, then looked right at her with those dead eyes.

"Maybe some other time," he said, his voice calm. Then he mouthed the word *bitch* at her, and she pushed through the front door out into the damp night air.

The next time she saw him he was being carried out of his house in a body bag.

She never told Lloyd about what had happened and never told the police, either. She felt guiltier about not telling the police, because it was possible that the information she had on Dustin might be relevant to the case. If he was going to rape her—and he was *definitely* going to rape her—then maybe he'd raped someone else before, and if that was the case, then that might have been a motive for the crime. But she never went to the police. She couldn't bring herself to do it, and eventually she told herself that what had happened that week had maybe never happened at all. It was just a foolish, terrifying moment that she needed to forget. But she couldn't forget it, and she poured all of her guilt and remorse into her obsession with who had killed Dustin.

Later, after her hospitalization and the ECT and the med changes, she sometimes wondered if she'd imagined the whole thing, that surreal, terrifying night with the boy from the Village Inn. The memory of it now felt more like a dream than any kind of reality. And some-